André Gide was a giant of twentieth-century French literature. An innovator of the novelistic form, he undertook a life-long exploration of morality in his work, and was a major influence on the writing of Jean-Paul Sartre and Albert Camus. Gide was awarded the Nobel Prize for Literature in 1947.

Julian Evans is a writer and translator. His most recent book is *Semi-Invisible Man: the Life of Norman Lewis*.

The Vatican Cellars
André Gide

An allegorical satire

translated from the French
by Julian Evans

Gallic Books
London

A Gallic Book

This edition published by arrangement with Alfred A. Knopf, an imprint of
The Knopf Doubleday Group, a division of Random House, LLC.
Copyright © Éditions Gallimard, Paris, 1914. First published in French by
Éditions Gallimard under the title *Les Caves du Vatican*.

This edition published in Great Britain in 2014 by Gallic Books, 59 Ebury
Street, London, SW1W 0NZ

English language translation copyright © Julian Evans, 2014

This book has been selected to receive financial assistance from English
PEN's "PEN Translates!" programme, supported by Arts Council England.
English PEN exists to promote literature and our understanding of it,
to uphold writers' freedoms around the world, to campaign against the
persecution and imprisonment of writers for stating their views, and to
promote the friendly co-operation of writers and the free exchange of ideas.
www.englishpen.org

ISBN 978-1-908313-69-0

Typeset by Gallic Books
Printed and bound by CPI Group (UK) Ltd, Croydon, CR0 4YY
2 4 6 8 10 9 7 5 3 1

Introduction

Les Caves du Vatican, first published in French in 1914 around the mid-point of André Gide's writing career, was banned by the Roman Catholic Church along with Gide's other works in 1952 – a year after the author's death, and five years after he was awarded the Nobel Prize for Literature.

To those familiar with the austere tone and intense moral explorations of Gide's earlier *récits* (short narratives), opening *The Vatican Cellars* to find a sprawling, rattling yarn may come as something of a surprise, as it did to many readers at the time. The book's satirical treatment of the credulity of believers, whether reliant on religion or other doctrine, shocked many critics, while its existential questions and especially the concept of the gratuitous act inspired the likes of the Surrealists and Sartre and Camus. Yet for all the book's perceived daring modernity, what is really striking looking back is just how funny it is.

Though it has continued to be available in the United States, where it is best known by the title *Lafcadio's Adventures* after one of its most memorable characters (though by no means the only one to have adventures), the 1925 English translation by Gide's contemporary and friend Dorothy Bussy has not been widely distributed in the UK for 25 years. This new translation, which deliberately modernises the text in line with Gide's own decision to adopt a more straightforward, vigorous style for the writing of the book, aims to bring this overlooked – and refreshingly light-hearted – classic to a larger audience in its centenary year.

BOOK ONE

ANTHIME ARMAND-DUBOIS

'Speaking for myself, my decision is made.
I have opted for social atheism, the atheism
that I have been expressing for the last
fifteen or so years in a series of works ...'
Georges Palante, from his column about philosophy
in the *Mercure de France*, December 1912

I

In 1890, in the papal reign of Leo XIII, the reputation of Dr X——, a specialist in rheumatic diseases, persuaded Anthime Armand-Dubois, freemason, to travel to Rome.

'What?' his brother-in-law, Julius de Baraglioul, exclaimed. 'You're going all the way to Rome to get your body looked after! I just hope that when you get there you'll realise how much sicker your soul is!'

To which Armand-Dubois replied, in a theatrically sorrowful voice, 'My poor dear friend, will you just look at my shoulders?'

Julius liked to oblige, and, despite his disapproval, looked up at his brother-in-law's shoulders. They were racked by spasms, as though shaken by deep, irrepressible laughter, and it was undeniably poignant to see Anthime's burly, half-crippled frame using up what was left of his physical strength in such a grotesque parody. Too bad! Both men had clearly made up their minds, and de Baraglioul's eloquence was not going to change anything. Perhaps time would? The whispered counsel of holy places ...

Looking profoundly discouraged, Julius said simply, 'Anthime, you cause me great sorrow.' The shoulders suddenly stopped jiggling, because Anthime was very fond of his brother-in-law. 'I shall just have to hope that in three years' time, when the pope has his jubilee, I shall come and find you improved in every way!'

At least Véronique would be accompanying her husband in an entirely different frame of mind. Every bit as devout as her sister Marguerite and Julius, she was looking forward to her extended stay in Rome as the fulfilment of one of her most cherished wishes. As one of those people who fill their flat, disappointed lives with countless small devotions, in her sterility she offered up to the Lord every attention that a baby would have demanded from her. Sadly she entertained almost no hope of leading her Anthime back to Him. She had known for a long time how much stubbornness that broad brow, knitted in perpetual denial, was capable of. Father Flons had warned her.

'The most unswerving resolves, Madame,' he had said

to her, 'are the worst. You must hope for nothing less than a miracle.'

She had even stopped letting it depress her. Within days of moving to Rome, husband and wife had, singly and separately, arranged their lives: Véronique around the household and her religious devotions, Anthime around his scientific research. And that was how they lived, side by side, disagreeing about everything, tolerating each other by turning their backs on one another. As a result, a kind of harmony reigned between them and an almost-happiness enveloped them, both finding in their toleration of the other's faults an unobtrusive outlet for their virtue.

The apartment they had rented with an agency's help offered, like most Italian accommodation, unforeseen advantages along with several remarkable drawbacks. Occupying the whole of the first floor of the Palazzo Forgetti, in Via in Lucina, it had an attractive terrace on which Véronique was instantly inspired to grow aspidistras, which were generally so unsuccessful in apartments in Paris, but in order to get to this terrace she had to go through the orangery that Anthime had immediately taken over as his laboratory. They therefore agreed that Anthime would allow his wife free passage at certain hours of the day.

As quietly as she could, Véronique would push open

the door and tiptoe furtively through, staring at the floor like a lay sister hurrying past a wall daubed with obscene graffiti, as she refused point-blank to contemplate the far end of the room where Anthime's enormous back, dwarfing an armchair against which he had leant his crutch, was hunched over heaven knows what evil experiment. Anthime pretended not to hear a thing. But as soon as his wife had walked back through the room he hoisted himself heavily out of his chair, dragged himself to the door and, full of spite, with his lips pressed tightly together, *clack!* he flipped the lock shut with an autocratic snap of his index finger.

It would soon be time for Beppo, his procurer, to come in by the other door and be given his instructions.

A boy of twelve or thirteen, dressed in rags and without parents or a fixed address, the urchin had come to Anthime's notice a few days after his arrival in Rome. Outside the hotel in Via di Bocca di Leone where the Armand-Dubois had first stayed, he had found Beppo trying to attract the attention of passers-by with a grasshopper nestling under a few blades of grass in a small fishing basket. Anthime had given him ten *lire* for the insect, then, using the tiny amount of Italian at his command, somehow let the boy know that he would soon be needing some rats at the apartment in Via in Lucina to which he was moving the next day. And not just rats: every crawling, swimming, scurrying, flying thing was a candidate to be documented. He worked on live animals.

Beppo, a born procurer, would happily have stolen the eagle or the she-wolf off the Capitol for him. His new job, indulging his appetites for roaming and petty larceny, delighted him. He was paid ten *lire* a day, and for that he also helped with domestic tasks. Véronique at first took a dim view of him, but the moment she saw him cross himself as he passed the Madonna at the building's north corner, she forgave him his rags and started to allow him to bring the water and coal, firewood and kindling through to the kitchen. She even let him carry her basket when he accompanied her to the market – that was on Tuesdays and Fridays, the days when Caroline, the maid they had brought with them from Paris, was too busy with the housework.

Beppo disliked Véronique but slavishly adored Anthime, who quickly allowed the boy to come up to his laboratory instead of painfully going down to the courtyard himself to take delivery of his victims. The laboratory could be reached directly via the terrace and a hidden staircase that led down to the courtyard. Surly and reclusive, Anthime felt his heart beat a little faster as he heard the light slap of bare feet on the tiles. He showed no sign: nothing was allowed to divert him from his work.

The boy did not knock on the glass-panelled door but

pawed at it and then, as Anthime stayed hunched over his table without answering, took a few steps forward and piped in his clear voice a *'Permesso?'* that filled the room with a sound like blue sky. His voice made you think of an angel – yet he was an executioner's assistant. What new victim had he brought with him in the bag he put down carefully on the sacrificial slab? Anthime, too engrossed, often did not open the bag immediately, merely giving it a quick glance. As soon as he saw it move, he was satisfied. Rat, mouse, songbird, frog, they were all grist to this Moloch's mill. Sometimes Beppo did not bring anything, but he came in anyway because he knew Armand-Dubois would be waiting for him even if he was empty-handed. And as the silent boy at the scientist's side craned forward to witness some appalling experiment, I should like to reassure the reader that the said scientist experienced no false god's glow of vanity at feeling the boy's astonished gaze settle, in turn, full of horror on the animal and then full of admiration on himself.

In preparation for his assault on *Homo sapiens* itself, Anthime Armand-Dubois was developing a theory in which all animal activity could be reduced to 'tropisms'. Tropisms! No sooner had the word been coined than no one talked about anything else. Whole swathes of psychologists acknowledged no higher power than *tropisms*. Tropisms! What sudden enlightenment burst forth from those syllables! Of course: animals were subject to exactly the same stimuli as the heliotrope whose flowers turn spontaneously towards the sun (a phenomenon easily reduced to a few simple laws of physics and thermochemistry). At last the cosmos was revealing a reassuring benevolence. A human being's most unexpected behaviour could now be explained solely in terms of total obedience to the new law.

To achieve his ends – to extract from his helpless creatures the proof of their simplicity – Armand-Dubois had invented a complicated arrangement of boxes containing tunnels, trapdoors, mazes and compartments: in some of these there was food, in others nothing or some respiratory irritant, and they had doors of different colours and shapes. These diabolical contraptions were soon to become all the rage in Germany and, known as *Vexierkasten*[1], would enable the new discipline of psycho-physiology to take a further step towards unbelief. In order to target a particular sense, or a part of an animal's brain, Armand-Dubois blinded some of them, deafened others, castrated, dissected, removed sections of grey matter and extracted this or that organ that you might have sworn was indispensable but which, for Anthime's edification, the animal had to go without.

His *Report on 'Conditional Reflexes'* had recently electrified Uppsala University. Bitter discussions had raged, in which top scientists from all over the world had taken part. But new questions had started filling Anthime's mind, and, leaving his colleagues to squabble, he was pursuing his investigations in new directions, ambitiously aiming to back God further and further into a corner.

Not content with accepting that all activity incurred a physical cost as a general principle, nor that an animal expended energy merely by the exertion of its muscles and senses, the question he strove to answer after each exercise was, how much? And so, as the ravaged creature attempted to recover, Anthime, instead of feeding it, weighed it. Any extra elements (such as feeding) would overcomplicate his experiments. Take for example this one: six rats – two blind, two one-eyed, two sighted – were kept without food, immobile, and weighed daily (the two sighted ones having their eyes strained continuously by a small mechanical mill). Having starved them for five days, what would their respective weight loss be? Each day at midday, Anthime Armand-Dubois triumphantly entered a new set of figures in the tables he had designed himself.

II

The jubilee was imminent. The Armand-Dubois were expecting the Baragliouls any day. On the morning the telegram came announcing their arrival that evening, Anthime went out to buy a necktie.

He did not go out often. In fact he went out as little as possible, because he was unable to move around easily. Véronique was happy to do his shopping for him or bring tradespeople to him to take orders from his selections. He no longer worried about fashion but, as simple as he wanted his new tie to be (a restrained bow of black silk), he still wished to choose it. The light-brown satin cravat he had bought for the journey and worn during their stay at the hotel kept escaping from his waistcoat (which he liked to wear cut low), and Marguerite de Baraglioul would think that the cream-coloured scarf he had replaced it with, held in place by a big old worthless cameo set on a pin, was far too casual. It had been a serious error to give up the small black ready-made bows he wore in Paris, and especially not to have kept one as an example. What styles would Rome have to offer? He decided not to choose until he had been to several shirtmakers on the Corso and the Via dei Condotti. Rounded ends were too informal for a man of fifty. No, what he needed was a nice straight bow in dull black silk …

Lunch was not until one. He came back around midday with his shopping, in time to weigh his animals.

He was not vain, but he felt the need to try on his necktie before settling down to work. There was a piece of a looking-glass lying there, which he had used for some of his tropism experiments. He propped it on the floor, against a cage, and bent over to see his reflection.

His hair was still thick and he kept it cut short. It had been ginger once, but now it was that variable greyish yellow of old silver-gilt. He had bushy eyebrows and a look in his eyes that was greyer and colder than the sky in winter. His whiskers, shaved high and cut short, had the same reddish tinge as his stiff moustache. He ran the back of his hand over his cheeks and under his big square chin and muttered, 'All right, all right, I'll shave this afternoon.'

He took the necktie out of its paper and placed it in front of him, unpinned his cameo and unwound his scarf. His powerful neck was confined by a medium-height collar cut low at the front, whose corners he turned down. And here, in spite of my earnest desire to describe only what is essential, I cannot pass over Anthime Armand-Dubois's cyst in silence. Until I have learnt to distinguish more skilfully between what is incidental and what is necessary, what else can I demand from my pen except accuracy and scrupulousness? In any case, who can say for certain that

Anthime's cyst had never played any part in, or influenced in any way, the decisions that he collected together under the heading of *free* thinking? He was willing to disregard his sciatica, but he could not forgive the Good Lord for the petty meanness of inflicting a cyst on him.

It had appeared out of nowhere shortly after he got married, and to begin with had been nothing more than an insignificant wart south-east of his left ear, on his hairline. For a long time he had been able to conceal the growth beneath his abundant hair, which he brushed over it in a curl. Even Véronique had not noticed it until one night, as she stroked his head, her hand had suddenly come up against it.

'Heavens! What have you got there?' she had exclaimed.

And almost as if, once identified, it had no reason to restrain its expansion, within a few months the cyst had become as big as a partridge's egg, then a guinea fowl's egg, then a hen's egg, where it paused as Anthime's receding hairline, struggling to perform its task, left it increasingly exposed. At the age of forty-six Anthime Armand-Dubois no longer needed to worry about looking appealing. He cut his hair short, and started to wear a style of detachable medium-height collar in which a kind of pocket hid and exposed the cyst at the same time. But enough about Anthime's cyst.

He put the necktie around his neck. In its middle there was a fastening ribbon that was supposed to be threaded through a small metal tube and clipped in place with a tiny lever. It was an ingenious device, but it took only the first poke of the ribbon for it to become detached from the tie, which slithered off his neck onto the table. He was forced to call Véronique, who came running.

'Be kind and sew this thing back on for me, will you?'

'Machine-made,' she muttered, 'awfully trashy.'

'It's true it wasn't sewn on at all well.'

Véronique always carried two needles, threaded with white and black respectively, pinned to the left breast of her tailored blouse. Standing by the French window, not bothering to sit down, she started the repair. Anthime watched her. She was a biggish woman with strong features and as stubborn as he was, but cheerful and smiling most of the time, so that even a faint moustache had not hardened her looks.

She's a good woman, Anthime reflected. I could have married a tease who cheated on me, a flibbertigibbet who ran out on me, a gasbag who drove me mad, a goose who infuriated me, or a shrew like my sister-in-law ...

And in a less irritable voice than usual he said, 'Thank you,' as Véronique, her work done, handed him back his tie.

His new necktie around his neck, Anthime is finally fully applied to his thoughts. No other voices can be heard, either outside or in his soul. He has weighed his blind rats. What is there to say? The one-eyed rats have not moved. He weighs the sighted pair – and jumps so sharply that his crutch clatters to the floor. Shock horror! His sighted rats … he weighs them a second time, but no, there is no getting away from it: since yesterday his sighted pair have *put on weight*!

A light suddenly goes on in his head.

'Véronique!'

Laboriously, having retrieved his crutch, he hastens to the door.

'*Véronique!*'

She runs to him again, ready to help. He stands in the doorway and asks grimly, 'Who has been interfering with my rats?'

No answer. He speaks slowly, enunciating each word, as though Véronique has lost the ability to understand plain French.

'While I was out, someone fed them. Was it you?'

Regaining some of her courage, she turns to face him, almost aggressively.

'You were letting those poor creatures starve. I didn't upset your experiment, I just gave—'

But he has grabbed her by the sleeve and, hobbling, he leads her over to the table and points to his pages of figures and observations.

'You see these pieces of paper – on which for the last

fortnight I've been collecting my remarks on these animals: the same ones that my colleague Potier is waiting to read out at the Académie des Sciences at its session on 17 May next. And on 15 April, that is, today, at the bottom of my columns of figures, what can I write? What am I to write?'

As she does not say a word, using the flat tip of his index finger like a pointer he prods the blank space on the paper.

'On this day,' he repeats, 'Madame Armand-Dubois, the researcher's wife, listening only to the urgings of her heart, committed the … what would you like me to put? Blunder? Reckless act? Folly?'

'You should write: had pity on these poor creatures, victims of a perverse curiosity.'

He draws himself up, mustering all his dignity.

'If that is the way you feel about it, Madame, you'll understand that I must ask you in future to use the courtyard staircase to go and look after your pot plants.'

'Do you think I ever come into your squalid room because I want to?'

'Then spare yourself the distress of entering it in future.'

And matching the act to his words as expressively as he can, he sweeps up his pages of records and rips them into small pieces.

'For the last fortnight' he said – although if we are honest, his rats have only been fasting for four days. But his exaggeration of his grievance must somehow have placated his anger, because at lunch he appears looking entirely untroubled and even sets aside his principles to the extent of holding out a hand of reconciliation to his other half. Possibly because he does not want to offer, any more than his wife does, a spectacle of discord to their invariably right-thinking Baraglioul guests, for which they would immediately hold Anthime's opinions responsible.

At about five o'clock Véronique exchanges her blouse for a tailored jacket of black cloth and leaves to meet Julius and Marguerite, due at Rome station at six. Anthime goes to shave. He has made the effort to replace his scarf with a formal necktie, and that ought to be enough. He recoils from ceremony and sees no reason why his sister-in-law's arrival should make him give up his alpaca jacket, his white waistcoat flecked with blue, and his drill trousers and comfortable black leather slippers that he wears everywhere, even to go out, his limp providing him with the perfect excuse.

III

The Baraglioul family – the *gl* is pronounced palatally, Italian-style, as in *Broglie* (duke of) – are originally from Parma. It was a Baraglioul – Alessandro – who became the second husband of Filippa Visconti in 1514, a few months after the annexation of the duchy of Parma to the Papal States. Another Baraglioul – also Alessandro – distinguished himself at the battle of Lepanto and was then murdered in 1580, in circumstances that are mysterious to this day. It would be straightforward, but not very interesting, to follow the family's fortunes until 1807, around the time Parma was annexed by France and Robert de Baraglioul, Julius's grandfather, moved to Pau in south-west France. In 1828 Charles X granted him a count's coronet – a title that his third son, Juste-Agénor (the elder brothers having died in their youth), was later to bear so nobly in his diplomatic career, where his sharp intelligence shone and his negotiating skills bore triumphant fruit.

Juste-Agénor de Baraglioul's second son Julius, who had lived a blameless life since his marriage, had had several passionate affairs in his youth. At least he could honestly claim that he had never ignored the urgings of

22

his heart, although the basic virtue of his nature, and a kind of moral elegance that pervaded everything he wrote, had always stopped his desires leading him down a slope on which his novelist's curiosity would undoubtedly have allowed them free rein. His blood ran placidly though not coldly in his veins, as a number of aristocratic beauties could have testified ... And I would not touch on it here if his first novels had not clearly hinted at it, which was one of the factors responsible for their widespread fashionable success. Their appeal to 'people of quality' had led to one of them being serialised in *Le Correspondant* and two others in *La Revue des Deux Mondes*. This was how, as though in spite of himself and at an absurdly young age, he had found himself swept towards the doors of the Académie: with his distinguished good looks, profoundly earnest expression and contemplative pallor he seemed made for it.

As for Anthime, he professed a deep scorn for the advantages of rank, wealth and looks that never ceased to distress Julius, but he did acknowledge that his brother-in-law possessed both a vein of natural goodness and a great lack of skill at discussion, which often let free thought win the day.

Sometime after six o'clock Anthime heard his guests' carriage stop at the door. He went to meet them on the landing. Julius came up first. In his Cronstadt hat and long overcoat with its silk lapels, he looked dressed for social calls rather than travelling. Only the tartan shawl draped over his forearm hinted otherwise. The long journey did not seem to have tired him at all. Marguerite de Baraglioul on the other hand, who was following him on her sister's arm, gave every appearance of exhaustion. Her bonnet and chignon were awry, her feet stumbled on the steps, her face was half hidden by the handkerchief she was holding like a compress to her face.

As she reached Anthime Véronique whispered, 'Marguerite has some coal dust in her eye.'

Their daughter Julie, a gracious little girl of nine, and the maid brought up the rear, keeping an anxious silence.

Marguerite's character being what it was, everyone knew it was not a good idea to make light of the situation. Anthime suggested that they send for an ophthalmologist but Marguerite, who knew the reputation of so-called Italian 'doctors', would not hear of it 'for the world', piping in a languishing whisper, 'Cold water. Just cold water. Oh!'

'Of course, my dear Marguerite,' Anthime went on, 'cold water will get rid of the irritation for a few seconds by rinsing your eye, but it won't get rid of the problem.'

Then, turning to Julius: 'Did you see what it was?'

'Not terribly well. As soon as the train stopped and I suggested looking at her eye, she got awfully tense—'

'Don't say that, Julius! You were awfully clumsy. The

first thing you did when you tried to lift up my eyelid was bend all my eyelashes back …'

'Would you like me to try?' Anthime said. 'Perhaps I'll be better at it.'

A porter was bringing up their trunks. Caroline lit a mirrored lamp.

'Well, my dear, you're not going to perform the operation in the hall, are you?' Véronique said, and led the Baragliouls to their room.

The Armand-Dubois apartment was laid out around the building's inner courtyard, overlooked by the windows of the corridor that led from the entrance hall to the orangery. Along this corridor doors gave onto the dining room, then the sitting room (an enormous ill-furnished corner room that the Armand-Dubois did not use), and two guest rooms that had been arranged, one for Julius and Marguerite de Baraglioul and the other, smaller one for Julie, next to the last bedroom, which was for the Armand-Dubois. Every room had a communicating door. The kitchen and two maids' rooms were off the other side of the landing and entrance hall …

'Please don't all crowd round me,' Marguerite wailed. 'Julius, will you do something about the luggage?'

Véronique persuaded her sister to sit in an armchair. She held the lamp while Anthime examined her.

'The problem is that it's inflamed. Do you think you could take your hat off?'

But Marguerite, possibly afraid that her disarranged hair would reveal a number of artificial aids, insisted she would take it off later: an ordinary carriage bonnet would not stop her from leaning her head against the back of the armchair.

'So, you'd like me to remove the mote in your eye before I take the plank out of mine?' Anthime said with a half-snigger. 'That sounds rather at odds with the teaching of the Scriptures to me.'

'Oh, please don't make me pay too dearly for your kindness.'

'I shan't say another word ... Here, the corner of a clean handkerchief ... I see what it is ... Keep calm ... good heavens! Look up! ... Got it.'

With the corner of his handkerchief Anthime removed an almost invisible piece of grit.

'Thank you! Thank you. Now can you leave me alone? This has given me the most awful migraine.'

While Marguerite was resting, Julius unpacking with the maid, and Véronique taking care of the dinner preparations, Anthime was looking after Julie in her bedroom. The last time he had seen his niece she had been very small, and he hardly recognised this tall young girl whose smile was already one of solemn innocence. As he sat trying to entertain her, talking to her as interestingly as he could about trivial and childish things, his attention was caught by a thin silver chain she wore around her neck. He immediately suspected that it had religious medallions attached to it, and, slipping his fat index finger indiscreetly inside her blouse, he hooked them out. Hiding his pathological dislike behind a display of astonishment, he said, 'Well now, what are these little things all about?'

Julie knew perfectly well that his question was not serious, but why should she be offended?

'What, Uncle? Haven't you ever seen medallions before?'

'Now you come to mention it, no, dear little one,' he lied. 'I must say they're not exactly pretty-pretty, are they, but I suppose they're for something?'

And because unquestioning piety is not incompatible with a touch of innocent mischief, in response the little girl pointed her finger at a photograph of herself tucked into the mirror above the fireplace and said, 'Look, Uncle, you've got a picture of a little girl who isn't pretty-pretty either. What's that for?'

Surprised to find such an impish sense of repartee, and with it clearly an equal dose of common sense, in a child he had hitherto thought of as a zealot, Uncle Anthime was briefly disconcerted. But he could hardly embark on a metaphysical discussion with a nine-year-old girl! He smiled. Julie seized her opportunity, holding out the holy tokens.

'This one,' she said, 'is St Julia, my patron saint, and this one is the Sacred Heart of Our—'

'You haven't got one of the Good Lord, then?' Anthime broke in, absurdly.

The child answered matter-of-factly, 'No, they don't make them of the Good Lord ... But this is the prettiest one: it's Our Lady of Lourdes, which Aunt Fleurissoire gave me. She brought her from Lourdes. I started wearing her the day Papa and Maman offered me to the Blessed Virgin.'

This was too much for Anthime. Utterly ignoring the indescribable charm that such images summoned up – the month of May, the procession of children in white and blue – he gave way to a manic urge to blaspheme.

'So the Blessed Virgin didn't want you, then, since you're still here with us?'

Julie said nothing. Had she already understood that the wisest response to some kinds of bad manners was not to respond at all? In any case, what could she say? In the silence that followed his taunting question it was not Julie but her freemason uncle who reddened – out of slight confusion, an unadmitted qualm that goes hand in hand with rudeness, a short-lived turmoil that he hid with a respectful kiss on his niece's innocent forehead to make amends.

'Why do you pretend to be so naughty, Uncle Anthime?'

Julie's instincts were entirely right: deep down, her

learned, unbelieving uncle was a gentle, kind-hearted person. So why this stubborn resistance?

At that moment Adèle opened the door.

'Madame is asking for Mademoiselle.'

It seemed that Marguerite de Baraglioul was wary of her brother-in-law's influence and did not wish to leave her daughter alone with him for long. Anthime dared say as much to her in a murmured aside a while later, as the family sat down to dinner. Marguerite turned a still faintly red gaze on him.

'Wary of you? My dear, Julie could convert a dozen cynics like you in less time than it would take you to make the tiniest impression on her soul. No. No, we're more robust than that, we believers. All the same, do remember she's a child … In an era as corrupt as this, and a country as shamefully governed as ours, she knows blasphemy is all she can expect to see around her. But it is sad that the first signs of impropriety she witnesses should come from her uncle, whom we should like to teach her to respect.'

IV

Would these words, so mild and wise, have the effect of calming Anthime?

Yes, during the first two courses (dinner, which was good but plain, was only three courses) and so long as the table talk ranged over uncontroversial subjects. Out of consideration for Marguerite's eye they discussed, first, ophthalmology (the Baragliouls pretended not to see how much Anthime's cyst had grown), then, out of kindness towards Véronique, Italian cuisine, with allusions to the excellence of her dinner. Then Anthime asked for news of the Fleurissoires, whom the Baragliouls had recently been to see at Pau, and of the Countess de Saint-Prix, Julius's sister, who was holidaying in the area, and finally of Geneviève, the Baragliouls' delightful older daughter, whom they would have liked to bring with them to Rome, but who steadfastly refused to take time off from the Hospital for Sick Children in Rue de Sèvres, where she went every morning to help heal the little ones' suffering. At this point Julius broadened the discussion by raising the question of the expropriation of Anthime's assets. This concerned his purchase of some land in Egypt on his first visit to that country as a young man – land that until recently had been worth almost nothing as a result of its poor location. Now, however, there was the prospect of the new Cairo–Heliopolis railway line crossing his property. There was no question that the Armand-Dubois's budget, which had been overstretched by risky speculation, badly needed such a windfall. Before leaving for Rome Julius had been able to speak to Maniton, the consulting engineer in charge of the project. He advised his brother-in-law not to get his hopes up too high: he might easily end up with nothing. Anthime listened. What he did not say was that he had placed the whole business in the hands of the Lodge, which never abandons its own.

Changing the subject, Anthime spoke to Julius about his candidature for the Académie and his chances. He smiled as he talked, finding the whole thing far-fetched, and for his part Julius also feigned a relaxed indifference, as if he had forgotten the whole idea. What was the point of mentioning that his sister, Countess Guy de Saint-Prix, had Cardinal André in her pocket and, ready to be called on, the fifteen Academicians who always voted with him? Anthime offered Julius a lukewarm compliment on his most recent novel, *The Air on the Heights*. To be honest, he had thought it was terrible, and Julius, who was not taken in, quickly said (to preserve his self-esteem), 'I felt quite sure you wouldn't like a book like that.'

Anthime, who had been ready to excuse the novel, was stung by Julius's implied disdain for his opinions and protested loudly that whatever views he, Anthime, held on other matters they never influenced his judgment about works of art and about his brother-in-law's novels in particular. Julius smiled with indulgent condescension and, to move the conversation on, asked how his brother-in-law's sciatica was, calling it 'lumbago' by mistake. What? Could he not ask how Anthime's scientific research was progressing instead? It would have been a pleasure to tell him. But no, he had to ask about 'lumbago'! He would be asking about his cyst next! But not his scientific research. Oh no. Apparently his brother-in-law was unaware of it: he preferred to act as if it didn't exist ... Anthime, hot under the collar and tormented by the very 'lumbago' Julius had mentioned, laughed and answered unpleasantly, 'Am I feeling better? ... Oh yes. Yes, yes! You'd be quite upset if I was, wouldn't you?'

Julius was bewildered. He earnestly asked his brother-in-law to tell him why he was suggesting he had such feelings.

'Good grief! You lot want to call a doctor the minute one of you gets ill, but when you get better it's nothing to do with medicine. It's because of all the prayers everyone said for you while the doctor was looking after you. Anyone who got better but didn't go to church, good grief... You'd think that was totally unfair and presumptious!'

'Would you rather stay ill than pray?' Marguerite asked pointedly.

And why was she poking her nose in? Usually she took no interest in conversations on general subjects: as soon as Julius opened his mouth she faded into the background. And this was man's talk. Enough self-restraint! He turned to her sharply.

'My dear woman, kindly understand that if there were a cure, there, *there*, can you see?' – he waved wildly at the saltcellar – 'right next to me, but that to make use of it I had to beg the Headmaster' – his mocking name for the Supreme Being on the days when he felt particularly bad-tempered – 'or pray for him to intercede, to overturn the established order of things, just for me – the natural order of causes and effects, the immemorial order – I wouldn't want his cure. I'd tell him, "Headmaster, no! Leave me in peace, you and your miracle, I don't want it."'

Emphasising each word, each syllable, he had raised his voice to a crescendo of fury. He was an appalling sight.

'You wouldn't want it … Why not?' Julius asked, with deliberate calm.

'Because it would force me to believe in Him who does not exist!'

Saying it he crashed his fist onto the table.

Marguerite and Véronique exchanged an anxious glance, then both looked at Julie.

'I think it's your bedtime, darling,' her mother told her. 'Be quick. We'll come and say goodnight to you in your bedroom.'

The little girl, scared stiff by her uncle's devilish appearance and shocking talk, fled.

'If I'm going to get better,' Anthime went on, 'I want it to be thanks to me and no one else. Full stop.'

'Do you? And what about the doctor?' Marguerite asked.

'I pay him for his treatment, so we're quits.'

In his most solemn voice Julius said, 'Whereas gratitude to God would bind you ...'

'Yes, dear brother-in-law, and that's why I don't pray.'

'Others have prayed for you, dearest.'

It was Véronique who said these words. She had been silent until now. At the sound of her gentle, familiar voice Anthime jumped and then lost control completely. Contradictory phrases poured out of him. To start with, no one had the right to pray for someone against their will or request a favour for them without them knowing: it was a betrayal. Véronique hadn't gained anything from it. So much the better! It would show her exactly how much her prayers counted! It was something to be proud of, was it? ... Then perhaps the problem was that she hadn't prayed hard enough?

'Don't worry, I'm still praying,' Véronique replied, as gently as before. Then, smiling steadily, as if she was out of range of the storm of his anger, she told Marguerite how each night without fail she lit two candles in Anthime's name, one on each side of the Marian shrine on the north corner of the building, the shrine where she had once caught Beppo crossing himself. The boy had a sort of cubbyhole just nearby, in a deep recess in the wall, where he would curl up and Véronique could count on finding him when she needed him. She could not reach the shrine on her own: it had been placed out of the reach of passers-by. But by hanging on to the stonework and a metal ring, Beppo, now a slim boy of fifteen, was able to reach up and place her lit candles next to the Madonna … And imperceptibly the conversation flowed away from Anthime, closing over him as the two sisters began to talk about the touching piety of ordinary people, which could make the most roughly carved statue also the most revered … Anthime felt himself sinking without trace. Good grief! Was Véronique not content with feeding his rats behind his back? Now she was lighting candles for him too! His own wife! And dragging Beppo into her clumsy charade … Ah! We'll soon see about that …

Blood rushed to his head. He felt he was suffocating. His temples pounded. With an immense effort he staggered to his feet, knocking over his chair. He emptied a glass of water over his napkin and mopped his forehead … Was he ill? Véronique ran to him. Brutally he fended her off and stalked to the door, slamming it behind him, and his uneven steps could be heard stamping down the corridor to the dull thump of his crutch.

His abrupt exit left our fellow diners saddened and

bewildered. For a while they sat in silence.

'My poor love!' Marguerite said finally. But the occasion once more exposed the difference between the two sisters' characters. Marguerite's soul was carved of that admirable stuff from which God rightly makes his martyrs. She knew it and longed to suffer. Life, however, unfortunately refused to grant her very much in the way of pain. Her days tended to overflow with bounty, forcing her to look for Christian fulfilment in enduring the most minor annoyances of daily life. She silently put up with situations that others found painless, scratched herself on the smoothest surfaces, and always made the most of the mildest inconvenience. No one was better at feeling snubbed than she was. But Julius always seemed to be working to reduce her opportunities to display her virtue. Was it any wonder that her attitude towards her husband was constantly dissatisfied and moody? If, on the other hand, she had a husband like Anthime, what might she not achieve! It made her cross to see her sister taking so little advantage of her good luck. And she was right: Véronique disregarded every unkindness. Sarcasm and mockery made no impression on her unfailingly cheerful and placid nature. They were like water off a duck's back – and she had probably come to terms with the solitude of her existence a long time before. As it happens, Anthime did not treat her badly and she did not mind him saying what he felt. She explained that the reason he spoke so loudly was because he was unable to move easily. He would get angry much less often if his legs were more mobile.

When Julius asked where he could have got to, she answered, 'His laboratory.'

To Marguerite, who asked if they should not go and see that he was all right – he might be unwell after an angry outburst like that – Véronique promised that it would be much better to let him calm down on his own and not pay too much attention to his dramatic exit.

'Let's finish dinner in peace,' she said.

V

But Uncle Anthime had not stopped at his laboratory.

Nor had he lingered on the terrace outside, bathed in the glow of a western sky. Why not? The evening's ethereal radiance might have soothed his mutinous soul, led him towards ... No. He was fleeing all persuasion. He had hobbled as fast as he could through the room where his six rats lay in the final stages of their suffering. Making his way awkwardly down the narrow spiral staircase, he reached the courtyard and lurched across it. To us, knowing how much effort each step cost him, and how much pain each effort, his unsteady haste seems tragic. Might we ever expect to see him expend his savage energy in a good cause, and if so when? Sometimes a groan escaped him through twisted lips, and his features convulsed. Where was his rebellious rage driving him?

The Madonna – from whose open hands grace and a reflection of celestial radiance streamed down to earth, who watched over the house and was even now perhaps interceding for the blasphemer – was not one of those modern statues moulded from Blafaphas's recently invented 'Roman plaster'[2] and shipped by the ton by the so-called art house of Fleurissoire-Lévichon. Simply and naïvely carved – a physical expression of ordinary people's adoration – she is all the more beautiful and eloquent to our eyes. The pale face, the radiant hands, the blue cloak were lit by a lantern that hung a short way in front of the niche from an overhanging zinc roof, which simultaneously protected the ex-votos fixed to the wall either side of the statue. A small metal door within arm's reach, to which the parish verger had the key, kept the lantern's coiled cord out of harm's way. Two candles also burnt day and night in front of the statue, placed there each afternoon by Véronique. At the sight of the candles, which Anthime knew had been lit for him, he felt his fury surge up again. Beppo, who was chewing a crust of bread and some fennel stems in his cubbyhole in the wall, came running to meet him. Without returning his cheerful greeting, Anthime grabbed him by the shoulder. Bending over him, what did he say to make the boy tremble so much? 'No! No!' he protested. Anthime took a five-*lire* note out of his waistcoat pocket. Beppo was indignant … Later he might rob, he might kill: who knew with what sordid stain misery would sully his brow in future? But to raise his hand against the Virgin who protected him? To whom he sighed each evening before he fell asleep, to whom every morning, as soon as he was awake, he smiled? … Anthime could try entreaty and corruption, he could try to browbeat him and threaten him, all he would get was a steadfast refusal.

Let us not, by the way, make the mistake of thinking it was the Virgin herself who was Anthime's target. It was Véronique's candles which specifically upset him. But Beppo's simple soul had no room for such subtleties, and in any case, now that the candles had been dedicated to her, no one had the right to extinguish them …

Exasperated by the boy's resistance, Anthime pushed him away. He would do it himself. Supporting himself against the wall, he grasped his crutch by its handle, drew back with all the force of his fury, and hurled it, leg first, into the air. The missile collided with the niche's wall and clattered to the ground, bringing with it a great fall of debris and plaster. Anthime retrieved his crutch and stepped back to see the niche … What the devil! The two candles were still burning. But what had happened to the Madonna? Where her right hand had been, all that was left was a rod of black metal.

For a moment, sobered by what he had done, the freemason stared at the aftermath of his act: to have indulged in such a petty attack … Too bad! He looked for Beppo. The boy had disappeared. Night was closing in. Anthime was alone. On the cobblestones he noticed a piece of the debris his crutch had knocked down and he picked it up: it was a small stucco hand. He shrugged his shoulders and put it in his waistcoat pocket.

With shame in his eyes and rage in his heart, the iconoclast turned away to walk back up to his laboratory.

He wanted to work, but the terrible exertion had finished him off. All he could think of was sleep. He reminded himself that he was not going to say goodnight to anyone ... At the door to his room, the sound of a voice stopped him. The neighbouring bedroom door was ajar. He limped through the shadows in the hall to where the voice was coming from ...

Like some instantly recognisable miniature angel, Julie was kneeling on her bed in her nightgown. At her bedside, in the light of the lamp, Véronique and Marguerite were also kneeling. A few feet away, at the end of the bed, Julius stood with one hand on his heart and the other covering his eyes, in a posture simultaneously devout and virile. The adults were listening to the little girl pray. A profound stillness enveloped the scene, bringing to Anthime's mind the memory of a particular still, golden evening on the bank of the Nile when he had watched – like this childish prayer rising in the air – a column of blue smoke rise vertically into a sky of flawless purity.

Julie was coming to the end of her prayers. Having run through the standard formulas, she began to pray spontaneously, out of the fullness of her heart. She prayed for the little orphans, for the sick people and poor people, for her sister Geneviève, for her Aunt Véronique, for her Papa, for her dear Maman's eye to get better very soon ... Listening to her, Anthime's heart tightened.

From the doorway, in a tone he intended to be ironic,

and loud enough to be heard at the far end of the room, he said, 'Isn't God to be asked for anything for your uncle?'

And Julie, to everyone's astonishment, without missing a beat, went on in an amazingly confident voice, 'And I pray, God, for you to forgive Uncle Anthime his sins too.'

Her words went like arrows to the atheist's heart.

VI

That night Anthime had a dream. Someone was knocking at his bedroom door. Not the door into the corridor or the interconnecting door: the knock came from another door, one he had not noticed in his waking hours and which led straight out into the street. Its strangeness made him feel afraid and at first prevented him from answering. A half-light allowed him to make out the outlines of objects in his room – a diffuse, ambiguous light like the glow of a nightlight, although there was no nightlight. As he was trying to work out where the light was coming from, the knock came again.

'What do you want?' he called out in an unsteady voice.

Then, as he heard the knock for the third time, an extraordinary sense of languor stole over him, a languor that somehow melted all his fearful feelings. (Later he would describe it as 'a sort of yielding tenderness'.) Simultaneously he felt he had no resistance left and that the door was going to give way. It opened noiselessly, and for a moment he could only see a dark doorway. Then, like a figure in a niche, the Blessed Virgin materialised in the space. Small and dressed in white, at first she resembled his little niece Julie, just as he had left her, her bare feet poking out below her nightdress, but a second later he recognised Her whom he had offended. By which I mean that this Virgin looked like the statue on the north corner – he could even make out the damage he had caused to her right forearm. But her pale face was even more beautiful and smiling than usual. Without him seeing her physically walk, she came towards him, as though gliding, and when she reached his bedside she said, 'Do you really think, you who have wounded me, that I need my hand to make you well again?'

And as she said it, she raised her empty sleeve over him.

It seemed to him now that the strange light in the room was emanating from her. But when the metal rod suddenly penetrated his side, he felt a terrible pain pierce him and woke up in darkness.

Anthime lay for perhaps a quarter of an hour before coming to his senses. All over his body he felt a strange sort of torpor and semi-consciousness, then an almost pleasant sensation of pins and needles that made him wonder whether he had ever really felt the sharp pain in his side. He could not quite grasp where his dream started and ended, or whether he was now awake, or whether he had in fact been dreaming just now. He felt himself, pinched himself, made sure he was really there, stretched an arm out of bed, and finally struck a match. Next to him

Véronique was asleep with her face turned towards the wall.

Sliding out from under the sheets and pushing back the blankets, he swivelled into a sitting position with the tips of his bare toes resting on his slippers. His crutch was there, propped against his bedside table. Leaving it untouched, he pushed himself upright with his hands pressed against the bed, then slipped his feet into the leather, stood up as straight as he could and, still uncertain, with one arm outstretched in front of him, the other behind, took a step, then a second one, next to the edge of the bed. Three steps. Then across the room ... Mother of God! Was he ...? Noiselessly he pulled on his trousers and slipped into his waistcoat and jacket ... Stop, reckless pen! What does the clumsy excitement of a paralysed body that has suddenly been cured matter, compared with the first fluttering wingbeats of a newly liberated soul?

When Véronique stirred from her sleep a quarter of an hour later, roused by some unknown sixth sense, she was at first anxious not to feel Anthime lying next to her. She became even more anxious when, striking a match, she saw his crutch, which his impaired mobility had made his constant companion, standing by his bedside table. The match burnt down to her fingers, for Anthime, wherever he had gone, had taken the candle with him. Véronique groped for her clothes, summarily dressing herself, and then, on leaving the bedroom, saw straight away the chink of light shining from under the laboratory door.

'Anthime! Are you there, dearest?'

No reply. But, straining her ears, Véronique could make out a curious sound. Anxiously she pushed open the door. What she saw rooted her to the spot.

Her Anthime was there, directly in front of her. He was neither sitting nor standing. The top of his head, which was level with the table, was illuminated by the full glow of the candle he had placed at the table's edge. Anthime the scientist, the atheist, who for years had not bent either his crippled knee or his rebellious will (and in his case it was striking how much mind and body were in tune with each other), Anthime was on his knees …

Anthime was kneeling, and in both hands he held a small fragment of plaster, a plaster hand that he was wetting with his tears and covering with frenzied kisses. To begin with he did not move, and Véronique, speechless at the mystery unfolding in front of her and not daring either to retreat or to step fully into the room, was just thinking that she ought to kneel down herself in the doorway, facing her husband, when he raised himself – miracle of miracles! – without effort and, walking over to her, took her in his arms.

'From now on,' he said, hugging her tightly as he looked down at her, 'from now on, my dearest, you'll be praying with me.'

VII

The freemason's conversion could not be kept secret for long. Before the end of the day Julius de Baraglioul had passed on the news to Cardinal André, who immediately broadcast it to conservative circles and the upper reaches of the French clergy. At the same time Véronique informed Father Anselmo, so that the news very quickly came to the ears of the Vatican.

Anthime Armand-Dubois had without doubt been the recipient of some special blessing. It was possibly unwise to claim that the Virgin had appeared to him in person, but even if he had really only seen her in a dream, the fact that he was cured was there for all to see, demonstrable, undeniable, assuredly a miracle.

However, although it might have been enough for Anthime to feel he was cured, it was not enough for the Church, which demanded a clear and full recantation from him, to be made in circumstances of unusual magnificence.

'Oh! Oh! I do beg your pardon!' Father Anselmo said to him a few days later. 'In the error of your ways you spent your whole life spreading heresy by every means – and now you're trying to wriggle out of your part in the lofty teaching that Heaven would like to draw from your example? How many souls have the false lights of your vain science managed to drive away from the one true Light! It's up to you to bring them back, and you would hesitate to do it? What am I saying: it's up to you? No, it's your absolute duty, and I shall not insult you by supposing that you don't feel it too.'

Anthime was not wriggling out of his duty. All the same, he could not help fearing the consequences. The substantial interests he possessed in Egypt were, as we have said, in the hands of the freemasons. What could he do without the Lodge's assistance? And how could he hope that it would continue to support someone who turned his back on it? Having once trusted the Lodge to restore his fortune, he now saw himself staring ruin in the face.

He confided his apprehension to Father Anselmo. The priest, who had not previously known about his status, was gleeful at the prospect of his recantation being even more newsworthy. Two days later Anthime's high rank in the Lodge was known to every reader of the *Osservatore* and the *Santa Croce*.

'You're going to ruin me,' Anthime said.

'Oh, on the contrary, my son,' Father Anselmo replied, 'we're bringing you salvation. As for your material needs, do not let them concern you: the Church will provide. I have talked at length about your case to Cardinal Pazzi, who is going to refer it to Rampolla. I may as well tell you that your recantation has already come to the Holy Father's attention. The Church will know how to compensate you for what you have sacrificed for her. She does not intend you to lose out. And while we're on the subject, don't you think you're overstating' – he smiled – 'the freemasons' influence in this business? I'm not saying I don't know that they're a force to be reckoned with – all too often! What I mean is, have you actually calculated what you fear their hostility might lose you? Let us have the figure, more or less, and ...' – his left index finger hovered near his nose with roguish good-naturedness – 'and have no fear.'

Ten days after the jubilee was celebrated, Anthime's recantation took place at the Gesù in circumstances of excessive pomp. There is no need for me to recount this ceremony, which was covered by all the Italian newspapers of the day. Father T——, the Jesuit Superior General's socius, made it the occasion of one of his most remarkable addresses. There was no doubt that the freemason's soul had been tormented to the point of madness, and the very excess of his hatred was a foretaste of love. The holy orator reminded his audience of Saul of Tarsus and discerned surprising similarities between Anthime's iconoclastic gesture and the stoning of St Stephen. And as the reverend father's eloquence swelled and rumbled down the nave like waves breaking and crashing into a sea cave, Anthime thought of his niece's girlish voice and in his secret heart thanked little Julie for having drawn to her unbelieving uncle's sins the merciful attention of Her whom he would serve in future, forsaking all others.

From that day forward, engrossed in these more lofty preoccupations, Anthime was scarcely aware of the commotion that surrounded his name. Julius de Baraglioul made sure that he suffered on his brother-in-law's behalf, and opened every newspaper with a pounding heart. The Catholic press's initial jubilation was soon followed by catcalls from the liberal papers: a substantial article in the *Osservatore*, 'A new victory for the Church', was answered by a diatribe in the *Tempo Felice* entitled 'Yet another fool'. Even the *Dépêche de Toulouse* prefaced Anthime's column, sent in the day before his cure, with a mocking introductory note. Julius responded in Anthime's name, with a letter both dignified and curt, to inform the *Dépêche* that the so-called 'convert' would no longer be among its contributors. The *Zukunft* pre-empted a similar exchange by writing Anthime a polite letter of thanks for his services. He accepted these developments with the serenity of expression which is a sign of the truly devout soul.

'Fortunately you'll be welcome at the *Correspondant*. I'll vouch for that,' Julius said drily.

'But, my dear fellow, what on earth would I write for it?' Anthime objected mildly. 'None of the things that kept me busy yesterday holds any interest for me today.'

Gradually silence fell on the affair. Julius had to return to Paris. Anthime, under pressure from Father Anselmo, meekly left Rome. Material ruin had followed hard on the heels of the Lodge's withdrawal of support, and with the visits that Véronique – confident in the Church's succour – had persuaded him to make having only resulted in wearying and finally exasperating the Vatican's higher officials, he had followed the priest's friendly advice to go and wait in Milan for the compensation he had been promised, plus whatever scraps of heavenly largesse might come his way, though these were growing rather stale in the waiting.

BOOK TWO

JULIUS DE BARAGLIOUL

'... because you should never refuse anyone
the chance to return'
Mémoires du Cardinal de Retȝ, VIII

I

On 30 March, at midnight, the Baragliouls arrived back in Paris and their apartment in Rue de Verneuil.

While Marguerite was getting ready for bed, Julius, carrying a small lamp and wearing slippers, went into his study, a room he always returned to with pleasure. It was soberly decorated: a few Lépines and a Boudin hung on the walls and on a revolving plinth in one corner stood a marble bust of his wife by Chapu, its whiteness a little dazzling. In the middle of the room was an enormous Renaissance table on which books, pamphlets and prospectuses had been piled up in his absence. On it there was also a tray of cloisonné enamel with several dog-eared visiting cards, and set apart from them, propped conspicuously against a bronze Barye sculpture, a letter on which Julius recognised his elderly father's handwriting. He immediately tore the envelope open and read.

My dear son,

My strength has faded greatly in recent days. Certain unmistakable signs are giving me to understand that it is time to pack my bags, and indeed I feel there is little to be gained by delaying much longer.

I know you are arriving back at Paris tonight and I count on your willingness to do me a service without delay. In view of certain arrangements of which I shall inform you as soon as the task is carried out, I need to know whether a young man by the name of Lafcadio Wluiki (pronounced 'Louki'; the w and i are almost silent) is still living at 12, Impasse Claude-Bernard.

I should be obliged if you would be so kind as to present yourself at this address and ask to see the above-named. (Being the novelist that you are, you will have no difficulty in finding a pretext to introduce yourself.) It is important to me to know

1) what the young man is doing

2) what he intends to do (does he have ambitions? On what scale?)

3) generally, tell me what means of support he seems to you to have, what sort of aptitudes, appetites and tastes ...

Don't try to see me for the time being: I'm in a bitterly bad mood. You can let me have the results of your enquiries in a short note. If I find myself disposed to talk, or if I feel close to my final exit, I shall let you know.

Affectionately yours,

JUSTE-AGÉNOR DE BARAGLIOUL

PS Do not under any circumstances allow it to be known that you have come on my behalf. The young man knows nothing about me and should continue to know nothing.

Lafcadio Wluiki is now nineteen years old. Romanian subject. Orphan.

I have had a look at your latest book. If you don't get into the Académie after that, then writing such codswallop is unforgivable.

It could not be denied: Julius's latest book was getting a bad press. Despite his tiredness, he skimmed through the newspaper cuttings, in which his name was quoted mostly unfavourably. Afterwards he opened a window and stood taking deep breaths of the misty night air. Julius's study windows looked out onto an embassy's garden with its pools of purifying shadow, in which eyes and mind could wash themselves clean of the vileness of the world and the streets. For a few moments he listened to the clear song of an invisible blackbird. Then he walked back to their bedroom, where Marguerite was already asleep.

Fearing insomnia, he took a small bottle of orange-flower water he often used from the chest of drawers. Attentive to the courtesies of the bedroom, he had taken the precaution of placing the lamp, with lowered wick, below where his wife might be bothered by it, but a faint tinkle of crystal as he put down his glass penetrated to the depths of Marguerite's sleep. Giving an animal moan, she turned towards the wall. Glad to have an excuse to believe she was awake, Julius went over to her and, while he was undressing, said, 'Do you want to know what my father says about my book?'

'My dearest, your poor father has no literary sense, you've told me a hundred times,' Marguerite murmured, only wanting to go back to sleep. But Julius was too hurt.

'He says I'm unspeakable for having written such codswallop.'

An extended silence followed, in which Marguerite sank into sleep again and lost all sight of literature, and Julius began to accept his solitary unhappiness. Then, out of love for her husband, Marguerite made a great effort and returned to wakefulness.

'I hope you're not going to fret about it.'

'I'm taking it quite coolly, as you can see,' Julius answered straight away. 'But I feel it's quite inappropriate for my father to express himself that way, more inappropriate for my father than for anyone else, and particularly about that book which, strictly speaking, is a monument to him in every respect.'

Had he not, in fact, retraced the elderly diplomat's

entire exemplary career in the book? And had he not balanced its novelistic excitements by underlining Juste-Agénor's dignified, calm and classical existence in both its aspects, political and domestic?

'Luckily you didn't write the book for him to be grateful to you.'

'He's insinuating that I wrote *The Air on the Heights* to get myself into the Académie.'

'What if you did? And what if you got into the Académie for having written a wonderful book?' She added, in a tone of pity, 'Anyway, let's hope the reviews show him how wrong he is.'

Julius erupted.

'The reviews! Oh yes! Let's talk about the reviews!' Turning furiously to Marguerite, as though they were all her fault, he went on with a bitter laugh, 'They're panning me, every one of them.'

Marguerite was at last wide awake.

'Are they really very bad?' she asked with concern.

'Yes, and the ones that aren't praise me with touching hypocrisy.'

'How right you were to despise all those journalists! But remember what Monsieur de Vogüé wrote to you the day before yesterday. "A pen like yours defends France like a sword."'

'"Against the barbarism that threatens us, a pen like yours defends France better than a sword,"' Julius corrected her.

'When Cardinal André promised you his vote recently, he reminded you that you had the whole Church behind you.'

'A fat lot of good it'll do me!'

'Dearest!'

'We've just witnessed with our brother-in-law what the lofty protection of the Church is worth.'

'Julius, you're becoming bitter. You've often said to me that you didn't work with any reward in view, or the approval of others, and that your own was enough for you. You've even written about it very beautifully.'

'I know, I know,' Julius said irritably.

The deep agitation he felt was not at all assuaged by her honeyed words. He went into the bathroom.

Why was he getting worked up like this? So pathetically, and in front of his wife? His distress wasn't the sort that a spouse could fuss over or sympathise with. He ought to keep it locked up in his heart, out of pride and self-restraint. 'Codswallop!' As he cleaned his teeth, he couldn't stop dwelling on the word, driving out any nobler thoughts. Good God! It was only a book. He would put his father's words out of his mind. At least he would forget that they had come from his father … An unwelcome self-questioning began to torment him for the first time in his life – he who up to now had received nothing but smiles and approval began to doubt the sincerity of those smiles, the value of that approval – the value of his writing – the reality of his thought, the authenticity of his life …

He went back to the bedroom, distractedly holding his tooth-mug in one hand, his toothbrush in the other. He put down the glass, half full of pink water, on the chest of drawers and dropped his toothbrush into it, and sat down at a little maplewood writing desk that Marguerite used for writing her letters. He snatched up his wife's pen-holder and a sheet of delicately perfumed, violet-coloured writing paper and started to write.

My dear father,
I found your letter on my return home this evening.
The errand you have entrusted me with will be carried
out to the letter tomorrow, I hope to your satisfaction,
so that I may thereby prove my devotion to you.

For Julius was one of those honourable men whose true greatness emerges when they feel most wounded. Leaning right back on his chair, he stayed in that position for a few moments, pen poised, weighing his words.

It hurts me to discover that you of all people should
doubt my disinterestedness, which …

No. Perhaps,

Do you imagine that I attach less importance to
literary probity than to …

The phrase would not come. Julius was in his nightshirt. Feeling that he was about to catch cold, he crumpled up the sheet of writing paper, picked up the tooth-mug and went to put it back in the bathroom, tossing the discarded writing paper into the slop bucket.

As he was getting into bed, he gently shook his wife's shoulder.

'So what do you think of it? My book?'

Marguerite half opened a mournful eye. Julius had to repeat his question. Half turning, she looked at him. Tight-lipped, with raised eyebrows beneath a mass of anxious wrinkles, he was a pitiful picture.

'Dearest, what is wrong with you? Do you honestly think your last book is less good than your others?'

It was not a proper answer. Marguerite was avoiding the question.

'Well, I don't think the others are any better than this one, if that's what you mean!'

'Oh, well then …!'

Losing heart in the face of Julius's huffiness, and feeling that her loving attempts to soothe him were being rejected, Marguerite turned away from the light and went back to sleep.

II

In spite of a certain professional curiosity, and the flattering illusion that nothing human was alien to him, Julius up till now had rarely strayed far from the habits of his class and hardly ever had dealings with anyone outside his milieu. It was more a case of lacking the opportunity than lacking inclination. On the point of going out the next morning, he realised that he was not wearing exactly the right clothes for such a visit either. His overcoat, starched shirt front and Cronstadt hat all conveyed an unavoidable impression of decency, restraint and distinction ... Although perhaps it was best, after all, that his dress should not encourage familiarity in the young man too soon. Words, he thought, conversation, that was the most suitable way to gain his trust. As he set off in the direction of Impasse Claude-Bernard, Julius mulled over the safest way to introduce himself and the kind of pretexts he might use to pursue his interrogation.

How could Count Juste-Agénor de Baraglioul be involved in the life of this Lafcadio person? The question buzzed around Julius's head, refusing to leave him alone. But he was not going to start speculating about his father's life just at the moment when he had finished writing it. He wanted to know only what his father eventually decided to tell him. In the last few years the count had become taciturn, but he had never been secretive. As Julius walked through the Luxembourg Gardens he was caught in a sudden shower.

Outside number 12, Impasse Claude-Bernard a hansom cab was stopped, in which Julius, as he passed, glimpsed the figure of a woman wearing an over-large hat and over-loud makeup.

His heart was beating fast as he gave Lafcadio Wluiki's name to the porter of the boarding house. The novelist felt as though he were about to plunge into an adventure. Then, as he climbed the stairs, the place's dreary appearance and minimal decoration repelled him, and his curiosity, finding nothing to stimulate it, flagged and was replaced by disgust.

On the fourth floor an uncarpeted hallway, lit only by the stairwell, turned sharp right a few steps from the landing. All along the hallway there were closed doors on both sides, but the last door was ajar. A thin shaft of daylight came through the opening. Julius knocked but there was no answer. Timidly he pushed the door open a little wider. There was no one in the room. He went back downstairs.

'If he's not there, he won't be long,' the porter said.

It was pouring with rain. In the lobby, opposite the stairs, was a door that opened into a waiting room. Julius was about to go in, but its rank smell and desperate appearance so repelled him that he decided he could just as easily let himself into the room upstairs and wait there for the young man to arrive. He went back upstairs.

As he turned the corner of the hallway for the second time a woman emerged from the room before the last one. Julius bumped into her and apologised.

'You're looking for ...?'

'Doesn't Monsieur Wluiki live here?'

'He's gone out.'

'Hah!' Julius said, in a tone of such sharp irritation that the woman asked him, 'Is your business with him urgent?'

Julius, who had only armed himself to confront an unknown Lafcadio, was disconcerted. But he saw that this was an excellent opportunity: this woman might know a good deal about the young man if he could persuade her to talk ...

'There's something I wanted to ask him about.'

'And who is it asking?'

Does she think I'm from the police? Julius wondered.

'I am Count Julius de Baraglioul,' he said in a mildly pompous voice, raising his hat an inch.

'Oh! Count ... I do beg your pardon for not having ... It's so dark in this hallway! Please be so kind as to go in.'

She pushed open the end door. 'Lafcadio's bound to be …
He's only gone as far as the … Oh! Allow me!'

And as Julius was about to enter, she dashed past him
into the room, making for a pair of ladies' knickers that
were hanging indiscreetly over a chair and which, not
managing to conceal them, she nevertheless attempted to
make less obvious.

'Such a mess in here …'

'Never mind, don't worry! I'm quite used to it,' Julius
said breezily.

Carola Venitequa was a plump young woman, or to
put it another way was slightly overweight but had a nice
figure and a healthy complexion, and average good looks
that were neither vulgar nor unattractive. She had gentle
eyes, like an animal's, and her voice was sweet and bleating.
She was ready to go out: a small soft felt hat perched on
her head and she wore a man's collar and white cuffs with
her short jacket, which was decorated with a sailor's bow.

'Have you known Monsieur Wluiki for long?'

'Perhaps I could ask him about the thing you wanted to
know?' she said without answering.

'It's … I really just wanted to know whether he was
very busy at present.'

'It depends on the day.'

'Because if he had a bit of free time, I was thinking of
asking him … to take on a small job of work for me.'

'What sort of work?'

'Well, that's exactly it ... I wanted first of all to learn a bit more about the kind of things he gets involved in.'

The question lacked guile, but Carola did not look like a woman who required subtlety. Meanwhile Count de Baraglioul had regained his assurance. He was now sitting on the chair from which Carola had spirited away the knickers, and she, standing close to him as she leant against the table, had just started to speak. Suddenly there was a loud noise in the hallway. The door opened with a crash, and the woman Julius had glimpsed in the cab downstairs appeared.

'I was sure,' she said, 'as soon as I saw him go upstairs ...'

Carola replied immediately, moving away from Julius, 'Don't be silly, it's nothing like that, dearest ... we were just chatting. My friend, Bertha Grand-Marnier, the Count de ... oh, I'm so sorry, here I am forgetting your name already!'

'It's not important,' Julius said stiffly, shaking the gloved hand that Bertha had offered.

'Now introduce me too,' Carola said.

'Listen, poppet, they've been waiting for us for an hour already,' Mademoiselle Grand-Marnier twittered, after introducing her friend. 'If you want to chat with Monsieur, bring him along. I've got a cab waiting.'

'But it's not me he came to see.'

'Then come on! Won't you dine with us tonight?'

'I'm afraid—'

'Forgive me, Monsieur,' Carola said, blushing and anxious to take her friend away as soon as possible. 'Lafcadio will be back any minute now.'

The two women went out, leaving the door open. The hallway's bare boards made every sound audible. You could not see anyone coming from the stairwell because of the passage's right-angle turn, but you could hear them coming.

'Well, perhaps the room will tell me more than the woman. Let's hope so,' Julius said to himself. Calmly he started to inspect it.

Unfortunately, almost nothing in the nondescript lodgings offered itself up to his untrained curiosity. There were no bookshelves and no pictures on the walls. On the mantelpiece was a copy of *Moll Flanders* in English in a nasty edition that was only cut two-thirds of the way through, and a copy of the *Novelle* of Anton Francesco Grazzini, alias Il Lasca, in Italian. The books intrigued Julius. Next to them, behind a bottle of spirits of peppermint, stood a photograph that disturbed him as much, if not more so. On a sandy beach a woman who was no longer very young but oddly beautiful was leaning on the arm of an emphatically English-looking man, slim and elegant in a lightweight suit. At their feet, on an upturned canoe, sat a strong-looking boy of about fifteen with thick, fair, tousled hair and a cheeky, mocking look. He was stark naked.

Julius picked up the photograph and moved over to the window to read in the bottom right-hand corner the faded words 'Duino, July 1886', which left him none the wiser, even though he remembered that Duino was a village on the Austrian shore of the Adriatic. Nodding, his lips pursed with disapproval, he put the photograph back. Under the mantelpiece in the cold hearth were stacked a packet of oat flour, a bag of lentils and another one of rice. Further along the wall a chessboard leant against it. Nothing in the room suggested to Julius the kind of studies or activities in which the young man might spend his time.

Lafcadio had apparently just had breakfast. In a small saucepan balanced on a spirit stove on the table there was one of those hollow, perforated metal eggs for making tea used by tourists who like to travel light, and there were crumbs around a cup that had been drunk from. Julius walked over to the table. It had a drawer, and the drawer had a key ...

I should not like what comes next to give a mistaken impression of Julius's character. He was one of the least indiscreet men imaginable: he respected the outer shell that everyone chooses to cloak their inner life in, and he held everyday decency in high regard. But being under his father's orders, he felt bound to set aside his scruples. He waited for a moment longer, listening intently, and then, hearing nothing – against his will, against his principles, but with a delicate sense of carrying out a duty – he pulled open the drawer, whose key had not been turned.

There was a Russia-leather notebook in the drawer. Julius picked it up and opened it. On the first page he read these words, in the same handwriting as on the photograph:

For Cadio to write his accounts in,
To my loyal companion, from his old uncle
FABY

and underneath, with almost no space between, in a faintly childish script that was neat, straight and regular:

Duino. This morning, 10 July '86, Lord Fabian joined us here. He brought me a canoe, a rifle, and this beautiful notebook.

The rest of the first page was blank.
On the third page, dated 29 August, was written:

Gave Faby 4 strokes.

And the next day:

Gave him 12 strokes ...

Julius realised that all he was looking at was a record of some swimming training. The list of days soon petered out, however, and following on from a blank page he read:

20 September. Left Algiers for the Aurès mountains.

Then a few more places and dates were jotted down, and this last entry:

5 October. Return to El Kantara. 50 km on horseback, without stopping.

Julius turned over several more blank pages, then the notebook seemed to start again. As if to give it a new title, these words were written at the top of the page in larger and more careful letters:

> *QUI INCOMINCIA IL LIBRO*
> *DELLA NOVA ESIGENZA*
> *E*
> *DELLA SUPREMA VIRTU.*

Tanto quanto se ne taglia.
BOCCACCIO [3]

At the discovery of moral ideas Julius's interest was

aroused: this was meat and drink to him.

But the next page disappointed him: the notebook reverted to a new set of accounts, although they were of a different sort. He read, without any more indication of places or dates:

> *For beating Protos at chess – 1* punta
> *For letting slip that I spoke Italian – 3* punte
> *For answering before Protos – 1* p.
> *For having the last word – 1* p.
> *For crying when I heard Faby had died – 4* p.

Julius, reading hurriedly, interpreted '*punta*' as being a unit of currency and decided that the list was merely a fussy, puerile calculation of merits and rewards. He turned the page and read:

> *This 4 April, conversation with Protos:*
> *'Do you understand what lies behind the words: BE UTTERLY RUTHLESS?'*

And there the writing stopped.

Julius shrugged, pursed his lips, nodded and replaced the notebook in the drawer. He took out his watch, stood, walked to the window and looked out. It had stopped raining. He walked to the corner of the room where he had leant his umbrella against the wall as he came in. At that moment he saw, leaning against the doorframe, half in shadow, a handsome fair-haired young man who was watching him with a smile on his face.

III

The adolescent in the photograph had hardly aged at all. Juste-Agénor had said nineteen years old, but most people would not have taken him for more than sixteen. Lafcadio Wluiki must have just arrived. As he put the notebook back in the drawer Julius had glanced at the doorway and not seen anyone, but how had he not heard him coming? Looking down involuntarily at the young man's feet, Julius saw he was wearing galoshes over his boots.

Lafcadio was smiling without a hint of hostility. He seemed amused, in an ironic way. He still had his cap on, but as soon as his eyes met Julius's he swept it off his head and bowed ceremoniously.

'Monsieur Wluiki?' Julius asked.

The young man bowed again without answering.

'Forgive me for sitting down to wait for you in your room. As a matter of fact, I wouldn't have come in if I hadn't been shown in.'

Julius spoke more quickly and loudly than usual, to prove to himself that he was not at all uncomfortable. Lafcadio's brow furrowed, almost imperceptibly. He walked over to Julius's umbrella and, picking it up without a word, took it out to drip in the corridor. Coming back into the room, he offered Julius a chair with a gesture.

'No doubt you're surprised to see me?'

Lafcadio calmly took a cigarette out of a silver cigarette case and lit it.

'I'll explain in a very few words the reasons that have brought me here, and which you'll grasp very quickly ...'

The more he talked, the more he felt his assurance ebbing away.

'So ... But, first of all, allow me to tell you who I am' – and, as if embarrassed at having to utter his own name, he took a visiting card out of his waistcoat pocket and offered it to Lafcadio who, without looking at it, put it down on the table.

'I am ... I've just finished a rather important piece of work, a little piece I haven't personally got time to make a fair copy of. You were mentioned to me as someone who has excellent handwriting, and it also occurred to me' – here Julius's gaze eloquently surveyed the bareness of the room – 'it occurred to me that perhaps you might have no objection to—'

'There is no one in Paris,' Lafcadio interrupted him, 'who could have talked to you about my handwriting.'

He looked pointedly at the drawer, from which Julius had unsuspectingly dislodged a tiny seal of soft wax, and, turning the key violently in its lock, dropped it in his pocket. 'No one who has any right to, I mean,' he went on, watching Julius's face reddening. 'In addition' – he

spoke slowly, almost oafishly, without any expression –
'I do not, so far, entirely perceive the reasons Monsieur'
– he glanced at the card – 'the reasons Count Julius de
Baraglioul can have for being particularly interested in
me. However,' – and his voice, mimicking Julius's, became
mellow and urbane – 'your proposition deserves serious
consideration by someone in need of funds, a fact that will
not have escaped you.' He stood up. 'Allow me if you will,
Monsieur, to bring you my answer tomorrow morning.'

The invitation to leave was clear. Julius felt that the
situation was too embarrassing to be prolonged. He picked
up his hat and paused.

'I would have liked to spend longer talking to you,' he
said awkwardly. 'Allow me to hope that tomorrow … I
shall expect you after ten o'clock.'

Lafcadio bowed.

As soon as Julius had turned the corner along the hallway,
Lafcadio pushed the door shut and bolted it. He ran to
the drawer, took out his notebook, opened it at the final,
indiscreet page and, at the place where he had stopped
several months earlier, wrote in pencil, in large, truculent
letters, very different from the previous entries:

*For letting Olibrius stick his filthy nose in this
notebook – 1* punta

He pulled a penknife out of his pocket. Its blade had been sharpened so much that all that was left was a sort of bradawl, which he held over the flame of a match and then, through his trouser pocket, stabbed into his thigh. He could not help wincing. But he was not satisfied. Standing at the table, below the new entry he wrote another:

And for showing him that I knew – 2 punte

This time he hesitated. He unfastened his trousers and pushed them down on one side. He looked at his thigh, where the small wound he had made was bleeding, and inspected some older scars around it, like vaccination scars. He held the blade over the flame again, then, rapidly, thrust it into his thigh twice.

'I never used to take so many precautions,' he murmured to himself, fetching the bottle of spirits of peppermint and sprinkling several drops on the wounds.

His anger had subsided slightly when, as he put the bottle back, he noticed that the photograph of him with his mother was no longer exactly where it had been. He grabbed it, gazed at it one last time with an expression of something like pain, and, with the blood rushing to his face, furiously tore it up. He tried to set fire to the fragments, but they were hard to burn, so he cleared the hearth of the bags he had stacked there and put his only two books in their place as firedogs, then wrenched the cover off his notebook, tore the pages into pieces and screwed them up, threw his photograph on top and set fire to it all.

With his face lit by the flames, he told himself that he was watching his memories go up in smoke with inexpressible contentment, but after they had been reduced to ashes and he got to his feet once more, his head swam a little. The room was filled with smoke. He went to his washstand and sponged his face.

At the table he picked up the visiting card he had dropped there and examined it more calmly.

'Count Julius de Baraglioul,' he repeated. '*Dapprima importa sapere chi è.*'[4]

He unwound the scarf he wore instead of a collar and tie, half unbuttoned his shirt, and stood at the open window to let the cool air wash over his torso. Then, suddenly itching to go out, he quickly dressed again, put on his shoes, found a decent felt hat to wear and, calmed and civilised as much as he could be, he shut the door of his room behind him and headed for Place Saint-Sulpice. There, in the Cardinal Library opposite the *mairie*, he would no doubt find the information he was looking for.

Walking through the arcades of the Odéon, his attention was caught by copies of Julius's novel on display. It had a yellow cover, the mere sight of which would have put him off completely on any other occasion. Today he felt in his pocket and tossed a five-franc piece onto the counter.

That'll make a good fire tonight! he thought, pocketing the book and his change.

At the library a *Dictionnaire des Contemporains* outlined Julius's indifferent career, mentioned the titles of his books, and praised them in terms so formulaic it extinguished any desire to read them.

'Terrible!' Lafcadio said ... He was about to close the dictionary when a phrase from the previous entry jumped out at him. A few lines above 'Julius de Baraglioul (Viscount)', in the biography of Juste-Agénor, he read the words 'Minister at Bucharest, 1873'. How could such a simple phrase make his heart beat faster?

Lafcadio's mother had presented him with five uncles, but he had never known his father. He had accepted that he was dead and always refrained from enquiring about him. As for the uncles (each a different nationality, three of them diplomats of one kind or another), he had quickly realised that none of them had any relationship with him apart from the one that the lovely Wanda cared to bestow on them. Lafcadio had just celebrated his nineteenth birthday. He had been born in Bucharest in 1874 or, to be precise, at the end of the second year of the Count de Baraglioul's posting.

Now, alerted by Julius's mysterious visit, how could he help seeing more than fortuitous coincidence in all of this? He tried to concentrate and read the whole of Juste-Agénor's biography, but the lines were dancing in front of his eyes. He did at least manage to glean from it that the Count de Baraglioul, Julius's father, was a man of considerable eminence.

The burst of anarchic glee that drummed in his heart was so loud he thought the whole world would hear it. He glanced furtively at his neighbours, regulars in the reading room, but they were all carrying on doing what they were stupidly doing … His flesh was decidedly solid and impervious. He made a quick calculation. 'If the Count was born in 1821, he would be seventy-two. *Ma chi sa se vive ancora?…*'[5] He put the dictionary back on the shelf and walked out.

A few light clouds buffeted by a stiff breeze were clearing from the blue sky. '*Importa di domesticare questo nuovo proposito*,'[6] quoted Lafcadio, who prized above everything his own freedom of action, and, despairing of bringing his tumultuous thoughts into any kind of order,

77

he decided simply, for now, to banish them from his mind. He took Julius's novel out of his pocket and tried hard to distract himself with it, but the book lacked all diversion or mystery, and nothing could have been less suited to offering him an escape.

'And it's the author of *that* that I'm going to play the secretary for tomorrow!' he could not help repeating to himself.

He bought a newspaper at a kiosk and went into the Luxembourg Gardens. The benches were soaking wet. He opened Julius's book, sat on it, and unfolded the newspaper to read the domestic news. Straight away, as if he had known exactly where to look, his gaze fell on the following item.

The health of Count Juste-Agénor de Baraglioul, which has given cause for grave concern in recent days, is said to be improving. His condition nevertheless remains unstable and he is only receiving close family members and friends.

Lafcadio jumped up from the bench. His mind was made up. Forgetting Julius's novel, he dashed to a stationery shop in Rue Médicis where he remembered having seen in the window an offer for 'Visiting cards while you wait, 3 francs a hundred'. He smiled as he ran. The audacity of his sudden new scheme amused him: it had been too long since his last adventure.

'How long will it take to print me a hundred cards?' he asked the stationer.

'You'll have them by this evening.'

'I'll pay double if you can do them by two o'clock.'

The shopkeeper pretended to examine his order book.

'We like to oblige … yes, you can collect them at two. What's the name?'

Without hesitation or blushing, but with his heart still racing, Lafcadio took the sheet of paper the stationer offered him and wrote

LAFCADIO DE BARAGLIOUL

'The ignoramus thinks I'm having him on,' he said to himself as he left, annoyed not to have received a more respectful bow from the stationer. Then, passing a shop window, he caught sight of his reflection and thought: I have to admit I don't look much like a Baraglioul. We'll have to see if we can make me look more like one by this afternoon.

It was nearly midday. Lafcadio, filled with a skittish elation, was not feeling hungry.

Let's walk for a bit, otherwise I'm quite likely just to float off somewhere, he thought. And let's stay in the road – if I use the pavements people will notice I'm a head and shoulders taller than them. Yet another of my superior qualities I have to hide. One has never finished perfecting one's technique.

He saw a post office and went in.

'Place Malesherbes ... this afternoon then!' he said to himself, copying Count Juste-Agénor's address out of the directory. 'But what's to stop me checking out Rue de Verneuil this morning?' (That was the address printed on Julius's card.)

Lafcadio knew and loved this part of Paris. Leaving the crowded streets behind, he took a circuitous route via Rue Vaneau, where his new-found excitement would have more room to breathe freely.

Turning off Rue de Babylone, he saw people running. Near Impasse Oudinot a crowd was gathering outside a two-storey house, from which sullen-looking smoke was billowing. He forced himself not to quicken his pace, in spite of his naturally athletic stride.

Lafcadio – dear friend – you need a reporter to do you justice here, not me. Don't expect my pen to relate a crowd's snatches of conversation, its exclamations and shouts ...

Slipping through the mass of onlookers like an eel, Lafcadio reached the front. There was a woman on her knees there, sobbing.

'My children! My little children!' she said again and again. She was being comforted by a girl whose simple and elegant clothes showed she was no relation. She was pale, and so pretty that Lafcadio felt an immediate attraction. He asked what had happened, and if she knew who the woman was.

'No, Monsieur, I don't know her. All I can tell is that her two small children are in that bedroom on the first floor, which the flames are going to reach any minute now: the stairs are already on fire. The firemen are coming, but by the time they get here the children will have been overcome by smoke ... Oh Monsieur, couldn't someone reach that balcony by climbing up the drainpipe? Some people said that thieves got in that way once before, but what thieves did in order to steal no one is prepared to do to save two children's lives. I've promised my purse as a reward, but no one wants to help. If only I were a man!'

Lafcadio had heard enough. Putting down his stick and hat at the young woman's feet, he dashed forward, grabbed the top of the wall without anyone's assistance, and, pulling himself up by his arms, hauled himself up to sit and then stand on the ledge and walk along it, avoiding the pieces of broken glass cemented into it.

The crowd's astonishment redoubled when, grasping hold of the drainpipe, he shinned up it, hardly putting his feet down for a second on the brackets that clamped it to the wall. Then he was at the balcony, with a hand on its railings. The crowd's fear subsided and, all apprehension gone, it stood back in admiration at his truly exemplary agility. He smashed the glass of the balcony doors with a shoulder and disappeared into the room ... The crowd waited in unspeakable suspense ... Finally they saw him reappear, holding a crying toddler in his arms. He had torn up a bedsheet and knotted it into a sort of rope. He attached the child and lowered it to its distraught mother. The second child was brought out and lowered to safety in the same way ...

When Lafcadio at last came down himself, the crowd cheered wildly, calling him a hero.

They think I'm a clown, he thought, furious to feel himself blushing and ungraciously and bad-temperedly waving away their applause. But when the young woman shyly held out his stick and hat and with them the purse she had promised, he took them with a smile and, after emptying the purse of the sixty francs it contained, offered the money to the poor mother who was still smothering her sons with kisses.

'Will you allow me to keep the purse to remind me of you, Mademoiselle?'

It was a small embroidered purse. He put his lips to it. The two looked at each other for a moment. The girl appeared flustered, and paler than ever. She looked as though she wanted to speak, but Lafcadio turned on his heel, parting the crowd with his stick and frowning so angrily that the cheers almost instantly died away and people soon stopped following him.

He returned to the Luxembourg Gardens and then, after a perfunctory lunch at Gambrinus's near the Odéon, went rapidly back to his room. He kept his savings concealed under a floorboard: three 20-franc coins and one of 10 were brought out into the light. He added up:

Visiting cards: 6 francs.

One pair of gloves: 5 francs.

One necktie: 5 francs (but what can I get for that price?).

One pair of shoes: 35 francs (shan't get much use out of them anyway).

Nineteen francs for contingencies.

(Lafcadio always paid in cash: he had a horror of being indebted.)

He went over to his wardrobe and took out a suit of soft dark Cheviot tweed, perfectly cut and hardly worn.

'Sadly I've grown since …' he said to himself, as he remembered the glittering period, not so long before, when the Marquis de Gesvres, the last of the five uncles, had dashingly taken him off to one of his outfitters after another.

Badly fitting clothes were anathema to Lafcadio, as much as a lie was anathema to a Calvinist.

'First things first. My uncle de Gesvres used to say that you could tell a man by his shoes.'

And out of respect for the shoes he was about to try on, he began by putting on clean socks.

V

Count Juste-Agénor de Baraglioul had not stepped outside his luxurious apartment in Place Malesherbes for five years. It was there that he had decided to prepare for death, wandering reflectively through its rooms stuffed with his collections or, more often, confined to his bedroom and submitting his aching shoulders and arms to the palliative benefits of hot towels and tranquillising compresses. An enormous caramel-coloured scarf enveloped his fine head in the style of a turban, one end of which hung down to the lace of his collar and the thick Havana-wool knitted waistcoat over which his luxuriant silver beard tumbled. His feet, tucked into Turkish slippers of white leather, lay on a hot-water bottle. One at a time he dug his pale, cold hands into a bath of hot sand that was kept burning by a spirit lamp underneath it. A grey shawl covered his knees. He certainly resembled Julius, but looked more like a portrait by Titian, and Julius's features were only a pale imitation of his father's, in the same way that the account he had given in *The Air on the Heights* was merely an expurgated version of his father's life, watered down to insignificance.

Juste-Agénor de Baraglioul was drinking herbal tea and

listening to a homily from Father Avril – his confessor, whom he had fallen into the habit of consulting frequently – when there was a knock at the door and his faithful Hector, who for twenty years had fulfilled the roles of footman, live-in carer and occasional adviser, brought in on a lacquered tray a small sealed envelope.

'The gentleman hopes that Monsieur le comte may be willing to see him.'

Juste-Agénor put down his cup, tore open the envelope and took out Lafcadio's card. He crumpled it agitatedly in his hand.

'Say that …' Then, controlling himself, he went on, 'A gentleman? You mean a young man? Exactly what kind of young man is he?'

'Someone Monsieur le comte may certainly receive.'

'My dear *abbé*,' the count said, turning to Father Avril, 'forgive me for having to ask you to interrupt our conversation for now, but make sure you come back tomorrow. No doubt I shall have a good deal to tell you then, and you will not go away disappointed.'

He kept his hand to his forehead as Father Avril withdrew by the drawing-room door, and then, finally raising his head, said, 'Show him in.'

Lafcadio entered the room with masculine assurance, his head held high. He stood in front of the old man and bowed deeply. Because he had promised himself that he would not open his mouth before he had counted to twelve, it was the count who spoke first.

'To begin with, Monsieur, there is no Lafcadio de Baraglioul,' the count said, ripping the card in half, 'and please be so good as to warn Monsieur Lafcadio Wluiki, since he is one of your friends, that if he persists in playing games with these visiting cards – if he does not tear them all up as I am doing with this one' – he shredded it into tiny scraps that he dropped into his empty cup – 'I shall immediately inform the police and have him arrested as a common fraud. Do I make myself clear? ... Now, come into the light so that I may see you.'

'Lafcadio Wluiki is your servant in everything, Monsieur.' Lafcadio's voice had taken on a deferential tone and shook a little. 'Forgive him for having chosen this means of introducing himself to you. Not one dishonest intention ever entered his head. He would very much like to convince you that he deserves ... at least your good opinion.'

'You're a strong-looking boy. But those clothes don't suit you,' the count went on, determined not to hear him.

'So I wasn't mistaken?' Lafcadio said, venturing a smile and indulgently submitting to his examination.

'Thank God he takes after his mother!' the old man murmured.

Lafcadio bided his time, then, staring fixedly at the

count and almost in a growl, said, 'Without speaking too obviously, is it entirely forbidden for me also to take after—'

'I was talking about your looks. Whether you only take after your mother or not, God will unfortunately not grant me the time to know.'

As he finished speaking, the grey shawl slipped off his knees onto the floor.

Lafcadio darted forward and as he crouched down felt the old man's hand gently on his shoulder.

'Lafcadio Wluiki,' Juste-Agénor went on, after Lafcadio had straightened up, 'my time is short. I shan't beat about the bush, it would be too tiring. I accept that you're not stupid, and I am glad to see that you're not ugly. Your ploy to see me was risky and shows a certain bravura which is not unbecoming. My first impression was of presumptuousness, but your voice and manner set my mind at rest. I have asked my son Julius to fill in the background for me, but I find that it doesn't greatly interest me, and matters less to me than having seen you. Now, Lafcadio, listen to me: no birth certificate, no other document exists that proves who you are. I have taken care not to leave you any possibility of recourse. No, don't bother to assure me of your feelings for me, it's pointless. And don't interrupt me. Your silence up till today is a guarantee that your mother kept her promise not to tell you about me. That's good. So in line with the commitment I made to her, you will discover the extent of my gratitude. Via my son Julius, as my intermediary, and legal difficulties notwithstanding, I will make over to you that part of my legacy that I told your mother I would apportion to you. That is to say, I shall favour Julius over my other child, the Countess Guy de Saint-Prix, by as much as the law allows me, and exactly the amount that, through him, I should like you to have. It will, I think, amount to … let's say 40,000 francs a year. I must see my notary this afternoon and go through the figures with him … Sit down if it's easier for you to hear me that way.' (Lafcadio had just put a hand out to the table to support himself.) 'Julius can contest any of this. The law is on his side. I'm counting on his honesty to do no such thing. Likewise I count on you never to bother Julius's family, in the same way that your mother never bothered mine. For Julius and his family, only Lafcadio Wluiki exists. I don't wish you to wear mourning for me. My boy, the family is a great and closed institution. You'll never be anything but a bastard.'

Lafcadio had not sat down, despite his father's invitation when he had seen him caught off balance. Having overcome his dizziness, he was now leaning on the edge of the table that held the cup and the lamp. His posture remained deeply respectful.

'Now tell me: you saw my son Julius this morning. He told you—'

'He didn't actually tell me anything. I guessed.'

'The clumsy … No, I don't mean you! … Are you to see him again?'

'He has asked me to be his secretary.'

'Have you accepted?'

'Do you want me not to?'

'… No. But I think it would be better that you do not … acknowledge one another.'

'I thought so too. But without exactly acknowledging him, I'd like to know him a bit better.'

'I don't suppose, however, that you have any intention of staying in such a junior role for long?'

'As long as it takes to get on my feet, no more.'

'And afterwards, what do you intend to do, now that you will be a man of fortune?'

'Monsieur, you're looking at someone who hardly had enough to eat yesterday. Give me a chance to get used to my appetite!'

Just then Hector knocked at the door.

'It's Monsieur le vicomte asking for you, Monsieur. Shall I show him in?'

The old man's brow furrowed. He did not say anything for a moment, but as Lafcadio discreetly prepared to take his leave the count exclaimed, so violently that the young man's heart went out to him, 'Don't go!'

Turning to Hector, the count added, 'It's too bad! But I made it perfectly clear to him that he shouldn't try to see me … Tell him I'm busy, tell him … I'll write to him.'

Hector bowed and left the room.

The old count kept his eyes closed for a few moments.

He seemed to be asleep, but through his beard his lips could be seen moving. Eventually he opened his eyes, held out his hand to Lafcadio and, in a voice that was completely changed, softened and as if broken, said, 'Hold my hand, my boy. Now you must leave me.'

'I have a confession I must make,' Lafcadio said hesitantly. 'In order to make myself presentable to you I have exhausted the last of my funds. If you don't help me, I'm not sure how I'll be able to eat this evening and I have no idea how I'll eat tomorrow … unless your son, Monsieur le vicomte …'

'Have this for now,' the old man said, opening a drawer and giving him 500 francs. 'Well, why are you still standing there?'

'I would also like to ask you … whether I may hope to see you again?'

'Indeed! I'll admit that that would not be without pleasure. But the reverend persons who look after my salvation keep me in a mood in which my pleasure comes second. If you're seeking my blessing, you shall have it at once' – and the old man opened his arms to embrace Lafcadio. But the boy, instead of throwing himself into the count's arms, knelt in front of him and rested his head on his knees, sobbing, overwhelmed by tenderness at the old man's affection and feeling his heart, with all its fierce resolves, melt.

'My boy, my boy,' the count stammered, 'I left it too late with you.'

When Lafcadio stood up his face was streaming with tears.

As he was about to leave he put the banknote in his pocket – he had not taken it immediately – and felt for the visiting cards. He held them out to the count.

'Here, this is the whole packet.'

'I trust you. You can tear them up yourself. Goodbye!'

'He would have been the best uncle of all,' Lafcadio murmured to himself as he retraced his steps to the *Quartier Latin*, 'with something extra special too,' he added, feeling a trace of melancholy. 'Tough luck!' He pulled out the visiting cards, opened the packet, and tore them in half in one go.

'I've never trusted drains,' he muttered, dropping 'Lafcadio' in one grating and waiting until he had passed two more before he dropped 'de Baraglioul'.

'Whatever! Baraglioul or Wluiki, it's time to erase the past and everything in it.'

On Boulevard Saint-Michel there was a jeweller's shop, where Carola kept him waiting every day. The day before yesterday it had been an unusual pair of cufflinks that had caught her eye in its showy window. They were made – joined together by a gold clasp and cut from an unfamiliar kind of quartz, a sort of smoky agate that was completely opaque although it looked transparent – to represent four cat's heads in a circular setting. Because Carola wore the masculine style of short jackets that we call tailored, as I have already said, with men's cuffs, and because she had whimsical taste, she had immediately coveted the cufflinks.

They were less amusing than odd. Lafcadio thought them horrible, and it would have annoyed him to see his mistress wearing them. But since he was leaving her ... Going into the shop, he bought them for 120 francs.

'A piece of writing paper, if you'd be so kind.' Leaning on the counter, he wrote on the piece of paper the jeweller had given him:

For Carola Venitequa
To thank her for having shown the unknown guest into my room, and requesting her never to set foot in it again.

He folded the paper and slipped it into the box the jeweller was packing the cufflinks in.

'No hurry,' he said to himself, on the point of handing the box to the porter at his lodgings. 'Let's spend one last night under this roof, and be satisfied this evening with not answering the door to Mademoiselle Carola.'

VI

The moral regime under which Julius de Baraglioul lived was both provisional and protracted, the same regime to which Descartes had submitted while he perfected the permanent system of rules that would govern his life and work in future. But Julius's temperament did not express itself with such intransigence, nor his thinking with such authority, that he had so far had great difficulty in conforming to social convention. All things considered, his clear priority was his comfort, of which his success as a man of letters was a large part. With his latest novel having flopped, he felt the pricking discomfort of failure for the first time.

He had been more than somewhat put out to find himself turned away at his father's. He would have been even more so to discover who had forestalled him in gaining access to the old man. And returning from Place Malesherbes to Rue de Verneuil, he resisted more and more feebly the outlandish suspicion that had been bothering him since he first went to Lafcadio's room. He too had tied facts and dates together. He too began to refuse to accept that this strange collision of circumstances was no more than a simple coincidence. In addition, Lafcadio's youth and grace had attracted him, and although it occurred to him that his father probably would deprive him of a portion of his inheritance in favour of this new bastard brother, he did not bear him any grudge. As he waited for him the next morning, he realised with surprise that he was feeling a rather tender and attentive curiosity about him.

As for Lafcadio, however prickly and withdrawn he was by nature, he found both the rare chance to talk, and the opportunity to ruffle Julius's feathers, tempting. Even Protos had not been someone he had ever taken into his confidence very much. How far he had come since those days! And after all he did not dislike Julius, however vapid he seemed. He enjoyed the idea that he was his brother.

As he was making his way to where Julius lived, the morning after Julius's visit to Impasse Claude-Bernard, a peculiar chain of events occurred. Out of a liking for detours, possibly guided by his unconscious, and also to pacify an unquietness of mind and body and keen to arrive fully in control of himself at his brother's, Lafcadio had gone the longest way round he could think of. Walking up Boulevard des Invalides, he had passed close to the scene of yesterday's fire and then continued via Rue de Bellechasse.

'34 Rue de Verneuil,' he repeated to himself as he walked. 'Four and three, seven: good number.'

He was coming out onto Rue Saint-Dominique, where it runs into Boulevard Saint-Germain, when he thought he saw on the other side of the boulevard the girl who, since the previous day, had constantly occupied his thoughts. He walked faster ... It was her. He caught up with her at the other end of the short Rue de Villersexel, then, thinking it was not very Baraglioul-like to accost her, made do with smiling as he bowed slightly and discreetly raised his hat to her. Walking quickly past, he felt the most sensible thing to do was dive into a tobacconist's while she, walking ahead once more, turned into Rue de l'Université.

Emerging from the tobacconist's, Lafcadio took the direction she had taken, looking left and right down the street. She had vanished.

Lafcadio, my friend, you are descending into cliché. If you have to fall in love, don't rely on my pen to portray the confusion of your heart ...

But no: he decided it would be undignified to start looking for her. Nor did he want to arrive too late at Julius's, and the detour he had made had left him no more time for procrastinating. Luckily Rue de Verneuil was close by, and Julius's building was on the first corner. Lafcadio called the count's name to the concierge and dashed up the stairs.

At the same time Geneviève de Baraglioul – for it was she, Julius's elder daughter, on her way back from the Hospital for Sick Children, where she went every morning – had reached her father's apartment in a great hurry. A good deal more agitated than Lafcadio by their second

95

meeting, she had gone in through the carriage entrance at exactly the same moment as Lafcadio had turned the corner into Rue de Verneuil, and she was just reaching the second floor when the sound of hurrying footsteps made her turn round. Someone was running upstairs faster than she was. She stood back to let them pass, and then, recognising Lafcadio – who had stopped dead, speechless, in front of her – she said in the most indignant tone she could muster, 'Don't you think it demeans you, Monsieur, to stalk me like this?'

'Oh God! Mademoiselle, what must you think of me?' Lafcadio blurted out. 'I don't suppose you'll believe me if I tell you that I didn't see you come into the building, and that no one could be more surprised than I am to find you here. But isn't this the address of Count Julius de Baraglioul?'

'What?' Geneviève said, blushing. 'Are you the new secretary my father is expecting? Monsieur Lafcadio Wlou— Your name's so strange I don't know how to say it.' As Lafcadio, reddening too, bowed, she went on, 'Since we have met again here, Monsieur, can I ask you to do me the great favour of not saying anything to my parents about yesterday's adventure, which I don't think is their kind of thing at all, or about the purse, which I told them I've lost.'

'Mademoiselle, I was likewise going to beg you not to say anything about the ridiculous role you saw me playing yesterday. I share your parents' feelings: I don't understand it and I completely disapprove of it. You must have thought I was a Newfoundland or something. I couldn't help it ... Forgive me. I still have things to learn ... I'll learn them, I promise you ... Will you give me your hand?'

Geneviève de Baraglioul, who had not admitted to herself that she thought Lafcadio very handsome, did not admit to him that, far from looking ridiculous, he was a hero in her eyes. She held out her hand, and he swept it impulsively to his lips. Then, smiling happily, she asked him to go back downstairs a few steps and wait till she had gone inside and shut the door before he rang the bell himself, so that no one caught sight of them together, and also particularly asked him not to reveal, under any circumstances, that they had met before.

A few minutes later Lafcadio was shown into the novelist's study.

Julius's greeting was welcoming, but he had no idea how to conduct relations with Lafcadio. The young man's hackles rose immediately.

'Monsieur, I must warn you before we go any further that I loathe gratitude as much as I hate obligations, and that whatever you may do for me you'll never manage to make me feel beholden to you.'

It was Julius's turn to feel ruffled.

'I'm not trying to buy you, Monsieur Wluiki,' he began huffily ... Then, realising they would walk out on each other if they carried on like this, they both stopped dead and after a moment of silence Lafcadio started again in a more conciliatory voice.

'What exactly is the work you wanted to entrust me with?'

Julius was evasive, pretending that the text was not yet completed to his satisfaction. However, it could be no bad thing for them to get to know each other better beforehand.

'Admit, Monsieur,' Lafcadio said lightly, 'that that was not why you were waiting for me yesterday, and that you were much more interested in looking at a certain notebook ...'

Julius was out of his depth now. He answered confusedly, 'I admit I was,' and then, with more dignity, 'I beg your pardon. If the situation could be revisited, I would not do it a second time.'

'There won't be a second time: I've burnt the notebook.'

Julius looked crestfallen.

'Are you very angry?'

'If I were still angry, I wouldn't be talking to you about it. Forgive my tone of voice just now as I came in,' Lafcadio went on, determined to press his point home. 'Even so, I should like to know if you also read a scrap of a letter that was in the notebook?'

Julius had not read any scrap of a letter, for the reason that he had not found any, but seized the opportunity to protest his innocence. His protestations amused Lafcadio, who enjoyed showing his amusement.

'As it happens, I got my own back a bit by reading your new novel.'

'Not really your kind of thing, I shouldn't have thought,' Julius said quickly.

'Don't worry, I didn't read it all. I have to tell you that I'm not terribly interested in reading. The only book I've really enjoyed was *Robinson Crusoe* ... Oh yes, there was *Aladdin* too ... I expect that disqualifies me utterly in your eyes.'

Julius gently put up his hand.

'I merely feel sorry for you: you're depriving yourself of great pleasures.'

'I've got plenty of others.'

'Perhaps not of such good quality.'

'Oh, I'm sure you're right!' Lafcadio laughed, his rudeness barely restrained.

'And one day you'll suffer the consequences,' Julius retorted, mildly put out by the turn the conversation was taking.

'By then it'll be too late,' Lafcadio finished sententiously, then abruptly changed his tone. 'Do you really like it? Writing, I mean?'

Julius almost stood to attention at this.

'I don't write to enjoy myself,' he said nobly. 'The pleasures I take in writing are on a higher plane than those I take in living. Although one does not exclude the other.'

'So people say.' Raising his voice sharply, after letting it drop apparently unintentionally, Lafcadio said, 'You know what spoils writing for me? All the corrections, the crossings out, the improvements you do.'

'Do you think you don't correct yourself, in life?' Julius asked, his eyes lighting up.

'You're missing the point. In life you correct yourself, so they say, you improve yourself. But you can't correct what you've *done*. It's the right to retouch everything that makes writing such a grey business and such ...' He did not finish. 'Yes. It's that that seems so brilliant about life to me: you have to paint it as it happens. You're not allowed to go back and paint over it.'

'Is there much to paint over in your life?'

'No ... not too much yet ... And as you can't ...' Lafcadio was silent for a moment, then said, 'Even so, it was because I wanted to paint over it that I threw my notebook on the fire! ... But too late, you see ... Anyway, go on, admit that you didn't understand much of what you read.'

But Julius would not admit it.

'Will you allow me to ask you a few questions?' he said, changing the subject.

Lafcadio got to his feet so brusquely that Julius thought

he was about to walk out, but instead he went over to the window and lifted the muslin curtain.

'Is that your garden?'

'No,' Julius said.

'Monsieur, up to now I have not allowed anyone to poke their nose into my life to the smallest degree,' Lafcadio went on, without turning round. Then, coming back to Julius, who was beginning to think he was hardly more than a boy: 'But today's a holiday. For once in my life, I'm going to give myself a day off. Ask your questions: I guarantee to answer all of them ... Ah! The first thing to tell you is that I've kicked out that girl who let you into my room yesterday.'

Julius felt he should put on a show of concern.

'Because of me! Believe me—'

'Oh, don't worry! I'd been trying to find a way to get rid of her for a while.'

'Were you ... er ... living with her?' Julius asked gauchely.

'Yes, for the sake of my health ... But as little as possible, and mainly in memory of a friend who was her lover before.'

'Was that Monsieur Protos?' Julius guessed, having firmly decided to swallow his indignation, his disgust, his reproofs, and only to show, on this first day, as much of his astonishment as was necessary to enliven his side of the conversation.

'Yes, it was,' Lafcadio answered, laughing. 'Would you like to know who Protos is?'

'Getting to know your friends a little might tell me something more about you.'

'He was an Italian by the name of … God, I've forgotten, and it's not important. His friends and even the masters at school never called him anything except Protos from the day he came first in Greek composition, out of the blue.'

'I can't remember ever coming first myself,' Julius said to encourage the flow of confidences, 'but I liked being around the ones who came first too. So Protos—'

'Oh, he did it for a bet. Before that he'd always been one of the last in the class, despite being one of the oldest, while I was one of the youngest, not that that made me work any harder. Protos was terrifically scornful of what our masters taught us, and then one day, after one of our class swots – a boy he loathed – had told him that it was all very easy to despise the things you're no good at – or something along those lines, I don't know what – Protos took offence, studied like mad for a fortnight, and did so well that in the next composition he came first – higher than the other boy – to everyone's complete amazement. Or rather, to everyone else's, since I already held him in too high a regard for it to surprise me much. He had said to me, "I'll show them it's not that hard," and I believed him.'

'It sounds as though Protos influenced you a fair amount. Am I right?'

'Perhaps. He impressed me. To tell the truth, I've only ever had one personal conversation with him, but I was so persuaded by what he said that the next day I ran away from school, where I was shrivelling up like a lettuce under a cloth, and walked all the way back to Baden – that was where my mother was living then with my uncle, the Marquis de Gesvres ... But we're starting at the end. I have the feeling you'd make a very bad interrogator.

'I have an idea. Let me tell you my life story, from the beginning. That way you'll learn much more than you would if you stuck to your questions – and perhaps more than you care to ... No thanks, I prefer mine,' he said, taking out his cigarette case and throwing away the cigarette Julius had given him as he arrived and which he had allowed to go out while he was talking.

VII

'I was born in Bucharest in 1874,' he began deliberately, 'and as you know, I believe, I lost my father a few months after I was born. The first man I remember being with my mother was a German, my uncle, Baron Heldenbrück. But as I lost him when I was twelve, I only have a rather vague memory of him. Apparently he was a financier, a very good one. He taught me his language and how to do arithmetic in such clever and roundabout ways that I enjoyed it hugely. He made me what he affectionately called his cashier, entrusting me with a small fortune in cash wherever we went together and putting me in charge of what we spent. Whatever he bought (and he bought a lot), he insisted that I add it up in the time it took me to pull the change or the notes out of my pocket. Sometimes he weighed me down with foreign money and I had to work out the exchange rate. Then there were discounts, interest, loans, and even share-dealing. I fairly quickly became quite clever at doing multiplications and even divisions of several sets of figures in my head, without paper. Don't worry' – he saw Julius starting to frown – 'it didn't give me a taste for money or for arithmetic. In fact, if you want to know, it's probably why I never keep accounts. The truth is that my early upbringing was all practical and positive, and none of it struck a chord with me ... Heldenbrück was also something of a genius where children's physical education was concerned: he persuaded my mother to let me go barefoot and bareheaded in all weathers, and leave me out of doors as much as possible. He gave me a cold bath himself every day, winter and summer. I enjoyed it greatly ... But you're not interested in those details.'

'Yes, I am!'

'Then he had to go to America on business and I never saw him again.

'In Bucharest my mother's salon attracted the most brilliant and, as far as I can judge from memory, the most varied people, but her closest friends then, who were there most often, were Prince Vladimir Bielkowski and Ardengo Baldi, who I never called my uncle, I don't know why. Russia's interests (I was going to say Poland's) and Italy's kept them both in Bucharest for three or four years. They taught me their language, in other words Italian and Polish, though not Russian which, even if I read it and understand it without too much difficulty, I've never been fluent in. Because of the people my mother received I was rather spoilt for company, and there was never a day when I didn't have the chance to use four or five languages, all of which I spoke without any accent and interchangeably by the time I was thirteen. All the same, it was French I spoke by choice, because it had been my father's language and my mother had been determined that I should learn it first.

'Bielkowski took great care of me, as did everyone who wanted to please my mother: I seemed to be the one they paid court to. But what he did was, I think, without ulterior motive, because he always gave in to his whims, as soon as they came over him and wherever they led him. He took care of me even more than my mother realised, and I never stopped feeling flattered by the special attachment he showed to me. He was outlandish in lots of ways, but he transformed our slightly stuffy existence into a kind of endless party. Actually that's inaccurate: he didn't give in to his whims, he raced to meet them in a hell-bent rush. He threw himself at his pleasure in a sort of frenzy.

'For three summers he took us to a villa – it was more like a castle – on the Hungarian side of the Carpathians near Eperjes, which we often used to drive to. But more often we went out on horseback, and there was nothing my mother enjoyed more than roaming the countryside and forest around the villa, which are very beautiful, wherever her fancy took her. For more than a year the pony that Vladimir gave me was the thing I loved most in the world.

'The second summer, Ardengo Baldi came to join us. It was then that he taught me to play chess. I'd been so well-versed in mental calculations by Heldenbrück that pretty soon I acquired the habit of playing without looking at the chessboard.

'Baldi and Bielkowski got on very well together. In the evenings in our lonely tower, basking in the silence of the park and the forest, the four of us stayed up late into the night, dealing the cards over and over again, because although I was still only a child – I was thirteen – Baldi (who hated being dummy) had taught me how to play whist. And to cheat.

'He was a juggler, a conjurer, an illusionist, an acrobat, and the first time he came to us my imagination was only just emerging from the long dormancy that Heldenbrück had imposed on it. I was thirsty for marvels, credulous and naïvely curious. Later Baldi taught me how to do his tricks, but no amount of penetrating their secrets could dispel the feeling of mystery I experienced when, on the first evening, I saw him calmly light his cigarette from the flame at the end of his little fingernail and then, having just lost at cards, pull out of my ear and nose all the roubles he needed to settle his debts. It literally terrified me, but it made everybody else roar with laughter as he kept saying, as calmly as anything, "Thank heavens this child is such an inexhaustible goldmine!"

'The evenings he was alone with my mother and me he was always inventing some new game, some new surprise or joke. He took off all our friends, pulled faces and made his own face completely unrecognisable, did people's voices, animal noises, musical instruments, produced the weirdest noises from somewhere, sang and accompanied himself on the gusle, danced, did somersaults, walked on his hands, vaulted tables and chairs and, with his shoes off, juggled with his feet, Japanese-style, spinning a screen or a side table on the tip of his big toe. He juggled even better with his hands: he'd make dozens of white butterflies appear out of pieces of torn-up tissue paper and I'd chase them round the room, blowing on them, while he'd keep them fluttering in the air above a flapping lady's fan. Objects that were near him lost mass and reality, even presence, or took on new, unexpected, weird meanings that were far removed from any sort of utility. "There are very few things that aren't fun to juggle with," he used to say. And he was so funny at the same time that I would be choking with laughter and my mother would shout at him, "Stop, Baldi! Cadio will never go to sleep." And actually my nerves must have been pretty calm not to be affected by all the excitement.

'I gained a tremendous amount from what he taught me. In fact, after a few months I could do more than one of his tricks better than he could, and even—'

'I can see that you've had a very well-balanced education indeed,' Julius broke in.

Lafcadio started to laugh, delighted by the novelist's appalled expression.

'Oh, none of it went in very far, don't worry! But it was high time Uncle Faby came on the scene, I agree. He became close to my mother when Bielkowski and Baldi were both summoned away to new postings.'

'Faby? The one whose handwriting I saw on the first page of your notebook?'

'Yes. Fabian Taylor, Lord Gravensdale. He took me and my mother to a villa he had rented near Duino, on the Adriatic. I grew up a lot there, physically. There was a rocky peninsula that jutted out from the coast, and that was the villa's grounds, all of it. I spent every day among the pine trees, on the rocks, down in the creeks, or swimming and paddling in the sea, living like a savage. The photograph you saw was from that time. I burnt it with the notebook.'

'It seems to me,' Julius said, 'that you might have presented yourself a little more decently for the occasion.'

'That was just what I couldn't do,' Lafcadio answered, laughing. 'Pretending that I needed to get a suntan, Faby kept all my clothes under lock and key, even my underwear ...'

'And what did Madame, your mother, have to say?'

'She thought it was funny. She said that if any of our guests were scandalised, all they had to do was leave, but it didn't stop anyone we invited from staying.'

'But all that time, your education, my dear boy!'

'It's true. I learnt so easily that my mother had neglected it a bit. She seemed suddenly to take notice as my sixteenth birthday was coming up, and after a wonderful trip to Algeria that Uncle Faby and I had together – I remember that trip as the best time of my life – I was sent to Paris and handed over to a sort of unfeeling jailer person who took charge of my schooling.'

'After enjoying such excessive freedom, I can easily comprehend that a period of constraint must have seemed very hard for you.'

'I'd never have put up with it without Protos. He had come to the same school, to help his French apparently, but he spoke brilliant French and I've never understood what he was doing there – or me for that matter. I was languishing, I really was. I didn't exactly make friends with Protos, but I turned to him as if he was the one who was supposed to deliver me from that hell. He was a lot older than I was and seemed even older than his age, with nothing childish left in his manner or tastes. He had extraordinarily expressive features when he felt like it, that could convey anything at all, and yet when his face relaxed he looked like an imbecile. One day, when I joked about it, he replied that in this world it was a good idea not to look too much like what one really was.

'He couldn't be satisfied with just looking ordinary. He wanted people to think he was dim. He liked to say that men's downfall lay in their preferring the parade to the exercise, and not knowing how to conceal their talents, but he only said it to me, not to anyone else. He didn't mix with the others – he didn't even mix with me, the only boy in the school he didn't despise. Whenever I could get him to talk, he spoke with extraordinary eloquence, but most of the time he said very little. Then he looked as if he was hatching dark schemes, which I'd have liked to know about. When I asked him, what are you doing in this place? his answer was, I'm starting my run-up! He claimed that in life the way to get through the most difficult situations was to be ready to tell yourself: don't give a damn! That was what I said to myself just before I ran away.

'I left with eighteen francs in my pocket and made my way to Baden in short stages, eating anything, sleeping anywhere ... I was a bit done in when I arrived, but mostly I was pleased with myself because I still had three francs – it's true that I picked up five or six on the way. My mother was there, with Uncle de Gesvres, who thought my escape was very funny and decided to take me back to Paris: he said he was inconsolable at the thought that Paris should have left me with bad memories. And the fact is that when I came back here with him I did see Paris in a different light.

'The marquis was addicted to spending, fast and furiously: it was an unrelenting need with him, a craving. You might say that he was grateful to me for helping to satisfy it and for increasing his appetite with mine. He was the exact opposite of Faby: he taught me to have a taste for clothes. I think I wore them pretty well – I had a good teacher in him. His elegance was perfectly natural, a kind of sincerity in action. We got on very well. We spent whole mornings together at shirtmakers', bootmakers', tailors'... he paid particular attention to shoes. People judged each other by their shoes, he said, as surely and more deeply than by the rest of their clothes or their facial features ... He taught me to spend without counting the cost and without worrying whether I'd have enough to satisfy my impulses, my desires or my stomach. It was a principle with him that you should satisfy your stomach last, for (I remember his words) desires and impulses make fleeting appeals, while hunger never goes away and only gets more insistent, the longer you keep it waiting. He also taught me not to appreciate a thing more because it happened to be expensive, or less if, by chance, it turned out not to cost you anything at all.

'That's where I was when I lost my mother. A telegram came, calling me back to Bucharest urgently. She was dead by the time I got to see her. I found out that after the marquis had left she had run up a lot of debts that her estate only just covered, so that I couldn't hope to inherit a single kopeck, a single Pfennig, a single Groschen. Straight after the funeral I went back to Paris, where I thought I'd find Uncle de Gesvres. But he had taken off for Russia without warning and hadn't left a forwarding address.

'I don't need to tell you everything that went through my mind. Of course I had a few skills up my sleeve, the sort that can be useful to get yourself out of a tight spot, but the more I thought I'd need them, the more I disliked the idea of resorting to them. Luckily, one night when I was roaming the streets, feeling a bit confused, I happened to meet the woman you saw, Carola Venitequa, who'd been Protos's mistress, and she took me in. A few days after that I received notification that a small allowance would be paid to me, rather mysteriously, at a notary's office on the first of each month. I can't stand explanations, so I started drawing it without trying to find out any more. And then you came …

'Now you know more or less everything I feel like telling you.'

'It's fortunate,' Julius said solemnly, 'it's fortunate, Lafcadio, that you have an allowance coming to you at this stage in your life. Without a profession, without an education, obliged to live from hand to mouth … I see that you were ready to do anything.'

'On the contrary, I was ready to do nothing,' Lafcadio responded, regarding Julius gravely. 'Despite everything I've told you, you still don't know me very well. Nothing makes me balk quicker than need: I've only ever gone after what can't be any use to me.'

'Paradoxes, for example. And do you believe they'll sustain you?'

'It depends on your stomach. You like to call the ideas that conflict with yours paradoxes … Personally I'd prefer to starve if all I had in front of me was the stew of logic I've seen you feed your characters on.'

'Let me—'

'The hero of your new novel, anyway. Is it true that you based him on your father? The care you take to ensure, in every situation and on every occasion, that he's consistent with you and with himself, that he's faithful to his obligations and his principles, to your theories in other words ... judge for yourself how that makes someone like me feel! ... Monsieur de Baraglioul, believe me, because I'm telling you the truth: I'm nothing if not inconsistent. And see how much I've been talking! Me, who only yesterday considered myself to be the most silent, the most unforthcoming, the most withdrawn of creatures. But it was good for us to become acquainted with each other without delay – so there'll be no need to go back to it. Tomorrow – tonight – I shall creep back into my shell.'

The novelist, thrown off balance by Lafcadio's words, made an effort to regain his composure.

'Be assured, first of all, that there is as little inconsistency in psychology as there is in physics,' he began. 'You are a being in the making and—'

He was interrupted by a knocking at the door. As no one showed themselves, it was Julius who left the room. Through the door he had left open, a confused sound of voices reached Lafcadio. It was followed by a deep silence. After he had been waiting for ten minutes, Lafcadio was preparing to leave when a liveried servant came into the room.

'Monsieur le comte says that he will not detain Monsieur le secrétaire any longer. Monsieur le comte has had some bad news about Monsieur his father and is sorry not to be able to take his leave of Monsieur.'

From the tone in which this was said, Lafcadio gathered that news had come that the old count had died. He steeled himself.

'All right!' he said to himself as he arrived back at Impasse Claude-Bernard. 'The moment has come. *It is time to launch the ship.*[7] Whatever direction the wind may blow from in future will be the right one. Since I cannot be close to the old man, it will make no difference if I go as far away from him as I want.'

As he passed the porter's room he handed the man the little box he had been carrying around since the previous day.

'Be so kind as to give this package to Mademoiselle Venitequa this evening when she comes back,' he said. 'And make up my bill.'

An hour later, with his case packed, he sent for a cab. He departed without leaving an address. His notary's would have to suffice.

BOOK THREE

AMÉDÉE FLEURISSOIRE

I

Countess Guy de Saint-Prix, Julius's younger sister, whom the death of Count Juste-Agénor had abruptly summoned to Paris, had not long been back at home at the elegant Château de Pezac, four kilometres outside Pau – a home which she had rarely left since becoming a widow and even less since her children had got married and settled down – when she received an unusual visit.

She had just returned from one of the morning rides that had become part of her daily routine, in a light dogcart she drove herself. She was informed that a Capuchin friar had been waiting for her in the drawing room for an hour. The unknown friar came recommended by Cardinal André, as a card from him, which was handed to her, confirmed. The card was in a sealed envelope. When she opened it, below the cardinal's name she read, in his wispy, almost feminine script, the following words:

Recommends to the particular attention of the Countess de Saint-Prix, Father J.-P. Salus, canon of Virmontal.

That was all, and it was enough. The countess not only willingly received members of the clergy, but Cardinal André also held her soul in his hand. Without further ado she hurried to the drawing room and apologised for keeping her visitor waiting.

The canon of Virmontal was a good-looking man. His noble features radiated a masculine vigour, although it was curiously at odds with the hesitancy of his gestures and his voice, just as his almost white hair seemed incompatible with his youthful, fresh complexion.

Despite the warmth of the countess's welcome, the conversation started awkwardly and was becoming bogged down in small talk: expressions of regret for the countess's recent bereavement, enquiries after Cardinal André's health, Julius's recent failure to be elected to the Académie. As they talked, the friar's voice became slower and slower and deeper and deeper, and his expression more and more doleful. He finally stood, but instead of taking his leave said, 'Madame la comtesse, I should have liked to speak to you, and on the cardinal's behalf also, about a serious matter. But this room is not soundproof, and the number of doors alarms me: I fear that we may be overheard.'

The countess adored confidences and melodrama. She invited the canon to follow her into a narrow boudoir that could only be reached from the drawing room and shut the door.

'Here we will be safe,' she said. 'You can speak freely.'

The priest sat down in a small, low armchair facing the countess. But instead of speaking, he pulled out a large handkerchief and started sobbing into it convulsively. Bewildered, the countess reached for a work basket on a console table near her, took out a bottle of smelling salts, was unsure whether to offer it to her guest, and finally decided to wave it under her own nose.

'Forgive me,' the priest said eventually, lifting a flushed face from his handkerchief. 'I know you to be too good a Catholic, Madame la comtesse, not to understand me very soon and share my emotion.'

The countess disliked outpourings of emotion. Her sense of decorum took refuge behind a lorgnette. The priest recovered himself and pulled his armchair a little closer.

'Madame la comtesse, I needed the cardinal's solemn assurance to make the decision to come and speak to you. Yes – the assurance he gave me that your faith is in no way one of those worldly convictions, a convenient covering for indifference—'

'Please come to the point, Father.'

'The cardinal has assured me that I may have total confidence in your discretion – the discretion of the confessional, if I may be so bold …'

'But, Father, forgive me. If this is a secret of which the cardinal is informed, a secret of such apparent gravity, how is it that he has not come to talk to me about it himself?'

The priest's smile alone might have shown the countess how misguided her question was.

'A letter! But, Madame, in these times any letter a cardinal sends is opened.'

'He could have entrusted the letter to you.'

'Yes, Madame, but who knows what might happen to a piece of paper? We are so closely watched. Moreover, the cardinal prefers to remain in ignorance of what I'm about to tell you, to have nothing to do with it ... Ah, Madame! The moment is approaching, but I feel my courage ebbing away and I do not know if—'

'Father, you do not know me and so I cannot be offended if you do not have greater confidence in me,' the countess said mildly, turning her head away and letting her lorgnette fall. 'I have the greatest respect for the secrets people entrust me with. God knows if I have ever betrayed the smallest one. But soliciting a confidence is not something I have ever had occasion to do ...'

She made a slight movement, as if to get to her feet. The priest put out his hand towards her.

'Excuse me, Madame, for stooping to point out that you are the first woman, the first, I repeat, who has been judged worthy by those who have entrusted me with the dreadful mission of warning you, worthy to be told this secret and to keep it to herself. And I am sorely afraid, I admit, when I consider how weighty, how burdensome this revelation is for a feminine intelligence.'

'People are apt to fall into great misapprehension as to the limitations of a woman's intelligence,' the countess almost snapped, and then, with her hands slightly raised, she concealed her curiosity beneath an air of distraction, resignation and vague ecstasy which she felt was a suitable demeanour for hearing an important confidential message from the Church. The priest pulled his armchair closer again.

But the secret that Father Salus was about to confide to the countess still seems to me today to be too baffling and too odd to venture to report it here without preparing the ground rather more carefully.

There are novels, and there is history. Intelligent critics have remarked that fiction is history which could have taken place, and history is fiction that did take place. We should acknowledge certainly that the novelist's art often overrules credibility, just as events sometimes defy it. Alas, certain sceptical spirits will disbelieve any situation whatsoever that strays from the ordinary and everyday. They are not the readers I am writing for.

Whether God's representative on earth could have been abducted from the Holy See and, by the intervention of the Quirinal, stolen from all of Christendom as it were, is an excessively thorny problem which I do not have the temerity to raise in these pages. But it is a *historical* fact that, around the end of 1893, rumours were circulating to that effect. It goes without saying that numerous devoted souls became deeply agitated. A pamphlet on the subject appeared in Saint-Malo and was suppressed.[8] The truth was that the freemasons were as reluctant for news of such an abominable abuse to spread widely as the Catholic Church was fearful of supporting, or could not face the ramifications of, the extraordinary appeals which instantly followed in the wake of the rumour. There is no doubt that countless pious souls made financial sacrifices (the total sum that was gathered or dissipated in this connection is estimated at roughly half a million francs), but it remained dubious whether all of those who received donations were genuine campaigners, or whether some were perhaps fraudsters. It is nevertheless certain that to carry off such an appeal, in the absence of religious conviction, demanded of those who undertook it a boldness, skill, tact, eloquence, knowledge of people and events, and vigour that only fellows such as Protos, Lafcadio's former friend, prided themselves on possessing. For here I forewarn the reader: it is he who has appeared on this day at the Château de Pezac under the likeness and borrowed name of the canon of Virmontal.

The countess, determined not to open her mouth again or to change either her manner or her expression before she was apprised of every detail of the secret, listened sphinx-like to the false priest, whose self-possession was gradually increasing. He was on his feet now, striding back and forth. To prepare his case better, he had gone back, if not to the roots of the affair exactly (hadn't the enmity between the Lodge and the Church, innate and essential, always existed?), then at least to certain events in the course of which more flagrant hostility had erupted. He first of all invited the countess to recall two letters addressed by the pope in December '92, one to the Italian people, the other more particularly to his bishops, in which he urged Catholics to be on their guard against the agitation of the freemasons. Then, as the countess's memory was hazy on this point, he delved further into the past and reminded her of the erection of the statue of Giordano Bruno, organised and carried out by Crispi, behind whom the Lodge had concealed itself until then. He told her about Crispi's fury at the pope's rejection of his overtures and refusal to negotiate (and by negotiation what else could he mean but submission?). He recounted the events of the tragic day: the two camps taking up their positions, the freemasons finally throwing off their mask, and as the entire diplomatic corps accredited to the Holy See was paying its respects at the Vatican, thereby displaying simultaneously its scorn for Crispi and its veneration for our Holy Father in his wounded state, the Lodge, banners flying, was out on the Campo dei Fiori at the site of the offending statue, celebrating the illustrious blasphemer.

'At the consistory that followed soon afterwards, on 30 June 1889,' the false priest went on (still standing, he was now leaning across the console table, his arms supporting him, his face close to the countess's), 'Leo XIII expressed his vehement indignation. His protests were heard by the whole world, and that Christian world trembled to hear him speak of turning his back on Rome! Yes, turning his back on Rome ...! Madame la comtesse, you know all of this already, it has caused you pain, and you, like me, cannot forget it.'

He resumed striding up and down.

'Eventually Crispi was overthrown. Could the Church breathe freely again? And so, in 1892, the pope wrote his two letters. Madame ...'

He sat down again, dragged his armchair vigorously towards the sofa, and gripped the countess's arm.

'A month later the pope was abducted and imprisoned!'

As the countess persisted in remaining tight-lipped, the canon released her arm and continued in a calmer voice.

'I shan't attempt to move you to pity for a captive's suffering, Madame: a woman's heart is always quick to be moved by the spectacle of others' misfortune. Allow me to address your intelligence, Countess, instead and invite you to consider the turmoil into which we, as Christians, have been thrown by the disappearance of our leader.'

A faint pucker was visible on the countess's pale brow.

'To have lost a pope is a frightful thing, Madame, there is no doubt about it. But even more frightful is a false pope! Because to conceal its crime – what am I saying? – to inveigle the Church into pulling itself apart and fatally weakening itself, in place of Leo XIII the Lodge has installed on the papal throne who knows what puppet of the Quirinal, who knows what pawn in the image of its holy victim, who knows what impostor? To whom, for fear of harming the true pontiff, we must feign submission, to whom – oh, the shame of it! – the whole of Christendom bowed at the jubilee.'

At these words the handkerchief he was twisting in his hands ripped.

'The false pope's first act was that all too well-known encyclical to France, at the memory of which every Frenchman's heart – every French man and woman worthy of the name – still bleeds. Yes, yes, I know, Madame, how your aristocratic heart, noble in every way, must have suffered to hear the Holy Church rejecting the holy cause of the monarchy and the Vatican – for all to see – applauding the Republic. Alas, Madame, be assured that your astonishment was justified. Be assured, Madame la comtesse! But reflect on what the captive Holy Father has suffered too, hearing that pawn and impostor proclaim *him* a republican!'

Throwing himself back in his chair, he gave a sobbing laugh.

'And what did you think, Countess de Saint-Prix, what did you think, as a corollary to that cruel encyclical, of the audience granted by our Holy Father to the editor of the *Petit Journal*? The *Petit Journal*, Madame la comtesse! Ahh!

The Lord have mercy! Leo XIII and the *Petit Journal*? You can see how impossible that is. Your noble heart has already told you loud and clear that it's not right!'

'But,' the countess exclaimed, unable to restrain herself any more, 'we must shout it out to the whole world!'

'No, Madame! We must keep it to ourselves!' the priest boomed forbiddingly. 'We must keep it to ourselves, for now. We have to keep it to ourselves in order to act.'

Then, begging her pardon, in a suddenly tearful voice he said, 'You see, I talk to you as I would talk to a man.'

'You're right to do so, Father. To act, you said. Tell me quickly: what have you decided?'

'Ah, I knew I would find in you that manly, noble impatience, so worthy of the Baragliouls' name. There is unfortunately, however, nothing to be more feared in the current climate than inopportune zeal. If a chosen few have indeed been informed of these abominable outrages, Madame, it is of the utmost importance that we be able to count on their absolute discretion and full and unswerving obedience to the signal they will receive at the appropriate moment. To act without us is to act against us. And in addition to the ecclesiastical disapproval that could result – let me not beat about the bush: excommunication – any individual initiative will be categorically disowned and denied by the rest of us. Yes, we are undertaking a crusade here, Madame, but a hidden crusade. Forgive me for insisting on this point, but the cardinal has directed me to warn you particularly of this – wishing himself to remain in ignorance of this story and refusing even to acknowledge what you are talking about, should you bring it up with him. As far as the cardinal is concerned, he has not seen me. Likewise, should events bring us together later, it is to be understood that you and I have never spoken to each other. Our Holy Father shall know who his true servants are, all in good time.'

Faintly disappointed, the countess persevered more timidly.

'So what—?'

'We are not idle, Madame la comtesse. We are not idle, have no fear. And I am authorised to pass on to you a part of our plan of action.'

He settled himself comfortably in his armchair, facing the countess. She had raised her hands to her face, and now she sat, leaning forward, her elbows on her knees and her chin resting on her palms.

He told her that the pope was not locked up in the Vatican but probably in the Castel Sant'Angelo, which, as the countess obviously knew, was connected to the Vatican by an underground passage, and that it would doubtless not be too burdensome to release him from his incarceration, if it were not for the near-superstitious fear his retainers had of freemasonry in all forms, even though their hearts were with the Church. It was this that the Lodge was banking on: the knowledge that His Holiness was being held confined kept those unhappy souls terrorised. Not one of his retainers would offer assistance without being provided with the wherewithal to travel far away, beyond the persecutors' reach. Substantial sums had been granted for that purpose by a number of people who were both devout and of recognised discretion. Only one more obstacle remained to be removed, but it would require more effort than all the others put together. For the obstacle in question was a prince, Leo XIII's jailer-in-chief.

'Do you remember, Madame la comtesse, what mystery still shrouds the double death of Archduke Rudolf, Crown Prince of Austria-Hungary, and his young wife, found breathing her last beside him – Marie von Vetsera, niece of Princess Grazioli, whom he had just married? Suicide, so they said. But the gun was merely there to pull the wool over people's eyes: the truth is that they were both poisoned! A cousin of the archduke, himself an archduke, was so hopelessly in love with Marie von Vetsera that he could not bear to see her give herself to another ... After this abominable outrage, the said Archduke Johann Salvator, son of Maria-Antonietta, Grand Duchess of Tuscany, left the imperial court of Franz Joseph. Finding himself discovered in Vienna, he went to the Vatican to throw himself on the pope's mercy and sway him by a personal appeal. He was pardoned. But on the pretext of a necessity for penitence, Monaco – Cardinal Monaco La

Valletta – locked him in the Castel Sant'Angelo, where he has been languishing for three years.'

The canon had given this account in a more or less neutral tone of voice. He paused for a moment, then, tapping his foot to punctuate his words, he said, 'That is who Monaco has appointed jailer-in-chief of Leo XIII.'

'What? The cardinal?' the countess exclaimed. 'So can a cardinal be a freemason?'

'Unfortunately,' the canon said reflectively, 'the Lodge has infiltrated the Church widely. I'm sure you can see, Madame la comtesse, that if the Church had known how to defend itself better, none of this would have happened. The Lodge was only able to seize hold of our Holy Father with the connivance of a number of highly placed attendants.'

'But this is appalling!'

'What more can I tell you, Madame la comtesse? Johann Salvator believed himself to be a prisoner of the Church, when in fact he was in the hands of the freemasons. He refuses to work towards our Holy Father's liberation unless he is allowed to make his escape at the same time, and the only country he can escape to is a very distant one, from where no extradition is possible. He is demanding two hundred thousand francs.'

At these words Valentine de Saint-Prix, having sat back and lowered her hands a few moments earlier, threw back her head, uttered a weak groan and lost consciousness. The canon darted towards her.

'Do not despair, Madame la comtesse.' He patted her inert hands. 'Don't worry!' He waved the bottle of smelling salts under her nose. 'Of those two hundred thousand francs we already have a hundred and forty.' And as the countess opened one eye: 'The Duchess of Lectoure has promised a maximum of fifty. We need to find another sixty.'

'You shall have them,' the countess murmured almost inaudibly.

'Countess, the Church was right to believe in you.'

He stood up very gravely, almost ceremonially, and paused for a moment.

'Countess de Saint-Prix,' he said, 'I have the most unshakeable confidence in your generous words. But reflect upon the nameless difficulties that will accompany, hinder, perhaps obstruct the giving of this sum, a sum, as I have said to you, that you would have to forget that you had given me, that I myself must be ready to deny ever having received, for which it will not be possible for me to offer you a receipt ... Prudence dictates that the only way I can receive it is from your hand to mine. We are being watched. My presence at your château may be remarked. Are we ever certain of our servants? Think of the Count de Baraglioul's election! I can never come back here!'

He remained standing, rooted to the spot, neither stirring nor speaking, and the countess understood.

'But, Father, as you may well imagine, I certainly don't

have such an enormous sum immediately available. And even …'

The priest fidgeted impatiently, and she did not dare add that it would almost certainly take her some time to find it (for she hoped very much that she would not have to provide the whole sum from her own funds).

'What to do?' she murmured.

Then, as the canon's frown became darker: 'I do have a few pieces of jewellery upstairs …'

'Pooh, Madame! Jewels are mere keepsakes. Can you see me turning into a bric-a-brac merchant? And do you think I want to raise the alarm by going around asking for the best price? I should be risking compromising both you and our crusade.'

His deep voice was gradually changing, becoming harsh and violent. The countess's own voice quavered.

'Wait a moment, Canon. I'll see what I can find upstairs.'

She returned a few moments later. Her tense hand gripped some crumpled blue notes.

'Fortunately I've just had some rents. I can let you have six and a half thousand francs straight away.'

The canon gave a shrug.

'What do you expect me to do with that?'

And with a mixture of sadness and scorn, and a noble gesture of dismissal, he waved the countess away.

'No, Madame, no! I shan't take your notes. I shall only take them with the others. Upstanding people do not leave sums outstanding. When will you be in a position to hand over the whole sum?'

'How long can you let me have? ... A week?' the countess asked, thinking how she could pass the hat around.

'Countess de Saint-Prix, can it be that the Church has made an error? A week! I have only one thing to say to you. THE POPE IS WAITING.'

Then, raising his arms to the heavens, he said, 'What? You have the incalculable honour of holding his deliverance in your hands, and you are delaying? Be careful, Madame, that on the day of your own deliverance the Lord does not do the same to you and keep your insufficiently virtuous soul waiting, languishing on the threshold of paradise!'

He was threatening and terrible now. Abruptly he brought the crucifix of his rosary to his lips and and murmured a swift prayer.

'Then ... at least allow me the time to write to Paris?' the distraught countess pleaded.

'Send a telegraph! For your banker to transfer the sixty thousand francs to the Crédit Foncier at Paris, which will telegraph to the Crédit Foncier at Pau to pay you the amount forthwith. Child's play.'

'I have some money at Pau, on deposit,' she said timidly.

'At a bank?'

'At the same Crédit Foncier.'

His indignation knew no bounds.

'Ah, Madame, why must you send me all round the houses to find this out? Is this your idea of eagerness? What would you say now if I were to refuse your support …?'

Striding across the room, hands clasped behind his back and as though hostile henceforth to anything that he might hear, he added, 'There is more than half-heartedness going on here' – he made little clicks with his tongue to underline his disgust – 'there is something close to duplicity.'

'Father, I beg you …'

For several moments the priest continued to stride, his frown deep and unmoving. Finally he said, 'I am aware that you know Father Boudin, with whom I am lunching this very day' – he pulled out his watch – 'and whom I am about to be late for. Make out your cheque to him. He'll cash it and be able to pass the sum on to me immediately. When you next see him, just tell him it was "for the expiatory chapel". He's the soul of discretion and knows the ways of the world: he won't press you. So! What are you still waiting for?'

The countess, prostrate on the sofa, raised herself, moved mechanically to a small writing desk which she opened, and took out an oblong olive-green chequebook and filled out the top page in her straggling handwriting.

'Pardon me for having browbeaten you a touch just now, Madame la comtesse,' the priest said in a much softer voice, taking the cheque she held out to him. 'But so much is at stake!'

Slipping the cheque into an inside pocket, he added, 'It would be inappropriate to thank you, would it not? Even in the name of Him in whose hands I am no more than a most unworthy instrument.'

He gave a brief sob and stifled it in his big handkerchief. Recovering himself with a restless stamp of his heel, he muttered a rapid phrase in another language.

'Are you Italian?' the countess asked.

'Spanish! The depth of my feelings betrays me.'

'But not your accent. Truly, you speak such pure French …'

'You are too kind, Madame la comtesse. Forgive me if I leave you abruptly. Thanks to our combined plan, I shall be able to reach Narbonne this very evening, where the archbishop is waiting for me with profound impatience. Farewell!'

He had taken the countess's hands in his and, standing back, was looking fixedly at her.

'Farewell, Countess de Saint-Prix.' He put a finger to his lips. 'And remember, a word from you can bring everything down around our ears. Everything!'

No sooner had he left than the countess ran to her bell pull.

'Amélie, tell Pierre he is to have the carriage ready immediately after lunch, to go into town. Ah! And one more thing … Ask Germain to get on his bicycle and take this note that I'm about to give you to Madame Fleurissoire straight away.'

Bent over the writing desk, which she had not closed, she wrote,

Dear Madame

I'm coming to see you this afternoon. You can expect me around two o'clock. I have something of very grave importance to tell you. Can you arrange it so that we'll be alone?

She signed the letter, sealed the envelope and handed it to Amélie.

II

Madame Amédée Fleurissoire *née* Péterat, the younger sister of Véronique Armand-Dubois and Marguerite de Baraglioul, answered to the extravagant name of Arnica. Philibert Péterat, a botanist who had acquired a certain notoriety during the Second Empire as a result of his marital mishaps, had promised himself since childhood that he would give any children he might have the names of flowers. He was aware that some of his friends found Véronique, the name he baptised his first daughter, slightly peculiar, but when he heard it insinuated, after he had baptised his second Marguerite, that he was backing down, giving in to public opinion, rejoining the crowd, he resolved, so offended was he, to bestow upon his third-born a name so deliberately botanical it would shut up the gossips once and for all.

Shortly after Arnica's birth Philibert, his character having soured, separated from his wife, quit Paris and moved south to Pau. His wife would stay on in Paris for the winter, but with the first fine weather would travel south herself to Tarbes, where she had been born, and where she would look after the two older girls in the old family home.

Véronique and Marguerite got used to dividing their year between Tarbes and Pau. As for little Arnica, overlooked by her sisters and her mother, a little simple-minded it was true, and more pitiable than pretty, she stayed, summer and winter, with her father.

The little girl's greatest joy was to go botanising in the countryside with her father, but he, in his maniacal way, surrendering to his melancholy mood, would often leave her at home and go off alone on a lengthy hike, come back dead-tired and flop into bed as soon as the meal was over without gratifying his daughter with even a smile or a word. In his more poetic moments he played the flute, interminably repeating the same tunes. He spent the rest of his time drawing minutely detailed pictures of flowers.

An old servant nicknamed Réséda who looked after the cooking and cleaning took care of the child and taught her the little she knew, with the result that by the time she was ten years old Arnica could barely read. People's reactions finally brought Philibert to his senses. Arnica was sent to school at Madame Sémène's, a widow who drummed the basics into a dozen young girls and a few very small boys.

Arnica Péterat, trusting and defenceless, had never imagined that her name might cause amusement.[9] On her first day at school she experienced the shocking revelation of how ridiculous it sounded. Under the steady stream of jeers she bent like slow-moving aquatic weed. She blushed, went pale and wept, and Madame Sémène, in punishing the whole class together for unacceptable conduct, achieved the clumsy feat of injecting malice into an initially innocent joke.

Skinny, weedy-looking, anaemic and bewildered, Arnica stood, arms dangling at her sides, in the middle of the small classroom. When Madame Sémène pointed and said, 'Third bench on the left, Mademoiselle Péterat,' the class, ignoring their teacher's reprimands, erupted in sniggers again more loudly than before.

Poor Arnica! Life seemed to stretch out in front of her like a dismal avenue lined with mockery on one side and insults on the other. Fortunately Madame Sémène did not remain indifferent to her unhappiness, and she found a refuge in the widow's generous bosom. When classes were over she willingly stayed behind, rather than go home and find that her father had not returned yet. Madame Sémène had a daughter, a girl with a slight hunchback but a kind nature, who was seven years older than Arnica. In the hope of landing a husband for her, Madame Sémène held Sunday evening 'at homes' and twice a year organised small Sunday tea parties, complete with recitals and dancing. Some of her former pupils attended out of a sense of gratitude, chaperoned by their parents, and a few youths without money or prospects came because they had nothing better to do. Arnica was present at all these get-togethers, a flower without radiance and shy to the point of invisibility – yet destined not to remain entirely overlooked.

When she was fourteen Arnica lost her father. Madame

Sémène took her in. Her sisters, older than she was, no longer came to see her except on rare occasions. It was, however, in the course of one of these brief visits that Marguerite first met the man who was to become her husband two years later: Julius de Baraglioul, then twenty-eight years old and spending a holiday at the home of his grandfather Robert de Baraglioul, who, as aforementioned, had settled near Pau in the aftermath of the duchy of Parma's annexation by France.

Marguerite's glittering marriage (as it happens, the *demoiselles* Péterat were not entirely without fortune) made her sister even more remote in Arnica's overawed eyes. She thought it highly unlikely that any count, any Julius, would ever bend over her to breathe her perfume. Most of all she envied her sister for having succeeded in escaping the ill-starred name of Péterat. 'Marguerite' was a charming name. How much more charming it sounded with 'de Baraglioul'! Was there any name that 'Arnica' could be married to and not sound ridiculous?

Repelled by the material world, her muddled, undeveloped soul turned to poetry. At sixteen, dangling corkscrew-shaped ringlets framed her wan face and dreamy blue eyes stared in permanent surprise out of the black-and-white contrast of her hair and skin. Her colourless voice was not at all coarse. She read poetry and did her utmost to write it. Everything that helped her escape from real life was poetic in her eyes.

At Madame Sémène's *soirées* there were two young men

who always came together and seemed to be connected by an intimate friendship that had bound them since childhood: one slightly twisted and not very tall, not so much thin as scrawny, with hair that was more faded than blond, and with an impressive nose and a shy look. This was Amédée Fleurissoire. The other, who was fat and stubby, with thick black hair that grew low on his forehead, had a strange habit of carrying his head at a permanent angle, leaning towards his left shoulder, and walking around with his mouth open and right hand held out in front of him. I am describing Gaston Blafaphas. Amédée was the son of a monumental mason and businessman who supplied funerary sculptures and memorial wreaths. Gaston's father was a successful pharmacist.

(Bizarre though it may seem, the name of Blafaphas is widely distributed in the villages of the lower Pyrenees, though written in diverse ways. To take just one example, in the small town of Sta——, to which the writer of these lines was once summoned for the purpose of some legal business, he came across a Blaphaphas (a notary), a Blafafaz (hairdresser), a Blaphaface (*charcutier*), who, when he asked them, failed to acknowledge any common link between each other and looked down on the others' inelegant spelling of the name with scorn. But these philological asides will only be interesting to a relatively limited group of readers.)

What might Fleurissoire and Blafaphas have been

without one another? It is hard to imagine. At break times at their lycée they were always seen together: teased and tormented unmercifully, they consoled each other, helped each other to be patient, gave each other support. The other boys called them 'the Blafafoires'. To both of them their friendship seemed their one lifeline, their oasis in life's pitiless desert. Neither experienced a joy that he did not instantly want to share with the other. To put it another way, there were no joys for either of them, except what each shared with the other.

Being extremely average students, despite a mitigating diligence, and fundamentally averse to every sort of culture, the Blafafoires would have stayed at the bottom of their class permanently without the help of Eudoxe Lévichon, who, in return for a trickle of small fees, corrected and even did their homework for them. The Lévichon boy was the younger son of one of the town's main jewellers. (Twenty years earlier, soon after his marriage to the only daughter of another jeweller, a Monsieur Cohen – at the moment when, with his business taking off, he left the lower town to open new premises not far from the casino – this jeweller, Albert Lévy, had decided it would be a good idea to combine the two names as he had combined the two businesses.)

Blafaphas was a sturdy boy, but Fleurissoire's constitution was delicate. With the onset of puberty Gaston's features became swarthy and he looked as if the rising sap might make his whole body erupt in a new growth of hair, while Amédée's more sensitive epidermis resisted, became red and angry and burst out in pimples, as though the hair was determined to make the maximum fuss about sprouting. Blafaphas *père* recommended laxatives, and every Monday Gaston brought a flacon of antiscorbutic mixture to school in his briefcase, which he furtively handed to his friend. They also used ointments.

Around this time Amédée caught his first cold, a cold that, despite Pau's wholesome climate, he could not shake off all winter, and which left him with an annoying susceptibility to bronchial ailments. For Gaston it was an opportunity to offer his friend new treatments, and he showered him with liquorice, jujube lozenges, cough mixture, and eucalyptus throat pastilles made by Monsieur Blafaphas himself, according to the recipe of an elderly priest. Amédée, who was prone to catarrh, had to get used to never going out without a scarf.

Amédée had no other ambition than to follow in his father's footsteps. Gaston, however, despite his indolent exterior, did not lack initiative: since starting at the lycée he had thrown himself into all sorts of small inventions, most of them recreational: a fly trap, scales for marbles, a security lock for his desk (which held no more secrets than his heart did). Innocent as the first applications of his efforts were, they were to lead him into the more serious research that occupied him afterwards, the first outcome of which was the invention of a 'hygienic smoke-absorbent pipe for smokers with delicate chests and others', which stayed on show in the window of his father's pharmacy for a long time.

Amédée Fleurissoire and Gaston Blafaphas fell in love with Arnica simultaneously. It was bound to happen. What was most admirable about their blossoming passion – which both immediately confessed to the other – was that, far from dividing them, it joined them closer together than ever. And Arnica certainly did not, at least at the outset, give either one of them serious cause for jealousy. Neither of them, in any case, declared himself, and Arnica would never have guessed that both carried a candle for her, despite their quavering voices when they met her at one of Madame Sémène's Sunday *soirées* and she offered them cordial or verbena or camomile tea. And as they went home later that evening, both of them praised her modesty and grace, expressed concerns about her pallor and, emboldened, planned their next meeting with their beloved ...

They decided that they would both declare their love the same evening, together, and submit to her selection. Arnica's simple heart, new to love in every way and completely taken by surprise, thanked the heavens and begged her two suitors to allow her time to reflect.

To tell the truth, she did not favour one more than the other and was only interested in them because they were interested in her at a time when she had given up hope of ever interesting anybody. For six weeks, as she grew increasingly perplexed, she allowed herself to be more and more carried away by the compliments of her twin admirers. And as, during their night-time walks, mutually calculating each other's standing, the Blafafoires recounted at length to each other, entirely unabridged, the slightest words, looks, smiles that *she* had granted them, Arnica, alone in her bedroom, was writing on scraps of paper that she subsequently took great care to burn in the flame of her candle and repeating incessantly, one after the other, 'Arnica Blafaphas?' 'Arnica Fleurissoire?', paralysed by indecision at the atrociousness of both names.

Suddenly, one day when there was dancing at Madame Sémène's, she chose Fleurissoire. Hadn't Amédée just called her *Arníca*, putting an accent on the penultimate syllable of her name and making it sound Italian? (Inadvertently, as it happened, and probably as a result of Mademoiselle Sémène's piano-playing, supplying rhythm to the mood at that moment.) And the name *Arníca* – her name – seemed suddenly rich with an untapped music, as able to express poetry and love as any other name … The two of them were alone in a little side room next to the sitting room, and so close to each other that when a swooning Arnica bowed her head, heavy with gratitude, her forehead rested on Amédée's shoulder. With the utmost seriousness he took Arnica's hand and kissed the tips of her fingers.

When Amédée announced his happiness to his friend on their way home, Gaston, unusually for him, did not say anything, and as they walked past a streetlamp it looked to Fleurissoire as if his friend was crying. However excessive his naïvety was, could he really have imagined that his friend would share his happiness to this ultimate extent? Disconcerted and abashed, he hugged Blafaphas (the street was deserted) and swore to him that, great as his love was, their friendship far exceeded it, that he did not intend it to be diminished one iota by his marriage, and that rather than feel Blafaphas suffer from jealousy of any kind, he was ready to promise on his honour never to take advantage of his conjugal rights.

Neither Blafaphas nor Fleurissoire was made of particularly ardent stuff, but Gaston's masculinity was somewhat more to the forefront of his thoughts. He went on saying nothing and let his friend promise.

A short time after Amédée's wedding, Gaston, who had sought consolation by burying himself in work, discovered his 'Plastic plaster'. At first his invention seemed to offer no particular benefits, but it revived Eudoxe Lévichon's dormant friendship with the Blafafoires, for a good reason. Lévichon immediately foresaw the potential advantages to the religious statuary business of the new material which, with a remarkable feeling for future opportunities, he christened 'Roman plaster'. The company of Blafaphas, Fleurissoire & Lévichon was founded.

The business was set up with a declared capital of sixty thousand francs, of which the Blafafoires modestly contributed ten thousand between them. Lévichon generously supplied the remaining fifty, refusing to allow his two friends to burden themselves with debt. It is true that of the fifty thousand, forty were lent by Fleurissoire, drawn on Arnica's dowry, to be repaid in ten years at four and a half per cent compounded – which was more than Arnica had ever hoped for, and which secured Amédée's small fortune against the considerable risks that the new enterprise would inevitably face. The Blafafoires for their part brought the support of their family connections and those of the Baragliouls, which in turn – after their Roman plaster had been tried and tested – elicited the backing of numerous influential churchmen. These clergy, in addition to substantial orders of their own, persuaded numerous small parishes to turn to Blafaphas, Fleurissoire & Lévichon to cater to the growing needs of the faithful, whose increasingly sophisticated artistic knowledge demanded finer works than those that had until recently satisfied the homely faith of their forebears. To this end, a number of artists whose quality the Church had approved and who had been commissioned to work in Roman plaster finally saw their artworks accepted by the Salon's jury. Leaving the Blafafoires at Pau, Lévichon established himself in Paris, where, as he had a gift for making himself sociable, the company's activities soon expanded substantially.

What could have been more natural than Countess Valentine de Saint-Prix turning to Arnica to enlist the help of Blafaphas & Co. in the secret cause of the pope's rescue? Or her trusting in the Fleurissoires' great piety to make a contribution to the amount she had promised? Unhappily, because of the minimal sum invested by them at the outset of the undertaking, the Blafafoires' share of the profits was correspondingly small: two-twelfths of the official profits and none at all of the rest. The countess had no inkling of this, as Arnica, like her husband, was terribly reticent when it came to talking about money.

III

'Dear Madame! What's wrong? Your note frightened me.'

The countess toppled into the armchair that Arnica pushed towards her.

'Oh, Madame Fleurissoire … oh, please may I call you dear friend? … This awful thing, which touches you too, can only bring us together. Oh, if you only knew!'

'Say it! Say it! Don't leave me in suspense any longer.'

'I won't, but what I've just heard, and am about to tell you must remain a secret between us.'

'I have never betrayed a single confidence,' Arnica said dolefully (because no one had ever confided in her till now).

'You won't believe it.'

'I shall! I promise,' Arnica pleaded.

'Oh!' the countess groaned. 'Oh, would you be very kind and get me a cup of … anything … I can feel my energy draining away.'

'Would you like verbena? Lime tea? Camomile?'

'Anything … Tea is probably best … I refused to believe it, to begin with.'

'The kettle has just boiled in the kitchen. It won't take any time at all.'

As Arnica busied herself with tea, the countess's expert eye appraised her drawing room. It was dispiritingly plain. Some green rep-covered chairs, a red velvet armchair, another (which she was sitting on) in a vulgar tapestry pattern, a table, a mahogany console, a woollen rug in front of the fireplace, and on the mantelpiece, either side of an alabaster clock under a glass dome, two big vases in alabaster fretwork, also under domes. On the table was an album of family photographs and on the console a figure of Our Lady of Lourdes in her grotto, made of Roman plaster (miniature version). Everything in the room depressed the countess, and she felt her heart sink.

But no giving up yet: perhaps they were pretending to be poor, perhaps they were just stingy ...

Arnica returned with a teapot, a bowl of sugar and a single cup on a tray.

'I'm putting you to a lot of trouble.'

'Oh, it's no trouble at all! ... All I'll say is that I prefer to do it now. Later I may not have the strength.'

'Very well then,' Valentine began when Arnica had sat down. 'The pope—'

'No! Don't say it! Don't say it!' Madame Fleurissoire said, holding her hand up and, with a feeble wail, falling backwards, her eyes shut.

'My dear! My poor, dear friend!' the countess said, patting her wrist. 'I knew my secret would be too much for you to bear.'

Arnica eventually opened an eye and murmured sadly, 'So he's dead?'

Valentine, leaning towards her, hissed in her ear, 'Imprisoned!'

Amazement brought Madame Fleurissoire to her senses, and Valentine began her long account, stumbling over the dates and getting the sequence of events mixed up, and yet one fact remained, certain and indisputable: the Holy Father had fallen into the hands of infidels. A crusade was being secretly organised to rescue him, and in order to see it successfully through, what was needed above all was a great deal of money.

'What is Amédée going to say?' Arnica wailed, dismayed.

He was not expected back until the evening, having gone out for a walk with his friend Blafaphas …

'Whatever you do, make sure he knows he must keep the secret,' Valentine repeated several times as she said goodbye to Arnica. 'Kiss me, my dear, and be brave!' Arnica, getting muddled, offered the countess her damp forehead. 'Tomorrow I'll drop in to hear what you think you can do. Discuss it with Monsieur Fleurissoire. But remember that the Church is involved! … And remember what I said: only to your husband! You promise me. Not a word! Don't you? Not a word.'

The Countess de Saint-Prix left Arnica in a state of despondency bordering on inanimation. When Amédée came back from his walk she said to him almost mechanically, 'My dear, I have just heard some excessively sad news. Our poor Holy Father has been imprisoned.'

'Out of the question!' Amédée replied dismissively.

Arnica burst into noisy sobs.

'I knew it, I just knew you wouldn't believe me!'

'Come, come, darling,' Amédée went on, shrugging off the overcoat he insisted on wearing, rain or shine, for fear of the temperature suddenly dropping. 'Do think about it! Everyone would know if the Holy Father had really been abducted. We'd be reading about it in the papers ... Who could have locked him up?'

'Valentine says it's the Lodge.'

Amédée stared at her, thinking she might have gone mad. He said carefully, 'The Lodge ... What Lodge?'

'How do you expect me to know? Valentine promised not to speak about it.'

'And who told her all this?'

'She said I mustn't tell you ... A canon, who was sent by a cardinal, with his card ...'

Arnica did not understand anything about world affairs and had only remembered a muddled picture of what Madame de Saint-Prix had told her. The words 'captivity' and 'imprisonment' conjured up dark, semi-romantic images to her, and the mention of a 'crusade' was infinitely thrilling, so that when Amédée, at last stirred to a reaction, suddenly started to talk about setting out for Rome, she envisaged her husband in helmet and breastplate, saddled up … By now he was pacing back and forth across the room.

'First things first,' he said. 'We haven't got any money to give … And do you imagine that would be enough for me, to donate money? Do you think I could sleep easily because I'd done without a few banknotes? … My dearest, if what you tell me is true, then something utterly dreadful has happened, which will give us no rest until we act. Truly dreadful. Do you understand?'

'Yes, of course I do, truly dreadful … But will you try and explain to me … Why?'

'Oh Lord! Do I have to spell it out to you at this moment?' Amédée, perspiration beading at his temples, appealed with raised arms to heaven. 'No, no,' he went on, 'it's not money that's needed. We must give ourselves, body and soul. I'll go and consult Blafaphas. We'll see what he has to say.'

'Valentine de Saint-Prix made me promise not to talk to anyone about it,' Arnica ventured meekly.

'Blafaphas isn't anyone, and we'll emphasise that he absolutely has to keep it to himself.'

'How do you intend to go away without anyone knowing?'

'People will know that I'm going away, but they won't know where I'm going.'

Turning to her, in a dramatic voice he implored, 'Arnica, darling … let me go.'

She started sobbing again. Now she was the one insisting on Blafaphas's advice. Amédée was about to go and fetch him when he appeared, tapping on the drawing-room window to be let in, as he always did.

'That is the oddest story I have ever heard in my life,' he exclaimed, when they had told him everything they knew. 'No, but honestly! Who would ever have expected such a thing?' Abruptly, before Fleurissoire had mentioned his intentions, he added, 'Dear friend, there's only one thing for us to do – we have to go there.'

'You see,' Amédée said, 'it's his first thought too.'

'I unfortunately can't go, because of my poor father's ill health,' was his second.

'It doesn't matter. It will be better if I go on my own,' Amédée went on. 'We should be more noticeable if there were two of us.'

'But will you know what to do when you get there?'

Amédée drew himself up and raised his eyebrows, as if to say, I shall do my best, what do you expect!

Blafaphas continued, 'Will you know who to go and see? Where to go? ... In fact, what are you actually going to do there?'

'First, to find out what is going on.'

'Because, well, what if it turns out that none of this is true?'

'But that is precisely the point. I can't rest until I know for certain.'

To which Gaston immediately exclaimed, 'Neither can I!'

'Dearest, don't rush into anything,' Arnica objected mildly.

'I'm not rushing. I've thought it all through: I'll leave secretly …'

'When? You haven't got anything ready.'

'This evening. What is so important for me to take?'

'But you've never been anywhere. You won't know what to do.'

'You'll see, little one. I'll come back and tell you all my adventures,' he said, with an affectionate chuckle that made his Adam's apple bob up and down.

'You'll catch cold. You will.'

'I shall wear your scarf.'

He stopped pacing to lift up Arnica's chin with the tip of his index finger, the way adults do with babies when they want them to smile. Gaston maintained a reserved expression. Amédée went over to him.

'I'll rely on you to look up the trains. You can tell me when I can get a good train to Marseille, in third class. Yes, yes, I'm determined to travel third. Anyway, write down a detailed timetable for me, with all the places I'll need to change marked on it – and where I can get refreshments – as far as the frontier. After that I shall be well and truly on my way. I'll work things out, and God will guide me to Rome. Write to me there poste restante.'

The importance of his mission was perilously close to overheating his brain. After Gaston had left he continued to stride up and down the room. Basking in solemnity and warm gratitude, he kept murmuring to himself, 'That such a task should fall to me!'

He had discovered his mission in life at last. Oh, Madame, I entreat you, don't hold him back! There are so few beings on this earth who succeed in finding out what they are here for.

In the event, the only concession Arnica extracted from her husband was that he would stay and spend that night with her, Gaston having underlined the train that left at eight the following morning as the most practical on the timetable he brought round that evening.

Next morning the rain was pouring down. Amédée flatly refused to let Arnica or Gaston accompany him to the station. So no one gave a farewell glance to the comical-looking traveller with the protuberant eyes, a dark-red scarf wound around his neck, carrying in his right hand a grey canvas suitcase to which his visiting card was pinned, in his left an elderly umbrella, and on his arm a brown-and-green checked shawl, who was borne away on the train to Marseille.

IV

At about this time an important sociology conference called Count Julius de Baraglioul back to Rome. He was not invited in a professional capacity as such (having beliefs rather than qualifications where social policy was concerned), but he was delighted at the prospect of mixing with a number of eminent experts in the field. And as Milan was on the way – where, as we know, the Armand-Dubois had gone to live at Father Anselmo's suggestion – he decided to use the journey to spend a day or two with his brother-in-law.

On the same day that Fleurissoire left Pau, Julius rang Anthime's doorbell.

He was shown into a wretched three-room apartment – if you can count as a room the dark space under the roof where Véronique was boiling a few vegetables (their staple diet) for herself and Anthime. A hideous metal reflector cast a wan version of daylight through the window from a small courtyard outside. Julius, holding his hat rather than put it down on a dubious-looking waxed tablecloth that covered an oval table, and remaining standing because of his dislike of oilcloth upholstery, grasped Anthime's arm and exclaimed, 'You cannot stay here, my poor friend.'

'And why exactly do you feel sorry for me?' Anthime said.

At the sound of voices Véronique had come running.

'Dear Julius, would you believe that that's the only thing he can say in the face of all the so-called favours and abuses of trust that we have been victims of.'

'Who persuaded you to come to Milan?'

'Father Anselmo. In any case we couldn't keep the apartment in Via in Lucina.'

'What did we need it for?' Anthime said.

'That's hardly the point. Father Anselmo promised you compensation. Does he know the conditions you're living in?'

'He pretends not to,' Véronique said.

'You must complain to the Bishop of Tarbes.'

'That's what Anthime has done.'

'What did he say?'

'He's an excellent man. He vigorously encouraged me in my faith.'

'And haven't you appealed to anyone else since you moved here?'

'I narrowly missed seeing Cardinal Pazzi, who had shown some interest in me and to whom I'd recently written. And he did come to Milan, but he sent a message via his footman—'

'That he regretted that an attack of gout had confined him to his room,' Véronique finished.

'But this is disgraceful!' Julius exclaimed. 'Rampolla must be made aware of all this.'

'Made aware of what, my dear friend? It's quite true that I'm a little short at present, but what else do we really need? When I was well-off, I strayed, I was a sinner. I was ill. Now here I am, cured. Before, you had every reason to feel sorry for me. You know all of this anyway: worldly goods turn us away from God.'

'But look, those worldly goods are yours by right. I grant you that the Church is right to instruct us to scorn them, but not that it should deprive you of them.'

'Now you're talking,' Véronique said. 'I am so relieved to hear you say it, Julius. The way he accepts everything makes me seethe. I can't convince him to stand up for himself. He's allowed himself to be fleeced like a lamb and said thank you to everyone who's put their hand in his pockets, because they were doing it in the Lord's name.'

'Véronique, it grieves me to hear you speak like that. Everything we do in the Lord's name is well done.'

'If you enjoy being credulous ...'

'In "credulous" you'll find "credo", dear friend.'

At this Véronique turned to Julius.

'Will you listen to him? He's like that from morning to night. All he ever comes out with now are these ghastly homilies. And when I've been working my fingers to the bone, going to the market, cooking and cleaning, there is Monsieur, quoting his Gospels and telling me I'm doing far too much and should be considering the lilies of the field.'

'I help you as much as I can, dearest,' Anthime replied in a serene voice. 'I've suggested to you plenty of times that as I'm so light on my feet these days I can go to the market or do the cleaning for you.'

'That's hardly men's work. No, you get on with writing your sermons, and just try and make them pay a bit better.' Then in an increasingly irritable tone (she who had once been so smiling!) she added, 'It's a complete outrage! When you think what he used to be paid for those ungodly columns he wrote for *La Dépêche*. And now *Le Pèlerin* pay him chicken feed for his sermons and he still manages to give away three-quarters of it to the poor.'

'Then he's a genuine saint!' Julius exclaimed, appalled.

'And how he drives me mad with his saintliness! … Look: do you know what this is?' and she walked into one of the room's dark corners and came back with a wicker cage. 'These are two rats that Monsieur the scientist blinded a little while ago.'

'Good Lord, Véronique, why do you have to keep bringing that up? You yourself used to feed them when I was carrying out experiments on them … Yes, Julius, in my days of infamy I blinded these poor rodents out of vain scientific curiosity. Now I look after them. It's natural that I should.'

'I only wish the Church would find it equally natural

to do for you what you're doing for those rats, having blinded you in just the same way.'

'Did you say blinded? Is that really the Julius I used to know? Torn the scales from my eyes, my friend, the scales from my eyes.'

'I'm talking to you about reality. The state the Church has left you in is, to my mind, quite unacceptable. It made some commitments to you, and it must honour those commitments for the sake of its reputation and our faith.' Turning to Véronique, he said, 'If you have so far received nothing, you must appeal to a higher quarter, and then higher still if necessary. Did I say Rampolla? It's to the pope himself that I intend to appeal on your behalf, to the pope – who is fully aware of your conversion. A miscarriage of justice as serious as this must be taken to the top of the Church. I'm leaving for Rome tomorrow.'

'You'll stay and have dinner with us, won't you?' Véronique asked, rather nervously.

'Forgive me, my stomach is none too robust,' and Julius, whose nails were very well cared for, stared at Anthime's short, thick, blunt-ended fingers. 'On my way back from Rome I shall call in for longer, and then I shall also be able to tell you about the new book I'm working on, Anthime.'

'I've been rereading *The Air on the Heights* recently and I thought it was much better than it seemed at first reading.'

'I feel sorry for you. It's a failure. I'll explain why when you're in a fit state to hear me and to appreciate the curious preoccupations that fill my mind now. I've got too much to say. Not another word today.'

Urging the Armand-Dubois not to give up hope, he left them.

BOOK FOUR

THE MILLIPEDE

> 'And I can only think well of those
> who seek and, seeking, suffer.'
> Pascal, *Pensées* (Section VI, 421)

I

Amédée Fleurissoire had left Pau with five hundred francs in his pocket, which he felt ought certainly to be enough for his journey, despite the additional expenses the Lodge's wickedness would no doubt put him to. If by any chance the sum was not enough and he found himself forced to extend his stay for longer than he expected, he would turn to Blafaphas, who was keeping a small additional amount available in case he needed it.

Because no one at Pau was to know his final destination, he had first bought a ticket as far as Marseille. From Marseille to Rome a third-class ticket would only cost thirty-eight francs forty and would even give him the option of breaking his journey en route, which he decided he would definitely take advantage of, not because he was keen to satisfy his curiosity for foreign places (which had never been strong) but because of his need for sleep, which was extraordinarily insistent. Put it another way, there was nothing he feared more than insomnia, and since it was vital for the Church that he should arrive at Rome fighting fit, he decided to overlook the two days' delay and minor additional hotel expenses ... What did they amount to, compared to having to spend a night on a train, a sleepless night for sure and a particularly unhealthy one, bearing in mind the proximity of other travellers breathing all over him? And then if one of them decided to open a window to let in some fresh air, he would definitely catch a cold, there was no doubt about it ... So he would spend the first night at Marseille and a second night at Genoa, in one of those comfortable but not too smart hotels that are always to be found in the streets around stations, and arrive at Rome on the evening of the day after tomorrow.

In fact he was enjoying the prospect of the journey and of making it alone, at last. At the age of forty-seven he realised he had only ever lived under the supervision of others, being escorted everywhere either by his wife or by Blafaphas. Ensconced in the corner of his compartment, he smiled a goat-like smile, with the tips of his teeth showing, and wished himself an excellent adventure.

As far as Marseille everything went well. On the second morning he made a false start. Deeply engrossed in the copy of *Baedeker's Central Italy* that he had just bought, he got on the wrong train, heading for Lyon, and only noticed he was going backwards at Arles, as the train was pulling out. He had to stay on until Tarascon, then retrace his steps back to Marseille. There he caught an evening train that took him as far as Toulon, rather than spend another night at Marseille, where he had been bothered by bedbugs. Yet his room, with its view of the Canebière, had not looked unappealing, nor the bed either, and he had flung himself confidently down on it after folding his clothes, bringing his accounts up to date, and saying his prayers. He had been ready to drop and had fallen asleep instantly.

Bedbugs have very particular manners. As long as a candle remains lit, they will make no move. As soon as it is snuffed out and the room goes dark, they rush forward. Their destinations are by no means random. Most make straight for the neck, their favourite place, while some head for the wrists and the odd one prefers the ankles. It is not fully known why they inject into the sleeper's skin an oily, burning substance whose irritation is magnified by the slightest rubbing.

The itching that woke Fleurissoire was so intense that he relit his candle and hurried over to the mirror to examine a blotchy red area under his lower jaw that was dotted with indistinct small white spots. But the candle's light was weak, the mirror's silvering was tarnished, and his eyes were foggy with sleep ... He lay down again, still rubbing, snuffed out the candle, and relit it five minutes later as the burning sensation became intolerable. Leaping over to his washstand, he wetted his handkerchief in the water jug and pressed it onto the inflamed area which, apparently ever expanding, had now reached his collarbone. He thought he must be ill and started to pray, and when he had finished snuffed out the candle again. The respite offered by the cool compress was too short to allow our sufferer to go back to sleep, and to the atrocious itching there was added the discomfort of a soaking-wet nightshirt collar, which his tears were not helping. Suddenly he sat up in horror: bedbugs! They're bedbugs! ... He was amazed he had not thought of them earlier, but he only knew them by reputation, and how could he have associated the effect of a specific bite with this diffuse burning sensation? He bounded out of bed and lit his candle for the third time.

Having a theoretical and anxious temperament, he, like many people, had several false preconceptions about bedbugs, and, with an icy disgust, at first started to look for them on his body, found not a trace, thought he must be mistaken, and again felt he must have succumbed to some illness. There was nothing on the sheets either. But before he lay down again it occurred to him to lift up his bolster. There he saw three minuscule blackish lozenges, which swiftly vanished into a fold of the sheet. It was them!

Placing his candle on the bed, he moved in stealthily,

flattened the sheet and found five concealed there, which, partly out of disgust and partly because he did not dare squash them against his nail, he tipped into his chamber pot and peed on. He watched them struggle for a few moments, feeling satisfied and victorious, and relief crept over him. He lay back and snuffed out the light.

The itching almost immediately redoubled, on the back of his neck now. Exasperated, he relit the candle and this time took off his nightshirt to examine its collar. Eventually he made out some almost invisible bright-red dots running along the edge of the seam, which he crushed against the cotton, where they left tiny smears of blood: horrible beasts, they were so tiny he could hardly believe they were proper bedbugs. But once he had disposed of these, he lifted up his bolster again just in case and unearthed an enormous one, probably their mother. Encouraged and excited, almost enjoying himself, he took the bolster off the bed, untucked the sheets, and began to search methodically. By now he had begun to see bedbugs everywhere. In the end he only captured four, after which he lay down again and was able to enjoy an hour of peace.

After an hour, the burning sensation began again. He set out to hunt the culprits down once more and then, infuriated, gave up and told himself that in fact the itching calmed down fairly quickly as long as he didn't rub it. At dawn the last of the beasts, replete, left him alone. He was fast asleep when the boy came to wake him up for his train.

*

At Toulon it was fleas.

He must have picked them up on the train. All night he scratched himself, tossing and turning and robbed of sleep. He could feel them jumping along his legs, tickling the small of his back, injecting him with fever. Exuberant welts appeared on his sensitive skin wherever they bit him, which he made worse by scratching himself uncontrollably. He snuffed out and relit his candle many times, got out of bed, took off his nightshirt and put it back on without managing to kill a single one. He might glimpse one for an instant, but it would immediately leap from his grasp, and even if he managed to capture it, after he thought he had squashed it dead between his fingernails it would suddenly swell back to its normal size and spring away as safe and energetic as before. He found himself wishing he had bedbugs again. He became infuriated, and his frayed nerves and the maddening pointlessness of the hunt ended up ruining any chance of sleep.

All the following day his angry bites of the night before went on itching, while new tickling sensations indicated that he was still infested. The extreme heat increased his discomfort considerably. The carriage was crowded with workers who drank, smoked, spat, belched and passed around saveloy sausages that had such a strong smell Fleurissoire felt on more than one occasion that he was going to be sick. He did not, though, dare to leave the compartment before the train reached the border because he was afraid the workmen would see him get into another carriage and be offended. In the new compartment to which he eventually moved, a plump wet-nurse was changing her child's nappy. He tried to ignore her and go to sleep, but his hat kept getting in the way. It was one of those flat hats made of white straw with a black ribbon – what people call a boater. If he left it in its proper position, its stiff brim stopped his head from resting against the back of his seat, but if he raised it slightly so that he could lean back, the seat tipped it forward over his eyes, and if he pushed it backwards the brim became trapped between the seat and the back of his neck and the whole thing lifted off his forehead like a steam valve. He eventually decided to take it off altogether and cover his head with his scarf, leaving its ends dangling over his eyes to keep out the light. At least he had taken precautions for the coming night: that morning, at Toulon, he had bought a tin of insect powder, and tonight, however expensive it might be, he would not hesitate to book into one of Genoa's best hotels, because if he did not get a good night's sleep tonight, what sort of wretched physical state would he be in when he arrived at Rome, a prey to the first freemason to cross his path?

The omnibuses of Genoa's finest hotels were lined up outside the station. He went straight to one of the most luxurious-looking, refusing to allow himself to be intimidated by the disdain of the valet who took his cheap suitcase from him, insisting that it should not be placed on the carriage roof and demanding that it be left on the seat cushion next to him. In the hotel lobby the desk clerk put him at his ease by speaking to him in French, and he cast caution to the winds: not content with just asking for 'a very good room', he enquired about the cost of a number of rooms that were suggested to him and resolved that he would not find anything under twelve francs acceptable.

The room at seventeen francs which – after inspecting several – he finally settled on was spacious, clean and unpretentiously elegant. The bed stood out from the wall, a brass bed that was definitely uninhabited, to which his pyrethrin powder would have been an insult. The washstand was concealed in a sort of enormous cupboard. Two large windows opened onto a garden. Amédée, leaning out into the dusk, stared at the dark, indistinct masses of foliage for a long time, letting the balmy air soothe his fevered brow and put him in the mood for sleep. Above the bed a canopy of muslin fell gauzily over three sides of it, and at the front neat cords like the reefing lines of a sail lifted it up in a graceful swag. Fleurissoire recognised that this was what people called a mosquito net, an item he himself had always disdained to use.

After he had washed, he lay down delightedly in the cool sheets. He left one of the windows open, not wide open, naturally, for fear of catching a cold or conjunctivitis but pushed back just far enough for the night breezes not to blow over him directly. He brought his accounts up to date, said his prayers, and turned off the light. (The hotel had electric lighting that was switched off by turning a small electrical switch.)

He was just getting off to sleep when an all but inaudible humming reminded him of a precaution he had failed to take, that of not opening the window until he had switched the light off, because light attracted mosquitoes. He also remembered having read somewhere about the Lord deserving praise for having bestowed on that tiny creature a particular and very recognisable tune, intended to warn the sleeper that he was about to be stung. He arranged the muslin curtain so that it fell impenetrably all around him. How much better this is, after all, he thought as he was dozing off, than those little cones of pressed hay that Blafaphas's father sells, the ones with that bizarre name, 'Fidibus', that you light on a metal saucer and they give off a haze of narcotic smoke, but before the mosquitoes have succumbed they have half asphyxiated the sleeper too. Fidibus! What an odd name! Fidibus … He was just dropping off when a stinging sensation on the left side of his nose woke him. He rubbed it with his hand, and as he was rubbing the affected spot felt another sting on his wrist. He became aware of a mocking buzz somewhere near his ear ... Horrors! He had shut the enemy up with him, inside his sanctuary. He reached for the light switch and turned it on.

Yes, the mosquito was there, waiting high up inside the net. Amédée was slightly long-sighted and he could make out every detail. The insect was flimsy to the point of absurdity, resting on four silken legs with the final pair trailing behind it, slender and almost curly. How dare it? Amédée stood up on his bed. How could he crush it against billowing muslin? ... Too bad! He slapped the net with the flat of his hand, so hard and so sharply that he thought he had ripped it. The mosquito could not have survived. He looked for its corpse and could not find it, but he felt a sharp prick on his bare calf.

At this point he felt that the least he could do was protect as much of himself as possible, so he retreated under his sheets and stayed there for perhaps fifteen minutes, baffled and immobile, not daring to turn off the light. Eventually reassured by neither glimpsing nor hearing his adversary, he reached for the switch and the room was dark. The humming music started again.

He put an arm outside the sheet, keeping the hand close to his face. Each time he thought he felt a mosquito settle purposefully on his forehead or his cheek, he gave himself a vigorous slap. And each time immediately afterwards he heard the insect's whine start up all over again.

He finally had the idea of wrapping his scarf around

his head. This made it difficult for him to breathe properly and failed to stop him being stung on the chin.

At last the mosquito either retired (by now no doubt replete) or Amédée became so overcome by sleep that he could not hear it. He unwound his scarf and dozed fitfully, scratching himself as he slept. The next morning his nose, which was naturally aquiline, looked like the appendage of a drunkard. The sting on his calf had swollen to the size of a boil, and the one on his chin had acquired a volcanic appearance. The barber to whom he took himself for a shave before he left Genoa, in order to arrive in Rome looking reasonably respectable, was enjoined to be particularly careful in its vicinity.

II

At Rome, as Fleurissoire hesitated outside the station with his suitcase in his hand, so tired, disoriented and bewildered that he felt robbed of his powers of decision and it was all he could do to brush off the hotel porters touting for business, he was lucky enough to come across a *facchino* who spoke French. Baptistin was a young Marseillais, bright-eyed and still smooth-chinned. Recognising a compatriot, he offered to act as his guide and carry his suitcase.

Fleurissoire had spent a large part of the long journey with his nose in his Baedeker. Almost straight away a kind of instinct, a foreboding, an inner alarm diverted his pious concerns from the Vatican itself, concentrating them instead on the Castel Sant'Angelo, the former mausoleum of the Emperor Hadrian and renowned jail whose hidden dungeons had housed so many famous prisoners in the past and which was connected, so people said, to the Vatican by an underground passage.

He studied the map. 'That is where I need to find somewhere to stay,' he decided, pointing his forefinger at the Lungo Tevere Tor di Nona, facing the Castel Sant'Angelo on the other side of the river. And by a providential happenstance that was where Baptistin had intended to take him: not onto the Lungo Tevere itself, which is really only a roadway, but nearby, to Via dei Vecchiarelli ('of the little old men'), the third street past the Ponte Umberto leading down to the embankment. He knew a quiet house there – if you leant out of its third-floor windows you could just see the Mausoleum – where some very kind ladies spoke every language, and one in particular spoke French.

'If Monsieur is tired we might take a cab. It's a long way … Yes, the air's cooler this evening because it's been raining. A bit of a walk's good for you after a long journey … No, the suitcase isn't too heavy, I can easily carry it that far … In Rome for the first time! Is Monsieur from Toulouse by any chance? … No, from Pau. I should have recognised the accent.'

Chatting, they made their way along Via del Viminale, then Via Agostino Depretis, which joins the Viminale to the Pincio, and then onto the Via Nazionale to get to the Corso, after which, having crossed it, they dived into a labyrinth of nameless alleys. The suitcase was not so heavy that it prevented the *facchino* from setting an athletic pace, which Fleurissoire had some trouble keeping up with. He jogged at Baptistin's heels, dog-tired and dripping with perspiration.

'Here we are,' Baptistin announced, just as Fleurissoire was about to beg him to stop.

The street, or rather the alley, of the Vecchiarelli was narrow and dark, so dark that Fleurissoire hesitated to set foot in it. Baptistin, however, had already gone into the second house on the right, whose door opened only a few metres from the Lungo Tevere. At the same moment Fleurissoire saw a *bersagliere* emerge, and the smart uniform that he had already noticed at the frontier reassured him, because he had confidence in the army. He took a few steps more, and a woman appeared in the doorway who looked very much like the boarding house's landlady. She smiled pleasantly at him. She was wearing a black satin apron, bangles and a sky-blue taffeta choker, and her jet-black hair, piled high on top of her head, sat heavily on an enormous tortoiseshell comb.

'Your suitcase's been taken up to the third, love,' she said to Amédée, who was mildly taken aback to be addressed so familiarly and thought it must be an Italian custom, or perhaps an ignorance of spoken French.

'*Grazia!*' he said, smiling back at her. '*Grazia!*' This was 'thank you', the only Italian word he knew, and one he felt it was polite to give a feminine ending to, when thanking a lady.

He climbed the stairs, catching his breath at each landing and trying to revive his flagging spirits at the same time, because he was worn out and the uninviting stairwell was doing its best to discourage him. There were landings every ten steps, where the stairs paused, twisted and continued three times before reaching the next floor. From the first landing's ceiling, facing the front of the building, there hung a canary's cage that could be seen from the street. On the second landing a mangy cat was about to gulp down a hake skin that it had dragged there. On the third was the toilet, whose door was wide open, showing the cubicles and, next to each seat, a yellow-coloured earthenware holder in the shape of a top hat, from whose brim the handle of a small brush stuck out. Here Amédée hurried on up without stopping.

On the first floor a gasoline lamp smoked next to a big glazed door on which the word *Salone* was inscribed in frosted letters, but the room in question was dark. Through the glass Amédée could just make out a mirror in a gilded frame that hung on the wall facing him.

He was about to reach the sixth or seventh of these landings when another soldier, a gunner this time, who had just emerged from one of the second-floor rooms, bumped into him as he took the stairs two at a time and then stepped round him, laughing and muttering some Italian excuse, having grasped Fleurissoire to make sure he stayed upright, because Fleurissoire had a drunken look about him and was so tired he could hardly stand. Reassured by the first uniform, he was more troubled by the second.

These soldiers are going to make a lot of noise, he thought, it's lucky my bedroom is on the third. I prefer the idea of having them underneath me.

He had just left the second floor when a woman in a gaping dressing gown and with her hair undone came running towards him from the far end of the corridor. She called out to him.

'She thinks I must be someone else,' he said to himself, and hurried on up, averting his gaze so as not to embarrass her by having glimpsed her in a state of such undress.

On the third floor, completely out of breath, he found Baptistin. The boy was talking in Italian to a woman of indeterminate age who reminded him extraordinarily of Blafaphas's cook, in a slimmer version.

'Your suitcase is in number 16, third door. Be careful of the bucket in the corridor as you go past.'

'I put it outside because it was leaking,' the woman explained in French.

The door to number 16 was open. A candle on the table lit the room and threw a faint glow into the corridor, where, outside the door of number 15, a metal slop-bucket stood in the middle of a shining puddle of liquid on the tiles. Fleurissoire skirted it gingerly. A sharp smell emanated from it. His suitcase was visible on a chair. As soon as he walked into the room its stuffy atmosphere started to make him feel dizzy, and, throwing his umbrella, shawl and hat down on the bed, he flopped into an armchair. His forehead was running with perspiration and he thought he was about to pass out.

'This is Madame Carola, the one who speaks French,' Baptistin said.

They had both come into the room.

'Open the window a bit, will you,' Fleurissoire moaned, unable to get up.

'Oh! He's so hot,' Madame Carola said, dabbing his pale, sweating face with a little perfumed handkerchief that she plucked from her cleavage.

'Let's push him a bit nearer the window.'

Each taking one side of the armchair, they lifted Amédée, unresisting and semi-conscious, to where he could breathe in the varied stenches of the street instead of the corridor's stale reek. The cooler air brought him round. Fumbling in his waistcoat pocket, he pulled out the rolled-up five-*lire* note he had got ready for Baptistin.

'I'm very grateful to you. You can leave me now.'

The *facchino* left.

'You shouldn't have given him that much, love,' Carola said.

Amédée thought it must be an Italian custom to be so familiar. All he wanted to do at that moment was go to sleep, but Carola did not seem at all anxious to leave, and so, politeness getting the better of him, he started a conversation.

'You speak French as well as a French person.'

'That's not surprising, I come from Paris. What about you?'

'I'm from the south.'

'I guessed that. As soon as I saw you I said to myself: That gentleman must be from the provinces. Is it your first time in Italy?'

'My first.'

'You're here on business.'

'Yes.'

'It's a gorgeous city, Rome. Lots to see.'

'Yes … Though tonight I'm a bit tired, if you don't mind,' he said, adding by way of explanation, 'I've been travelling for three days.'

'That's a long time to get here.'

'And I haven't slept for three nights.'

At these words Madame Carola, with that sudden Italian familiarity that Amédée still could not help being startled by, pinched his chin.

'You scallywag!'

Her reaction brought some blood back to Amédée's cheeks. Anxious to rebut the unwelcome insinuation immediately, he began to talk at length about bedbugs, fleas and mosquitoes.

'You won't get any of that here. You can see for yourself how clean it is.'

'Yes. I hope I shall sleep very well.'

She still did not leave. He levered himself awkwardly out of the armchair and started to undo the top buttons of his waistcoat, saying hesitantly, 'I think I'll go to bed now.'

Madame Carola realised his embarrassment.

'You want me to leave you alone for a bit, I can see,' she said tactfully.

As soon as she had left the room Fleurissoire turned the key in the lock, pulled his nightshirt out of his suitcase and got into bed. But evidently the lock's bolt had not gone home, because he had not snuffed out his candle before Carola's face reappeared around the half-open door, behind the bed, close to the bed, smiling …

An hour later, when he came to again, Carola was lying beside him, in his arms, completely naked.

He extracted his left arm, which was beginning to go numb, from underneath her and pulled away. She was asleep. A feeble glow from the street below filled the room, and Carola's regular breathing was the only sound. After a moment, feeling an unfamiliar sensation of languor that had spread all the way through his body and into his soul, Amédée Fleurissoire swung his thin legs out of bed and, sitting on the edge of the mattress, wept.

As his sweat had done an hour or two before, his tears bathed his face and mingled with the grime of the railway carriage. They flowed without a sound and without stopping, in a slow stream from deep down inside, as though from a hidden spring. He thought about Arnica and Blafaphas. If they could see him now … Never again would he dare take his place at their side. Then he thought about his honourable mission, for ever compromised. Half to himself he wailed, 'It's all over! I'm not worthy any more … It's all over, finished!'

The strange sound of his sobbing and wailing woke Carola up. By this time he was on his knees at the foot of the bed, hammering on his frail chest with little blows of his fists, and Carola, amazed at what she saw, heard his teeth chattering and him repeating between sobs, 'Every man for himself! The Church is collapsing …'

Eventually, unable to restrain herself, she said, 'What's got into you, lovey? Have you lost your marbles?'

He turned to her.

'I beg you, Madame Carola, please go away … I absolutely must be left alone. I'll see you in the morning.'

Then as, after all, he did not blame anyone except himself, he kissed her softly on the shoulder.

'What we did, what we've done here, you can't have any idea how awful it is. No, no, you can't! You can't ever have any idea.'

III

Under the pompous title of the 'Crusade for the Pope's Deliverance' the web of fraud spread its dark ramifications across one French *département*, then another. Protos, the bogus canon of Virmontal, was not its only perpetrator, any more than the Countess de Saint-Prix was its only victim. And not all of the victims collaborated as readily, just as not all the perpetrators displayed equal skill. Even Protos, Lafcadio's old friend, had had to watch his step after his latest operation: he lived in continual apprehension that the clergy – the real clergy – would find out about the affair, and he expended as much ingenuity in covering his tracks as he did in pushing ahead with new projects. But he was resourceful and had admirable backup: throughout its ranks, the fraudsters' band (which was known by the name of 'the Millipede') was characterised by an impressive unanimity and discipline.

Warned by Baptistin of the stranger's arrival the same evening, and moderately alarmed to find out that he came from Pau, Protos hurried to find Carola at seven the next morning. She was still asleep.

The information he was able to glean from her, her confused account of the night's events and of the anguish of the 'pilgrim' (her nickname for Amédée), his protestations and tears, left Protos in no doubt. His preaching at Pau had definitely borne fruit, though not the kind of fruit he would have wished. They would all have to keep an eye on this naïve crusader, who in his blunderings might nevertheless stumble across the whole thing …

'All right! Let me get past,' he told her curtly.

The demand might have sounded bizarre, since Carola was still in bed, but Protos and the bizarre were no strangers to each other. He planted one knee on the mattress, lifted the other over Carola and twisted so nimbly that, with a quick nudge of the bed, he had inserted himself into the gap between it and the wall.

Carola was clearly well used to the manoeuvre, because she merely asked, 'What are you going to do?'

'Change into a priest,' Protos answered just as casually.

'Are you coming back out this way?'

Protos hesitated for a moment.

'You're right. It's more natural.'

As he said it, he bent down and activated a secret door hidden in the retaining wall and so low that the bed hid it completely. As he was about to go through the door, Carola caught hold of his shoulder.

'Listen,' she said urgently, seriously, 'I won't have you hurting this one.'

'Didn't I tell you I'm going to change into a priest?'

When he had disappeared Carola got out of bed and started to dress.

I don't really know what to think about Carola

Venitequa. The urgency of her last words makes me feel that perhaps her heart was not so deeply debauched as all that. Thus, sometimes, in the very midst of degradation, a curious emotional delicacy can come to light, in the same way a bright-blue flower can bloom on top of a dung heap. Essentially submissive and devoted, Carola, in common with many other women, needed a manager. Deserted by Lafcadio, she had instantly gone to look for her first lover, Protos – out of defiance, disappointment, a thirst for revenge. She had been through hard times in the course of her search – and Protos had no sooner taken up with her again than he had made her his creature once more. Because Protos liked to be in charge.

Another man might have raised Carola to a new level in life, rehabilitated her. The key thing was the will to do it. It seemed, however, that Protos had taken it as his mission to degrade her. We have witnessed the shameful services the gangster demanded from her – and to be honest it did not seem to take very much persuasion for her to comply with his demands – but when a soul rebels against the ignominy of its destiny, it often happens that its first tremors of revolt go unnoticed, even by itself, and that only with the blessing of love does the secret mutiny declare itself. Had Carola fallen for Amédée? It would be rash to claim that she had, but, debauched as she was, she had been moved by the touch of his purity, and the entreaty I have reported undoubtedly came straight from her heart.

Protos re-emerged. He was wearing what he had been wearing before. He held a pile of old clothes, which he dropped on a chair.

'Now what?' Carola said.

'I've been thinking. First of all I need to go to the post office and look at his letters. I don't need to be a priest till lunchtime. Pass me your mirror.'

He went over to the window and, bending over his reflection, applied a pair of brown moustaches, no longer than his lip and barely a shade lighter than his own hair.

'Call Baptistin.'

Carola had finished getting ready. She pulled a cord that hung by the door.

'I've told you before that I don't want to see you wearing those cufflinks again. They make people notice you.'

'You know who they were a present from.'

'Another reason not to wear them.'

'You wouldn't be jealous, would you?'

'Don't be a silly cow!'

Baptistin knocked on the door and came in.

'Now you try and take yourself up in the world a notch,' Protos said to him, pointing to the chair where the jacket, shirt and tie that he had brought with him from the other side of the secret door lay. 'You need to escort your customer around the city. I shan't relieve you of him until later in the day. Between now and then you mustn't lose sight of him.'

*

It was to San Luigi dei Francesi that Amédée went to confess his sins, not St Peter's, whose vastness he found crushing. Baptistin was his guide. Afterwards he led him to the post office. As might be expected, the Millipede had accomplices there too. The visiting card pinned to the canvas of Fleurissoire's suitcase had provided Baptistin with his name, which he had supplied to Protos, who had had no difficulty in getting a helpful employee to pass him a letter from Arnica, and no scruples about reading it.

'How very odd!' Fleurissoire exclaimed when he himself came to collect his post an hour later. 'Very odd! You'd think someone had opened this envelope.'

'Happens all the time here,' Baptistin said impassively.

Fortunately Arnica was prudent and had confined herself to very discreet references. In any case the letter was very short: she simply recommended Amédée, on the advice of Father Mure, to go and see Cardinal San Felice S.B. at Naples 'before trying to do anything yourself'. It would be hard to imagine vaguer, and thus less compromising, instructions.

Outside the Mausoleum of Hadrian, known as the Castel Sant'Angelo, Fleurissoire suffered bitter disappointment. The building's enormous mass rose from the centre of an inner courtyard, which was closed to the public and only accessible to visitors who had an official pass. It was a condition of entry that they were also accompanied by a member of the castle staff …

Needless to say, the excessive security measures confirmed Amédée's suspicions, but at the same time they enabled him to reflect on the extravagant difficulty of the task he had set himself. Having finally got rid of Baptistin, he wandered along the embankment, almost deserted at the end of the day, in the shadow of the outer wall that defended the approach to the castle. Outside the drawbridge at the entrance he walked up and down, feeling gloomy and dispirited, then turned away towards the bank of the Tiber and attempted to get a slightly better view from there over the top of the outermost wall.

He had not paid any attention until that moment to a priest (there are so many in Rome!) who sat on a bench not far from him and who, although apparently immersed in his breviary, had been watching him for some time.

This worthy man of the cloth had a long, flowing mass of silver hair, and his fresh, youthful complexion, the sure sign of a wholesome existence, contrasted oddly with that accompaniment of old age. From his face alone it was clear that he was a priest and, from some elusive quality of respectability that emanated from him, French.

As Fleurissoire was about to pass him for the third time, he abruptly got to his feet, came towards him and, in a voice that was filled with suppressed emotion, said, 'Can it be true? I'm not alone! Do you mean to say you're looking for him too?'

As he said it, he hid his face in his hands, and his sobs, held back for too long, erupted noisily. Quickly getting a grip on himself, he exclaimed, 'Rash, rash man that I am! Hide your tears! Stifle your sighs! …' Seizing Amédée by the arm: 'Let's not stay here, Monsieur, we are being watched. Already the emotion I was unable to hide has been noticed.'

Amédée followed him in dazed astonishment.

'But how,' he at last managed to say, 'how did you guess my reason for being here?'

'May the heavens have allowed only me to suspect it! But your anxiety, the gloomy looks you were giving this place – could they go unnoticed by someone who has been haunting it day and night for the past three weeks? Alas, Monsieur, as soon as I saw you, I don't know what premonition, what portent from on high allowed me to recognise as kin to mine your ... Careful! Someone's coming. For the love of God, pretend to be completely casual ...'

A grocery porter was coming along the embankment towards them. Immediately, without changing his tone of voice and as if seeming to continue a sentence, but at a slightly livelier tempo, the priest went on, 'So that's why these Virginia cigars, so appreciated by some smokers, will only light with a candle flame after you've pulled out the fine length of straw that runs through them and which leaves behind a narrow airway that allows the smoke to draw freely. A Virginia that doesn't draw properly is only fit to be thrown away. I can tell you, Monsieur, I've seen choosy smokers light up to half a dozen before they find one to their liking ...'

And as soon as the man had gone past he said, 'Did you see how he looked at us? We absolutely had to trick him into thinking we were ordinary visitors.'

'What?' Fleurissoire exclaimed, stunned. 'Are you saying that even that common-or-garden grocer's boy is one of the people we have to stand up to?'

'Monsieur, I am not in a position to prove it, but I presume so. The vicinity of the castle is particularly closely watched. Officers of a special police force patrol it continuously. So as not to arouse suspicion, they put on the most varied disguises. These people are so clever, so clever! And we are so gullible, so naturally trusting!

What if I were to tell you, Monsieur, that I very nearly jeopardised everything by not suspecting an ordinary *facchino* to whom I gave my modest bags to carry as far as my lodging house, the evening I arrived in Rome! He spoke French, and even though I've spoken Italian fluently since I was a child … You'll no doubt have felt the same emotion yourself, which I was unable to fight against, to hear my own mother tongue spoken on foreign soil … So this *facchino* …'

'He was one of them?'

'He was one of them. I was more or less able to prove it to my satisfaction. Fortunately I had not said more than a few words to him.'

'You fill me with consternation,' Fleurissoire said. 'The evening I arrived, which is to say yesterday evening, I myself fell into the hands of a guide to whom I entrusted my suitcase and who also spoke French.'

'Heavens above!' the priest said in a tone of dread. 'He wasn't by any chance called Baptistin, was he?'

'Baptistin: yes, that was him!' Amédée wailed, feeling his knees turning to jelly.

'You unhappy man! What did you tell him?'

The priest squeezed his arm.

'Nothing that I can remember.'

'Think! Think hard! Try to remember, in heaven's name!'

'No, honestly,' Amédée stuttered, terrified. 'I can't think that I told him anything.'

'What might you have let slip?'

'Nothing, honestly, I assure you. But you do very well to put me on my guard.'

'Which hotel did he take you to?'

'I'm not at a hotel. I've taken lodgings.'

'Never mind. But where did you end up, as it happens?'

'In a little street you certainly won't know,' Fleurissoire stammered, deeply embarrassed. 'It's not important. I shan't be staying there.'

'Take great care. If you leave in a rush, you'll only draw attention to yourself.'

'Yes, perhaps you're right: it'll be better if I don't leave straight away.'

'But how I thank the heavens that brought you to Rome today! A day later and I should have missed you! Tomorrow, no later than tomorrow, I have to be in Naples to see a saintly and important figure who is secretly working for our cause.'

'It wouldn't be Cardinal San Felice, by any chance?' Fleurissoire asked, quivering with emotion.

The astonished priest took two steps backwards.

'How do you know?'

Then, coming closer: 'But why should I be surprised? He's the only person in Naples with the will to grapple with our secret.'

'Do you ... know him well?'

'Do I know him? My dear Monsieur, it is to him that I

owe … Never mind. Were you thinking of going to see him?'

'Of course, if I must.'

'He is the best man …' With an impatient gesture he dried the corner of his eye. 'Naturally you know where to go and find him?'

'I suppose anyone in Naples will be able to tell me. Everyone must know him.'

'Of course! But it goes without saying, I hope, that you don't intend to tell the whole of Naples whom you have come to visit? And I don't imagine either that you have been instructed about his part in … the matter we both know about, and perhaps entrusted with some message for him, without having been briefed at the same time on how to approach him.'

'I'm sorry,' Fleurissoire began timidly, because Arnica had not sent him any such instructions.

'What? Do you mean that you intended to go and find him just like that? Just turn up at the archbishop's palace, perhaps?' The priest started to laugh. 'And then bare your soul to him without further ado?'

'I confess that—'

'But do you understand, Monsieur,' the priest went on in a sterner tone, 'do you understand that you would risk getting him imprisoned too?'

He was becoming so visibly annoyed that Fleurissoire did not dare answer.

'So vital a cause, entrusted to such amateurs!' Protos muttered, pulling one end of a rosary out of his pocket, thinking better of it, crossing himself nervously, and then turning back to his companion.

'May I ask you, Monsieur, who asked you to meddle in this affair? Whose bidding exactly are you doing?'

'Forgive me, Father,' Fleurissoire said in confusion, 'I am doing no one's bidding. I am just a poor soul in a state of anxiety, seeking on my own account.'

His humble words seemed to disarm the priest, who extended his hand to Fleurissoire.

'I spoke harshly to you ... but it is because such dangers surround us.' Then, after a momentary hesitation: 'Look, why don't you and I go together tomorrow?' Raising his eyes heavenwards: 'Yes, I dare call him my friend,' he went on, in a voice that rang with emotion. 'Let's stop and sit on this bench. I'll write a note that we will both sign, and which will warn him that we are on our way. If we post it before six (eighteen hours, as they say here) he will have it tomorrow morning and be waiting to receive us around midday. Knowing him, we shall even be able to lunch with him.'

They sat down. Protos pulled a notebook out of his pocket and, as Amédée watched him, wild-eyed, on a blank sheet wrote: '*How are you, you old bugger ...*'

Enjoying the shocked expression on his new acquaintance's face, he smiled calmly.

'I suppose you'd have written to the cardinal himself, if we had left you to your own devices?'

And, in a more relaxed tone, he set about explaining the situation to Amédée. Once a week Cardinal San Felice left the archbishop's palace by the back door, as it were, dressed as a simple priest, a humble chaplain by the name of Bardolotti, and set out for the slopes of Mount Vomero where, in an unremarkable villa, he entertained a few very close friends and received the secret letters that those in the know sent him under his false name. Even in such a plebeian disguise he could not feel secure: he was never certain that letters sent in the post were not opened and so begged his correspondents not to make any specific references or to allow any whiff of his eminence, any trace of respect, however small it might be, to be expressed.

Now that Amédée was in the know, it was his turn to smile.

'*You old bugger* ... Let's think! What indeed are we going to say to the dear old bugger?' the priest joked, his pencil poised in hesitation. 'I know! *I've got a real joker for you.* (Yes, yes! Leave it: I know the tone we need.) *Dig out a couple of bottles of Falernian and we'll glug them with you tomorrow. It'll be a laugh.* Here, you sign it too.'

'Perhaps it would be better if I didn't sign my real name?'

'Oh, yours doesn't need disguising,' Protos said, writing next to the name of Amédée Fleurissoire the word 'Cave'.

'Oh! Very clever!'

'What do you mean? Are you surprised to see me sign that name? All you can think of are the Vatican *caves*, the ones under Sant'Angelo. Well, know this, my good Monsieur Fleurissoire: *Cave* is a Latin word that also means BEWARE!'

This speech was delivered in such a superior and peculiar tone of voice that poor Amédée felt a shiver run down his spine. It only lasted a second. Father Cave had already resumed his previously affable tone and, holding out to Fleurissoire the envelope on which he had just written down the cardinal's apocryphal address, he said, 'Would you mind posting it yourself? It will be more prudent: letters written by priests get opened. And now we should go our separate ways: we mustn't be seen spending any more time together. Let's arrange to meet tomorrow morning, on the 7.30 train for Naples. Third class, obviously. I shall naturally not be wearing my cassock (the idea!). You will see just a simple Calabrian farm labourer. (Because of my hair, which I don't want to be forced to cut.) Farewell! Farewell!'

He strode away, giving little waves of his hand.

'The heavens be blessed for leading me to that excellent father!' Fleurissoire murmured, making his way back to his lodgings. 'What should I have done without him?'

And Protos muttered too as he walked off, 'Oh yes, you'll get your cardinal, in spades! ... The thing is that, left to his own devices, he was perfectly capable of going and finding *the real one*!'

V

After he complained to her of extreme tiredness, Carola let Fleurissoire sleep that night in spite of the interest he had stirred in her and the heart-melting tenderness she had felt when he had admitted his almost total lack of experience in matters of love – sleep, that is, as much as the unbearable itching he was suffering from so many bites all over his body – flea bites and mosquito bites – would let him.

'You *mustn't* scratch like that, lovey!' she told him next morning. 'You'll only make them worse. Look how inflamed that one is!' and she touched the pimple on his chin.

As he was getting ready to leave, she said, 'Here! Keep these to remind you of me,' and fastened onto her 'pilgrim's' cuffs the whimsical agate cufflinks that Lafcadio had given her and Protos had objected to.

Amédée promised to be back that evening, or the following morning at the latest.

'You swear to me that he won't come to any harm?' Carola repeated a moment later to Protos, who, already dressed, had arrived through the secret door. Having made himself late by waiting until Fleurissoire had already left before he appeared, he had to hail a cab and have himself driven to the station.

In his new disguise, wearing a jerkin, brown breeches and sandals laced over the top of blue socks, with his short pipe in his mouth and his weathered hat with its narrow, flat brim, he unquestionably looked almost nothing like a priest and much more the perfect outlaw from Abruzzi. Fleurissoire, pacing up and down on the station platform, took a moment to recognise him when he saw him arrive, a finger on his lips like St Peter Martyr, and then pass him without showing any sign that he had seen him and vanish into a carriage at the front of the train. But a moment later he reappeared at the door and, looking in Amédée's direction and half closing one eye, he surreptitiously waved to him to make his way over.

As Amédée was about to board the train, he whispered to him, 'Be so kind as to make sure that there's no one next door.'

There was no one, and their compartment was the last one in the carriage.

'I was following you at a distance,' Protos said. 'I didn't want to come any nearer for fear that we might be noticed together.'

'How did I not manage to see you?' Fleurissoire said. 'I looked behind me dozens of times to make sure that I wasn't being followed. Your conversation yesterday threw me into such a state of alarm! I see spies everywhere.'

'So it seems, all too clearly. Do you think it's natural to turn round every twenty paces?'

'What? Do you mean to say I look—'

'Suspicious. Sadly, yes. Let's spell it out: suspicious. The most compromising look there is.'

'And even then I couldn't spot that you were following me! ... On the other hand, since we talked, every passer-by I meet has something shifty about their appearance. I get anxious when they look at me, and I become convinced that the ones who don't look at me are pretending not to see me. I hadn't realised until today how rarely people's presence on the streets can be justified. There can't be more than four in every dozen whose occupation is obvious. You have made me think seriously about the world around me, I must say! You know, for a soul as naturally trusting as mine used to be, suspicion does not come easily. This is an apprenticeship for me ...'

'Hah! You'll get used to it in no time. You'll see how it becomes a habit after a while. Sadly it's one I have been forced to acquire ... The most important thing is to maintain a cheerful exterior. Now, a word of advice: if you're worried that you may be followed, don't turn round. Just drop your stick or your umbrella, depending on the weather, on the ground – or your handkerchief – and as you pick it up, with your head down, look between your legs at what's happening behind you, in a natural way. I suggest you practise that. But tell me, how do you think I look in this outfit? I'm worried that the priest may be showing through here and there.'

'You've no need to worry,' Fleurissoire said honestly. 'No one apart from me, I'm certain, would recognise you for what you are.' Studying him sympathetically, his head slightly to one side, he added, 'Obviously I can see through your disguise, when I look carefully, to something elusive beneath it that marks you as a man of the cloth, and behind the joviality of your tone there is the anguish that torments us both, but what wonderful self-control you must have to let so little of it show! As for me, I've got a long way to go, I can see. Your advice—'

'What odd cufflinks you're wearing,' Protos interrupted, amused to see Carola's present from Lafcadio on Fleurissoire's wrists.

'They were a gift,' Fleurissoire said, reddening.

The day was sweltering. Protos glanced out of the window.

'Monte Cassino,' he said. 'Do you see the famous monastery up there?'

'Yes, I see it,' Fleurissoire said distractedly.

'I see you're not very sensitive to landscapes.'

'I am, I am,' Fleurissoire protested, 'I am sensitive. But how do you expect me to take an interest in landscapes, so long as my anxieties are still with me? It was the same in Rome with all the sights. I didn't see a thing – I couldn't bring myself to look at anything.'

'How I understand you!' Protos said. 'It's been like that for me. I told you, while I've been in Rome I've spent all my time shuttling back and forth between the Vatican and the Castel Sant'Angelo.'

'That's a pity. But at least you knew Rome already.'

Our travellers continued to chat in this vein. At Caserta they got off the train and each went separately to buy some cold meat and something to drink.

'We'll do the same in Naples,' Protos said. 'When we get close to the cardinal's villa we'll split up, if you don't mind. You'll follow me at a distance, and as I shall need a little time, especially if he is not alone, to explain who you are and the object of your visit, you'll give me a fifteen-minute head start before you knock at the door.'

'I'll make use of the time to have a shave. I was in too much of a rush this morning.'

A tram took them as far as Piazza Dante.

'Here is where we'll separate,' Protos said. 'It's still some distance to the cardinal's, but it will be better if we start now. Walk fifty paces behind me, and don't watch me the whole time as if you were afraid of losing me. And don't turn round either: you'll only get yourself followed. Look cheerful.'

He walked on ahead. Fleurissoire followed with a half-lowered gaze. The narrow street sloped steeply upwards, and the sun blazed down. People sweated and were jostled by an ebullient crowd that bawled, gesticulated and sang, leaving Fleurissoire dazed and bewildered. Half-naked children danced around a barrel piano. A street barker had improvised a raffle for a tremendous plucked turkey on the spur of the moment, two *centesimi* a ticket, and he was hoisting it above the crowd. To add authenticity, Protos bought a ticket and vanished into the crowd. Prevented from moving forward, Fleurissoire thought for a moment that he had lost him for good, then saw him again, having made his way through the throng, skipping up the hill with the turkey under his arm.

Gradually the houses became more spaced out and lower, there were fewer people, and Protos slowed his pace. He stopped outside a barber's window and, turning back to Fleurissoire, winked at him, then, twenty steps further on, stopping again in front of a small, low door, he rang the bell.

The barber's shop front was not particularly attractive, but Father Cave had no doubt had his reasons for indicating it. For one thing, Fleurissoire would have had to retrace his steps some way to find another, which would probably turn out to be just as unappealing as this one. The door had been left open because of the sweltering heat. A coarse-weave cotton curtain kept the flies out and let air in. You had to lift it to enter, so he lifted it and went in.

The barber was certainly an expert at his work: having soaped Amédée's chin, with the corner of a towel he carefully wiped the lather off the angry pimple his apprehensive customer had pointed out to him and exposed it to the light. What blessed drowsiness! What a delicious warm feeling of drifting away in this quiet little shop! Head back, almost horizontal in the barber's leather chair, Amédée let himself go. Oh, to forget, even if it was just for a short while! Not to have to think about the pope, mosquitoes, Carola! To imagine himself back at Pau, next to Arnica, to imagine himself elsewhere, no longer to know exactly where he was … He closed his eyes, then, half reopening them, glimpsed, as if in a dream, on the wall opposite him a woman with her flowing hair emerging from the Bay of Naples and bearing from beneath its waves, together with a voluptuous sensation of coolness, a sparkling bottle of hair restorer. Below this poster were other bottles standing on a marble shelf next to a cosmetic stick, a powder puff, tweezers, a comb, a lancet, a pot of pomade, a crystal jar in which several leeches floated lazily, a second jar containing a single ribbon-like tapeworm, and finally a third, without a lid, that was half full of a gelatinous substance and on the clear side of which was pasted a label with the single word written in flamboyant capitals: ANTISEPTIC.

To perfect his work, the barber was spreading over Amédée's newly shaved face another, creamier lather and, with the glinting edge of a second razor whose sharpness he tested on the palm of his other hand, adding the finishing touches. Amédée had forgotten his appointment now, had forgotten that he would have to leave the barber's chair, was dropping off … Just then, a Sicilian entered the barber's, his loud voice shattering the silence, and the barber, drawn into conversation, started shaving less attentively and, with a flowing stroke of his razor – *tssp!* – sliced off the head of the pimple.

Amédée yelped and was about to clasp his hand to the cut, where a large bead of blood had already welled.

'*Niente! Niente!*' the barber said, holding his arm and, still talking, rummaging in a drawer for a piece of yellowed cotton wool that he dipped into the ANTISEPTIC and pressed onto the spot.

Without caring now whether the passers-by turned to stare at him, where did Fleurissoire make for as he ran back down towards the city? For the first chemist's he came to: here he is, showing his injury. The man of medicine smiles, a greenish-looking old man who does not seem very wholesome himself, and, taking a small circle of gauze out of a packet, passes it over his broad tongue and …

Dashing back out of the shop, Fleurissoire gagged with disgust, tore off the damp gauze and, squeezing his pimple between two fingers, made it bleed as much as he could. Then, with his handkerchief wetted with saliva, his own this time, he rubbed it thoroughly. He looked at his watch and, panicking, set off back up the road at a sprint, arriving at the cardinal's door sweating, panting, bleeding and red in the face, a quarter of an hour late.

VI

Protos answered the door with a finger to his lips.

'We aren't alone,' he said quickly. 'As long as the servants are there, say nothing that might put them on their guard. They all speak French. Not a word or gesture that could give anything away. And for heaven's sake no "Cardinal" this, "Cardinal" that: your host is Ciro Bardolotti, the chaplain. And I'm not "Father Cave", just "Cave" plain and simple. Understood?' Abruptly changing his tone and slapping Amédée on the shoulder, he shouted, 'Well, well, it's him! Amédée's here! I say, old boy, you took your time getting shaved. A few minutes more and, by Bacchus's beard, we'd have sat down without you. The turkey on our spit's already starting to brown.' Lowering his voice, he said, 'Oh, dear sir, how painful it is to play-act! Like a stab to my heart!' Then, shouting, 'What do I see? You're cut! Dorino! Run to the barn and bring back a cobweb: there's no better remedy for wounds ...'

Clowning, he shoved Fleurissoire across the hall to a courtyard garden terrace where, under a trellis of vine, lunch had been set out.

'My dear Bardolotti, allow me to introduce Monsieur de la Fleurissoire, my cousin, the rascal I told you about.'

'You are most welcome, dear guest,' Bardolotti said with an expansive gesture, not rising from the armchair where he sat but pointing at his bare feet, which were submerged in a bowl of water.

'A good foot bath stimulates my appetite and draws the blood from my head.'

He was an odd-looking, rather tubby little man whose babyish features offered little indication of age or sex. He was dressed in alpaca, and nothing about his appearance suggested high rank. You would have had to be extremely observant or else in the know, as much as Fleurissoire was, to detect a well-concealed, cardinalesque unction beneath his jovial exterior. He leant sideways on the table, fanning himself nonchalantly with a triangular paper hat made from a sheet of newspaper.

'Er ... I'm deeply honoured ... er... what a ... lovely garden!' Fleurissoire stuttered, embarrassed as much by speaking as by staying silent.

'Enough soaking!' the cardinal exclaimed. 'Done, done, done! Will someone take this bowl away? Assunta!'

A comely, curvaceous young woman came running, scooped up the bowl and went to empty it over a flower bed. Breasts that were bursting out of her corset wobbled under the light material of her blouse. Smiling, she lingered at Protos's side, and Fleurissoire found the glow of her bare arms disturbing. Dorino put several *fiaschi* on the table, which had no cloth, and the sun danced as it shone through the boughs of vine, dappling the dishes with shifting rays of sunlight.

'No standing on ceremony here,' Bardolotti said, putting the paper hat on. 'You catch my drift, dear sir.'

In an authoritative voice, stressing each syllable and banging his fist on the table, Father Cave repeated in turn, 'No standing on ceremony here.'

Fleurissoire gave a knowing wink. Did he catch their drift? Of course he did, and there was no need to repeat it, but he searched in vain for some phrase that could simultaneously say nothing and yet express everything.

'Say something!' Protos hissed. 'Make a few puns. Their French is very good.'

'Come! Sit down,' Ciro said. 'My dear Cave, split this watermelon and cut it into Turkish crescents for us. Monsieur de la Fleurissoire, are you one of those who prefers pretentious northern melons, Sucrins and Prescotts – you know what I mean, those cantaloupe things – to our dripping Italian melons?'

'There is no variety better than this one, I'm sure, but may I pass? I'm feeling a little fragile,' Amédée said, his stomach still turning over with revulsion at the memory of the chemist.

'Some figs then, at the very least! Dorino's just picked 'em.'

'No, no figs either, I'm very sorry.'

'That's bad! Bad! Make puns,' Protos hissed in his ear,

adding aloud, 'Let's put this little chap back in sorts with some wine and get him ready for the turkey. Assunta, serve our excellent friend, will you?'

Amédée was obliged to toast and drink much more than he was used to. With the heat and fatigue taking their toll, he started to feel befuddled. His jokes came more easily. Protos made him sing and his audience went into raptures at his reedy voice: Assunta wanted to kiss him. Simultaneously, an indefinable anguish stirred in the depths of his beleaguered faith: he was laughing in order not to cry. He admired Cave's easy manner, his naturalness … Who, apart from Fleurissoire and the cardinal, would ever have guessed he was playing a part? Bardolotti himself, for that matter, was matching the priest's power of dissimulation and self-possession, laughing, applauding, nudging and winking at Dorino as Cave, tipping Assunta backwards, buried his face in her cleavage, and when Fleurissoire leant towards Cave, half bursting with despair, and murmured, 'How you must be suffering!' behind Assunta's back Cave took his hand and squeezed it silently, his head turned away and his gaze raised towards heaven.

Then, abruptly getting to his feet, Cave clapped his hands.

'Enough! Now we're to be left alone! No, you can clear away later. Go away. *Via! Via!*'

He made sure that neither Dorino nor Assunta were

staying behind to eavesdrop and returned to the table with his expression suddenly serious, his face longer, as the cardinal, running his hand over his features, erased at a stroke all their profane and spurious gaiety.

'Do you see, Monsieur de la Fleurissoire, my child, do you see to what we are reduced? Oh, this charade! This shameful charade!'

'It makes us recoil with horror,' Protos said, 'from even the purest pleasures and the most wholesome gaiety.'

'The Lord will be grateful, my poor dear Father Cave,' the cardinal replied, turning to Protos, 'the Lord will reward you for helping me drain this cup,' and, as if symbolically, he emptied his half-full glass in a single gulp, while the most painful revulsion was painted on his features.

'What?' Fleurissoire exclaimed, leaning forward. 'Can it be that even in this refuge and beneath this borrowed attire Your Eminence has to—'

'My son, just call me Monsieur.'

'I beg your pardon. Between ourselves—'

'I quake even when I am alone.'

'Can't you choose your servants?'

'They choose them for me, and the two you saw—'

'Oh, if I were to tell him,' Protos interrupted, 'where they are off to at this very moment to report every detail of our conversation!'

'Can it be that at the palace—'

'Sshh! No big words, you'll get us arrested! Try to remember it's Ciro Bardolotti, the chaplain, that you're talking to.'

'I am at their mercy,' Ciro groaned.

Protos, leaning forward across the table with his arms folded, twisted round towards him.

'And what if I were to tell him that they don't leave you alone for a single hour, day or night!'

'Yes, whatever disguise I assume,' the bogus cardinal went on, 'I can never be sure there isn't some agent of their secret police on my tail.'

'What? Do the people here know who you really are?'

'You misunderstand him entirely,' Protos said. 'You happen to be, as I am God's witness, one of the few individuals who can take pride in knowing that there is a connection between Cardinal San Felice and plain Father Bardolotti. But can you also comprehend this – that their enemies are not the same? – and that while the cardinal within his palace must defend himself against the freemasons, Chaplain Bardolotti finds himself spied on by—'

'The Jesuits!' the chaplain interrupted forlornly.

'I hadn't got round to telling him that part yet,' Protos said.

'No!' Fleurissoire wailed. 'Not the Jesuits against us too! Who would have imagined it? The Jesuits! Are you absolutely certain?'

'Think about it for a moment: it will seem entirely natural when you do. Understand that the Holy See's new policies, all conciliation, toleration and compromise, are just the sort of thing they like, and that the latest encyclicals are right up their street. Perhaps they don't know that the pope who promulgated them isn't the real one, but they'd be devastated if he were replaced.'

'If I understand you correctly' – Fleurissoire nodded – 'that means the Jesuits are the freemasons' allies.'

'What makes you say that?'

'But that's what Monsieur Bardolotti has just said.'

'Don't put absurd words into his mouth.'

'I'm sorry. I don't understand very much about politics.'

'That's why you shouldn't go looking any further than what we tell you. Two great forces are facing each other: the Lodge and the Society of Jesus, and as we, who know what is happening, cannot call for the support of either without revealing ourselves, we have both of them against us.'

'You see! What do you think of that?' the cardinal asked.

Fleurissoire did not think anything about anything. He felt completely flummoxed.

'All against one!' Protos added. 'The way it always is when one is in possession of the truth.'

'Oh, how happy I was when I was ignorant,' Fleurissoire groaned. 'Alas, from now on I shall never ever be able to be ignorant again!'

'He hasn't told you everything yet,' Protos continued,

putting his hand gently on Fleurissoire's shoulder. 'Prepare yourself for the worst ...' Leaning towards him, in a low voice: 'Despite all precautions, the secret has leaked out. There are reports of confidence tricksters taking advantage of it, especially in France's more pious *départements*, and going from one household to the next and pocketing for themselves, in the name of the Crusade, the money that should be going to our struggle.'

'How dreadful!'

'Added to which,' Bardolotti said, 'by their actions they heap discredit and suspicion on *us*, obliging us to be ever more ingenious and circumspect.'

'Here, read this,' Protos said, holding out a copy of *La Croix* to Fleurissoire. 'It's from the day before yesterday. A short article that speaks volumes.'

'We cannot,' Fleurissoire read,

> too strongly warn devout souls to be on their guard against the manoeuvres of certain persons who are currently impersonating churchmen, in particular one supposed canon who claims to have been entrusted with a secret mission and who, exploiting the credulity of the faithful, seeks to extract donations for a charitable organisation known as the 'Crusade for the Pope's Deliverance'. The organisation's name alone demonstrates its absurdity.

Fleurissoire felt the earth give way under his feet.

'Who then can one trust? But what if I were to tell you in turn, Messieurs, that it may be to this fraudster, this bogus canon I mean, that I owe my presence with you here today!'

Father Cave regarded the cardinal with great seriousness, then thumped his fist on the table.

'Hah! I suspected as much,' he exclaimed.

'Everything,' Fleurissoire continued, 'now leads me to fear that the person who informed me of this business was herself a victim of the manoeuvres of this criminal.'

'That would not surprise me,' Protos said.

'You see now,' Bardolotti went on, 'what a difficult position we find ourselves in, between these confidence tricksters who have appropriated our struggle and the police who, wanting to arrest *them*, are in danger of mistaking *us* for criminals.'

'In other words,' Fleurissoire groaned, 'we have no idea where is safe any more. I see danger wherever I turn.'

'Are you still surprised, after hearing this, at the lengths we've gone to to be prudent?'

'And do you understand,' Protos continued, 'why neither of us hesitated a short while ago to clothe ourselves in sin and feign an appetite for the wickedest pleasures?'

'But still,' Fleurissoire stammered, 'you at least – you can cling to your feigning and know that it is to conceal your virtues that you simulate sin. Whereas I ...'

And as the wine's vapours mingled with gusts of sadness, and belches of drunkenness with hiccupping sobs, slumped at Protos's side, Amédée first threw up his lunch and then, ramblingly, related the story of his night with Carola and his mourning for his lost virginity. Bardolotti and Father Cave had great difficulty stopping themselves from collapsing into howls of laughter.

'But you have been to confession, my son?' the cardinal asked, full of solicitude.

'The next morning.'

'And the priest gave you absolution?'

'Much too easily. It's that that torments me the most … But could I confide in him, tell him he wasn't dealing with any ordinary pilgrim, reveal what had brought me to his country? … No! No. And now it's all over for me. The mission I was given demanded a spotless record. I was the man with that record. Now it's all over! I have fallen from grace.' Again he was racked by sobs, while he hammered his chest with little punches and repeated, 'I'm not worthy! I'm not worthy!' and then went on in a sort of toneless chant, 'Oh, you're listening to me now and you can see my distress, so judge me, sentence me, punish me … At least tell me what extraordinary penance, what punishment will wash away this extraordinary crime?'

Protos and Bardolotti looked at each other. Eventually Bardolotti, getting to his feet, patted Fleurissoire on the shoulder.

'Come, come, my son! Whatever has happened, you mustn't upset yourself like this. Yes, it is true, you have sinned. But confound it! You are as much needed as you were before. (You've made a mess of yourself. Take this napkin. Rub it!) But of course I understand your distress, and as you've appealed to us we would like to give you the chance to redeem yourself. (You're not doing it right. Let me help you.)'

'Oh, please don't trouble yourself. Thank you! Thank you,' Fleurissoire said, as Bardolotti, continuing to rub, went on.

'But of course I respect your scruples, and to prove it to you I want to offer you an initial task, a small one with no glory attached, but it will give you the opportunity to get back on your feet and put your faith to the test.'

'That's all I ask.'

'Dear Cave, do you still have that little cheque about your person?'

Protos pulled a piece of paper out of the inside pocket of his jerkin.

'Circumscribed as we are,' the cardinal went on, 'from time to time we find it hard to convert into cash the offerings sent to us by a few kind souls we approach in strictest confidence. Spied on by masons and Jesuits, police and fraudsters all at once, we cannot afford to be seen presenting cheques or money orders at post-office and bank counters where our persons might be recognised.

The confidence tricksters that Father Cave was telling you about this afternoon have thrown our collections into such discredit!' Protos drummed impatiently on the table here. 'In short, here is a modest cheque for six thousand francs which I ask you, my son, to cash on our behalf. It has been drawn on the Credito Commerciale of Rome by the Duchess di Ponte Cavallo. Although it was addressed to the archbishop the payee's name has been left blank for reasons of prudence, so that whoever presents the cheque may cash it. You need have no scruples about filling it in with your own name, which will not arouse any suspicions. Take care not to let it or ... What's the matter, dear Father Cave? You seem nervous.'

'Go on.'

'Not to let it or the cash be stolen. You'll bring me the cash in ... let's see: you're going back to Rome tonight, so if you take the six o'clock fast train tomorrow night you'll arrive back at Naples at ten o'clock and I shall be on the station platform waiting for you. Afterwards we shall see about employing you on some more elevated task ... No, my son, do not kiss my hand. You can see very well there is no ring on it.'

He touched the forehead of the half-prostrated Amédée in front of him, and Protos took hold of Amédée's arm, shaking it gently to raise him.

'Come on! We've got time for one for the road. I much regret that I shan't be able to accompany you back to

215

Rome, but various matters need to be taken care of here, and much better that we aren't seen together. Farewell. Let us embrace, dear Fleurissoire, and may the Lord keep you! I thank Him for having given me the chance to know you.'

He walked with Fleurissoire to the door, and as he left him said, 'So, Monsieur, what do you think of the cardinal? Is it not upsetting to see the wear and tear that persecution has wrought on such a noble intelligence?'

He returned to where the bogus cardinal was sitting.

'You stupid bugger! That was terrifically clever, that was! Getting your cheque endorsed by some moron who doesn't even possess a passport and who I'm now going to have to keep an eye on.'

But Bardolotti, feeling increasingly drowsy, let his head rest on the table, murmuring, 'We have to keep the oldies busy.'

Protos went to one of the villa's bedrooms to divest himself of his wig and farm labourer's outfit. He reappeared a few moments later, thirty years younger and looking like a shop assistant or a bank clerk of the most junior grade. He was cutting it fine to catch the train he knew Fleurissoire would also be taking, and left without saying goodbye to Bardolotti, who was sound asleep.

VII

Fleurissoire arrived back at Rome and Via dei Vecchiarelli that same night. He was extremely tired and convinced Carola to let him sleep.

The next morning, as soon as he was awake, his pimple felt strange to the touch. He studied it in the mirror and saw that a yellowish scab had formed over the headless wound. The whole thing looked gross. At that moment he heard Carola in the corridor outside, and called to her and asked her to examine the afflicted spot. She led him to the window where she could see better, and with her first glance reassured him.

'It's not what you think.'

In truth Amédée had not actually been thinking about *that*, but Carola's effort to reassure him achieved the opposite of the desired effect, because from the moment she had stated that it was *not that*, it was obvious that it *could have been that*. And was she, for that matter, and how could she be, sure that it was *not that*? In addition, that it *might be that* seemed entirely natural to Amédée, because he had sinned and therefore he *deserved it to be that*. It therefore had to be that. A shiver ran down his spine.

'How did it happen?' Carola asked.

Aah! What did the physical cause – a slip of the razor,

a chemist's spit – matter? The deeper cause, the cause that deserved this punishment, was what mattered. Could he decently tell her? Would she understand? She would probably make fun of him … He heard her repeat the question.

'It was the barber,' he answered.

'You should put something on it.'

Her solicitude banished his last doubts: what she had said about it at first had just been to reassure him, and he already saw his face and body consumed by pustules and himself an object of horror to Arnica. Tears welled in his eyes.

'So you do think that …'

'No, my pet, don't be silly. And stop working yourself into a state – you look like a one-man funeral. For one thing, if it was that, you wouldn't know anything about it yet.'

'I would, I would! … It's all over for me, can't you see? All over!' he repeated.

She felt sorry for him.

'Anyway, it's never like that when it starts. Do you want me to call the manageress? She'll tell you … No? Well, I think you ought to get out and enjoy yourself then, take your mind off it, have a glass of Marsala.'

She was silent for a moment. Finally, unable to restrain herself, she said, 'Listen, I need to talk to you about something serious. You didn't come across a kind of white-haired priest yesterday by any chance?'

How did she know? Stunned, Fleurissoire said, 'Why do you ask?'

'Well …' She still hesitated, and then, looking at him and seeing how pale he was, went on in a rush, 'Well, be very careful of him. Trust me, lovey, he's going to take you to the cleaner's. I shouldn't tell you this, but … be very careful of him.'

Amédée said nothing but got ready to go out, shaken to the core by her words. He was already on his way downstairs when she called after him, 'And make sure if you do see him again, you don't tell him I talked to you. You'd be signing my death sentence.'

Life was becoming decidedly too complicated for Amédée. His confusion was becoming physical: his feet felt frozen, his forehead was burning, and his thoughts buzzed wildly around his head. How could he be sure of anything if Father Cave himself was a hoaxer? … In which case, did that mean the cardinal was one too? Then what about the cheque? He took it out of his pocket, rubbed it between his fingers, reassured himself of its reality. No! No, it wasn't possible. Carola was wrong. And what did she know about the mysterious interests that were forcing poor Father Cave to play a double game, anyway? Doubtless the most likely explanation was that Baptistin, about whom the good father had specifically warned him, had some kind of grudge against him ... Too bad! He pulled himself together: from now on his eyes would be sharper, and he would not trust Cave, just as he already did not trust Baptistin, and who knew, even Carola ...?

'So there it is,' he said to himself, 'the consequence and the evidence of the original wrongdoing, of the Holy See stumbling on its path: everything started to fall apart then. Who can one trust, if not the pope? The minute that keystone is removed, no part of any other truth ever matters again.'

Amédée was walking with quick, short steps towards the post office, where he hoped there would be some news, truthful news, from home, in which he could place his battered trust at last. The foggy morning, with its blanket of light that made every object dissolve and look faintly unreal, reinforced his feelings of dizziness. He walked as if in a dream, doubting the solidity of the walls and the physical existence of passers-by, doubting more than anything his own presence in Rome ... He pinched himself, to try to wake himself from the dream and find himself back home at Pau, in his bed, with Arnica already up and bending over him, as she always did, and eventually asking him, 'Did you sleep well, my dear?'

The post-office clerk recognised him and, dispensing with formalities, handed him his wife's latest letter. '*I have just heard from Valentine de Saint-Prix*,' she wrote, *that Julius is in Rome too, for a conference. How glad I am to think that you and he will be able to meet! Unfortunately Valentine was not able to give me his address. She thinks he is staying at the Grand Hotel, but she's not sure. All she knows is that he is supposed to be being received at the Vatican on Thursday morning – he wrote to Cardinal Pazzi in advance to request an audience. He is coming from Milan, where he went to see Anthime, who is very unhappy because he has not received any of what the Church promised him after his recantation, and so Julius wants to go to see our Holy Father to ask for justice (because of course Julius does not know what has happened). He can tell you about his visit and then you can enlighten him.*

I hope you're taking every precaution against the air there and you're not tiring yourself out. Gaston calls on me every day, and we miss you very much. How happy I'll be when you tell us you are coming home …

And so on. Hurriedly scribbled in pencil across the fourth page were a few words from Blafaphas.

If you go to Naples, remember to find out how they make the hole in the macaroni. I am about to come up with a new invention.

A bugle blast of joy filled Amédée's heart, mingled with slight unease: Thursday, the day of Julius's audience, was today. He had not dared ask for his clothes to be washed, and he had run out of clean shirts. At least he was afraid he had. That morning he had put on yesterday's collar again, but at the news that he might be meeting Julius it had stopped seeming sufficiently clean, and the pleasure he might have taken in the possibility of seeing his brother-in-law was dashed. Going back to Via dei Vecchiarelli was not an option if he wanted to be in time to catch Julius as he emerged from his audience, which would be less awkward than paying him a visit at the Grand Hotel. He did what he could, by turning his cuffs. As for his collar, he wound his scarf over it, which had the advantage of more or less hiding his pimple too.

But what did the details matter? What was important was that Fleurissoire felt inexpressibly cheered up by Arnica's letter. The prospect of renewing contact with one of his relations, and with it his former life, put the monsters spawned by his traveller's imagination back in perspective. Carola, Father Cave, the cardinal: they floated in front of him like a dream suddenly interrupted by the crowing of a cock. Why on earth had he left Pau? What did this absurd fable, which had shattered his happiness, mean? Good Lord! There was a pope, and in a short while Julius was going to be able to say to him, 'I've seen him!' A pope: that was all that was necessary. Would

God have allowed such an outrageous substitution to take place? A substitution that he, Fleurissoire, would never have believed in, had it not been for his ridiculous pride in having a part to play in the affair.

Amédée walked with short, hurried steps, hardly able to stop himself breaking into a run. His confidence was flowing back at last, and the objects around him took on reassuring mass and scale, their natural place and a convincing reality again. He clutched his straw boater in his hand, and when he arrived at the basilica was overcome by such a feeling of exhilaration that he began by walking round its right-hand fountain, and as he walked in the lee of its spray, letting it moisten his upturned face, he smiled at its rainbow.

He suddenly stopped dead. There, nearby, sitting at the foot of the colonnade's fourth pillar, wasn't that Julius? But he paused as he was about to call out to him, for if Julius's appearance was respectable his behaviour was less so: Count de Baraglioul was bareheaded, his black straw Cronstadt next to him, hung on the chough's-head knob of his stick, which he had planted between two paving stones, and, heedless of the square's solemnity, he sat with his right foot resting on his left knee like some prophet in the Sistine Chapel, balancing a notebook on his right knee and sporadically writing, his pencil poised in mid-air before it swooped down onto the pages, gripped to the exclusion of everything else by the dictation of a train of thought so urgent that Amédée could have performed a headstand in front of him without Julius noticing. As he wrote he talked. The burbling of the fountain masked the sound of his words, but you could clearly make out the movement of his lips.

Amédée approached, walking discreetly around the back of the pillar. As he was about to tap Julius on the shoulder, his brother-in-law said loudly, 'AND IN THAT CASE, WHAT DOES IT MATTER!'

He recorded the words in his notebook with a gesture of finality, replaced his pencil in his pocket and, getting briskly to his feet, came face to face with Amédée.

'By the Holy Father, what are you doing here?'

Amédée, quivering with emotion, stammered, unable to speak. He clasped one of Julius's hands tightly between both of his. Julius looked him up and down.

'My dear friend, what a mess you look!'

Providence had not dealt kindly with Julius: of the two brothers-in-law he had left, one had turned into a fanatic and the other lacked both fortune and vitality. It was less than three years since he had seen Amédée but his brother-in-law had aged by more than a dozen: his cheeks had sunk, the deep crimson of his scarf made him look even paler, his chin was trembling, his fish eyes were rolling in a way that ought to have aroused sympathy but just looked clownish, and his journey of the previous day had left him with a strange hoarseness, so that his speech seemed to be coming from far away. He was, as we know, deeply preoccupied.

'So did you see him?' he said.

As was Julius.

'Who?' he asked.

In Fleurissoire's ears this *who?* tolled like a death knell and a blasphemy. Lowering his voice he elaborated.

'I thought you had just come from the Vatican?'

'Quite true. Forgive me, I was thinking about something else ... If you only knew what has happened to me!'

His eyes were shining: he looked as if he were about to jump out of his skin.

'Please,' Fleurissoire begged him, 'tell me about it later. Tell me about your visit first. I can't wait to hear ...'

'Are you really interested?'

'Soon you'll know just how much. Tell me, please, tell me!'

'Very well, then,' Julius began, gripping Fleurissoire's arm and leading him away from St Peter's. 'Perhaps you already know how Anthime was left destitute after his conversion. He's still waiting vainly for what the Church promised him in compensation for what the freemasons robbed him of. He has been taken for a ride, there are no two ways about it ... Well, you must take the whole business as you find it. Personally I consider it an utter farce, and yet thanks to it perhaps I can see the matter which concerns us more or less clearly, and which I urgently want to discuss with you. So – *a creature of inconsequence*! It's saying a lot … and no doubt that apparent inconsequence conceals a much more subtle and abstruse sequence. The important thing is that what makes him act is no longer a simple matter of personal interest, or, as one usually says, that his motives are no longer self-interested.'

'I'm sorry, I'm not following you very well,' Amédée said.

'True, true, forgive me: I'm getting off the subject. So, I had decided to try to settle Anthime's problems myself … You should see the apartment he's living in in Milan! I told him straight away, "You can't stay here." And when I think of poor Véronique. But he's turning into an ascetic, a genuine monk. He refuses to let you feel sorry for him, and you especially aren't allowed to blame the clergy. "Dear friend," I told him, "I grant you that the higher clergy are not to blame, but that is because they are not in the picture. Allow me to go and enlighten them."'

'I thought Cardinal Pazzi—' Fleurissoire tried to say.

'Yes. Nothing came of it. You see, with these high-ranking clerics each of them fears compromising himself. To take charge of the matter someone was needed who was not an insider: myself, for instance. Because, look, you have to admire the way discoveries come about, I mean the most important ones: you think there's been some sudden illumination, when actually, deep down, you hadn't stopped thinking about it. By the way, that's why for a long time I've been anxious both about my characters' excess of logic and about their inadequate characterisation.'

'I'm afraid,' Amédée said gently, 'that you're getting off the subject again.'

'Not a bit,' Julius went on, 'it's you who aren't following my train of thought. In short, I decided it should be our Holy Father himself to whom I should address my petition, and I was going to take it to him this morning.'

'And? Tell me quickly: did you see him?'

'My dear Amédée, if you're going to interrupt me all the time … Well! One has no idea just how difficult it is to see him.'

'No!'

'I beg your pardon?'

'I'll tell you in a moment.'

'Well, to begin with I had to give up completely the idea of handing over my petition. I had it in my hand. It was a perfectly respectable sheaf of paper, but in the second antechamber – or was it the third? I can't quite remember – a tall chap in a black and red outfit politely relieved me of it.'

Amédée began to laugh quietly, like a person in possession of certain facts, who knows what he knows.

'In the next antechamber I was relieved of my hat, which was placed on a table. In the fifth or sixth, where I waited at length in the company of two ladies and three prelates, a sort of chamberlain came to fetch me and led me into the adjoining room where, as soon as I was in the Holy Father's presence – as far as I could make out, he was perched on a sort of throne overhung by a sort of canopy – he gestured to me to prostrate myself, which I did, so that I couldn't see anything else.'

'Yet you didn't stay bowed down or staring at the floor for so long that you didn't—'

'My dear Amédée, you're talking with the benefit of hindsight. Haven't you ever experienced how respect makes us blind? And apart from the fact that I didn't dare raise my head, each time I started to talk about Anthime a sort of steward, who had a kind of ruler, gave me little sort of taps on the back of my neck that made me keep my gaze glued to the floor.'

'At least *he* talked to you, anyway.'

'Yes, about my book, which he admitted he had not read.'

'My dear Julius,' Amédée said after a moment's silence, 'what you have just told me is something of the utmost importance. So you did not see him, and the strongest impression I retain from your account is that he is strangely uneasy about being seen. Oh! It all, alas, confirms my cruellest fears. Julius, I must tell you now … but step this way, the street is so busy …'

An amused Julius followed him without protest into an almost deserted *vicolo*.

'What I am about to impart to you is so serious ... It is vital that you don't show any outward reaction. We should look as if we're talking about unimportant matters, but you must get ready to hear something awful. Julius, dear friend, he whom you saw this morning—'

'Whom I didn't see, you mean.'

'Precisely... is not *the real one*.'

'I beg your pardon?'

'I'm saying that you weren't able to see the pope for the outrageous reason that – I have it from a confidential and reliable source – the real pope has been abducted.'

This astonishing revelation had the most unexpected effect on Julius. He dropped Amédée's arm and, running ahead of him and zigzagging across the *vicolo*, shouted, 'No. No! Oh good heavens, no, not that, not that! No!'

Returning to Amédée, he said, 'What? I manage, by making the most strenuous effort, to rid my mind of all this. I convince myself that there is nothing to expect from that quarter, nothing to hope for, nothing to gain, that Anthime has been taken for a ride, we've all been taken for a ride, they're all snake-oil salesmen, and there's nothing left to do but laugh at it all ... And then? No sooner have I set down my burden and come to terms with it than you come and say: Stop there! There's been a misdeal. Deal again! Well, no, frankly! No! No mistakes, no misdeals! I'm sticking with the cards I've got. If that one's not the real one, I don't give a damn!'

Fleurissoire was disconcerted.

'But,' he said, 'the Church …' and he regretted that his hoarseness did not allow him to be as eloquent as he wanted. 'What if the Church herself has been taken for a ride?'

Julius stopped in front of Amédée, half turned towards him and, blocking his way, and in a contemptuous, cutting tone of voice that was completely unlike him, said, 'So what? What-does-it-matter-to-you?'

And suddenly Fleurissoire experienced a doubt, a new, shapeless, ghastly doubt that had vague origins in the depths of his unease: that Julius, Julius himself, this Julius he was talking to, Julius to whom his expectations and his battered faith had clung, this Julius was not the real Julius either.

'What? Is it really you saying those things? The person I was counting on? You, Julius? Count de Baraglioul, whose writings—'

'Don't talk to me about my writings, I beg you. True or false, I've heard enough about them this morning from your pope. And thanks to my discovery, I also very much intend that any future ones will be better. Which is why I'm impatient to talk to you about more serious matters. You'll lunch with me, I take it?'

'With pleasure, but I shall have to leave promptly. I'm expected at Naples this evening … Yes, for business that I shall tell you about. You're not taking me to the Grand Hotel, are you?'

'No, we'll go to the Colonna.'

Julius too was hardly eager to be seen at the Grand Hotel in the company of a derelict like Fleurissoire. At the Colonna, feeling drained and haggard, Fleurissoire was instantly intimidated by the patch of bright light in which his brother-in-law placed him, facing him and under his searching gaze. If indeed that gaze had settled on him. Instead he felt it scrutinising the edge of his deep-crimson scarf, at that shameful spot on his chin where the suspect pimple was erupting, and which he felt to be horribly exposed. And as the waiter was serving the hors d'oeuvres, Julius said, 'You ought to try sulphur baths.'

'It isn't what you think it is,' Fleurissoire protested.

'I'm delighted to hear it,' Baraglioul went on, not thinking anything. 'It was no more than a passing suggestion.' Then, leaning back squarely, in his most professional tone: 'All right! Now, dear Amédée, to my mind we have all since the days of La Rochefoucauld been no more than the trail to his comet, and yet profit is not what always leads men's motives, and there are acts that are disinterested—'

'I do hope so,' Fleurissoire interrupted with feeling.

'Please don't try to understand me before I've finished. By *disinterested* I mean gratuitous, and also that evil, or what we call evil, can be as gratuitous as good.'

'Well, in that case, why commit them?'

'Precisely! From indulgence, a compulsion to spend,

or to gamble. For it's my view that the most disinterested souls are not necessarily the best, in the *Catholic* sense of the word: on the contrary, the best Catholic soul is the one that keeps the best accounts.'

'And that always feels its debt to God,' Fleurissoire added sanctimoniously, attempting to keep up with the discussion.

Julius was visibly irritated by his brother-in-law's interruptions: he found them whimsical and absurd.

'A scorn for what is serviceable,' he went on, 'is no doubt a sign of a certain aristocracy of spirit ... So once they have broken free of God's regard, self-regard and self-interest, can we conceive of a soul that no longer keeps any accounts whatsoever?'

Baraglioul was expecting acquiescence, but Fleurissoire exclaimed vehemently, 'No, no, a thousand times no. We shall not conceive of it!'

Then, startled by the sound of his own voice, he leant towards Baraglioul.

'Let's keep our voices down. People are listening.'

'Fah! Who do you think would be interested in what we're saying?'

'Dear friend, I see you have no idea what people are like in this country. Personally, I'm beginning to get to know them. In the four days I've spent here I've gone from one adventure to another, all of them instilling in me, and rather forcefully I can tell you, a caution that's quite foreign to my character. Our movements are watched.'

'You're imagining it.'

'Oh, I wish I were! How I wish it were all in the mind. But what can one do? When falsehood takes over from truth, truth has no choice but to dissemble. Having been entrusted with this mission, which I'll tell you about in a moment, I find myself caught between the Lodge and the Society of Jesus. It's all over for me: I'm suspected by everyone, and I suspect everything I see and hear. What if I were to admit to you, dear friend, that just now, when you were mocking me for my distress, I started to wonder whether it was the real Julius I was talking to or, more likely, some impostor masquerading as yourself ... And what if I were to tell you that this morning, before we met, I even doubted my own reality, wondering if it was me here, in Rome, or whether I was perhaps just dreaming that I was here and was soon going to wake up in Pau, tucked up in bed next to Arnica with my everyday life all around me.'

'Dear friend, you must be running a temperature.'

Fleurissoire clutched his hand and said in a strangled voice, 'A temperature! You're right, I'm running a temperature. And it's a fever that can't be cured, that one doesn't want to be cured of. A fever, I'll admit, that I'd hoped would infect you too when you got to hear what I've just told you – a fever I'd hoped to transmit to you, so that we would burn together, dear brother ... But no! I've realised that the path that stretches out darkly before me is one I'm to follow alone – one I'm compelled to follow now, after what you've told me … Oh Julius, can it really be true? That one really doesn't see HIM? That he can't be seen?'

'Dear friend,' Julius replied, disengaging himself from Fleurissoire's excitable grip and placing a hand on his arm to calm him, 'dear friend, I shall confess to you something I did not dare say to you just now: that when I found myself in the Holy Father's presence … well, I became distracted …'

'Distracted!' Fleurissoire repeated in a stunned voice.

'Yes: suddenly I was startled to find myself thinking about something else.'

'Am I really to believe what you say?'

'Yes, because it was at exactly that moment that I experienced my revelation. "So," I said to myself – going back to my earlier idea – "so supposing this wicked act, this crime, were gratuitous, it would be impossible to attribute authorship to it, and the said author *would therefore be unassailable*."'

'No! You're back on that again,' Amédée sighed despairingly.

'Because the motive, the reason for the crime is the hook on which the criminal is caught. And if, as the judge will usually say, *Is fecit cui prodest* …[10] You know your law, don't you?'

'I'm sorry?' Amédée said, beads of perspiration forming on his brow.

At that moment their conversation was interrupted without warning: the messenger boy stood at their table with a plate on which there was an envelope with Fleurissoire's name written on it. Gaping in astonishment, Fleurissoire opened the envelope and on the piece of paper inside read these words:

> *You haven't a minute to lose. The train for Naples leaves at three. Ask Monsieur de Baraglioul to accompany you to the Credito Commerciale where he is known and can vouch for your identity. Cave.*

'You see? What did I tell you?' Amédée muttered, obscurely relieved by the note's arrival.

'I must say, that is more than unusual. How the devil did they know my name, and that I have business with the Credito Commerciale?'

'These people know everything, I tell you.'

'I don't like their tone. The person who wrote this note might at least have apologised for interrupting us.'

'What's the point? He's well aware that my mission has absolute priority … A cheque to be cashed … No, impossible to talk to you about it here. You can see for yourself that we're under surveillance.' He pulled out his watch. 'Yes, we've just got time.'

He called the waiter.

'Leave it to me,' Julius said, 'you're my guest. The Credito isn't far, if necessary we'll take a cab. No need to panic ... Ah yes, I also wanted to say to you that if you are going to Naples tonight, use this round-trip ticket. It's in my name, but it doesn't matter.' Julius liked to be helpful. 'I rashly bought it in Paris, thinking I'd be going further south, but I shan't be able to get away from this conference. How long are you thinking of staying?'

'As short a time as possible. I hope to be back by tomorrow.'

'Then I shall expect you for dinner.'

Thanks to the Count de Baraglioul's introduction, at the Credito Commerciale Fleurissoire cashed the cheque without difficulty and was handed six thousand-franc notes, which he slipped into the inside pocket of his jacket. On the way to the bank, and then to the station, he provided a muddled account of how he had come by the cheque, and of the cardinal and priest. Baraglioul listened with half an ear.

They made one more stop, at a shirtmaker's where Fleurissoire bought himself a new collar, although he did not put it on there and then, for fear of making Julius, who was waiting outside the shop, impatient.

'You're not taking any luggage?' Julius asked when he emerged.

Fleurissoire would have liked to collect his shawl and

his nightshirt and toilet things, but to have to reveal to his brother-in-law the Via dei Vecchiarelli …

'It's only one night!' he said carelessly. 'In any case we haven't got time to stop at my hotel.'

'Where are you staying, by the way?'

'Behind the Colosseum,' Fleurissoire answered evasively. He might just as well have said 'under a bridge'.

Julius stared at him again.

'What an odd chap you are!'

Did he really seem so odd? Fleurissoire mopped his forehead. Their cab stopped outside the station and they walked a few steps in silence.

'Well, it's time to say goodbye,' Baraglioul said, holding out his hand.

'You … you wouldn't come with me, would you?' Fleurissoire stammered shyly. 'I don't know why, but I feel a bit anxious about going on my own …'

'You came all the way to Rome on your own, didn't you? What can possibly happen to you? Forgive me for not coming onto the platform with you, but the sight of a train pulling out always leaves me feeling unspeakably sad. Farewell! *Bon voyage!* And bring me back my return ticket for Paris when you come to the Grand Hotel tomorrow.'

BOOK FIVE

LAFCADIO

'There is only one remedy. One thing alone
can cure us from being ourselves.'
'Yes; strictly speaking, the question is not
how to get cured, but how to live.'

Joseph Conrad, *Lord Jim*

I

Lafcadio, with Julius acting as intermediary and the assistance of a notary, had come into the 40,000 francs a year left him by Count Juste-Agénor de Baraglioul. Afterwards his chief concern had been for it not to show at all.

'Off gold plate, maybe,' he had said to himself, 'but you'll eat the same food.'

He had not taken into account, or not learnt yet, that from that moment on his taste in food would change. Or perhaps it was simply that, as he enjoyed giving in to indulgence as much as he enjoyed defeating his appetite, now that he was not oppressed by need any longer his resistance slackened. Let's put it plainly: having an aristocratic nature, he had never let necessity force him into an attitude – one that he might now have indulged, out of mischief, and playfulness, and for the fun of putting pleasure ahead of what was good for him.

In accordance with the count's wishes he had not worn black. A mortifying discovery had awaited him at the tailor of the Marquis de Gesvres, his last uncle, when he went there to order his new wardrobe. When he told the tailor he had come on the marquis's recommendation, the man produced several bills that his uncle had not bothered to pay. Lafcadio, who found such deception repugnant, pretended that the outstanding bills were the reason for his visit and settled them. What he ordered for himself he paid for in cash. The same thing happened at the bootmaker's. He felt it would be wise to choose a different shirtmaker.

I wish I had Uncle de Gesvres's address! Lafcadio thought. I would love to send him the receipted bills. He'd despise me for it but I am a Baraglioul, and as of today, you rascally marquis, I banish you from my heart.

There was nothing to keep him in Paris, or anywhere else. He travelled south at a leisurely pace to Italy, heading for Brindisi, with the idea that he would pick up a boat for Java there.

Alone in the carriage that was carrying him away from Rome, he had – despite the heat – thrown a plush fawn rug across his knees and was enjoying looking at his hands resting on it, sheathed in pale-grey suede gloves. Through the soft, almost fluffy cloth of his suit every pore of his body breathed well-being. His neck sat comfortably in a stand-up, lightly starched collar, around which was tied a bronze silk necktie, as thin as a bootlace, that lay flat against his pleated shirt. He felt well, supremely well, well in his suit, well in his shoes – soft moccasins stitched from the same suede as his gloves. In their soft prison his feet stretched, arched and felt alive. His beaver hat, pulled low over his eyes, distanced him from the landscape, and as he smoked a short clay pipe filled with dried juniper he let his thoughts wander naturally and unchecked.

That old woman, he thought, with a little white cloud above her head, and the way she pointed it out to me and said, 'That's not for today, that rain!'... and then I loaded her bag on my back (on a whim he had spent four days crossing the Apennines between Bologna and Florence, sleeping at Covigliajo on the way) and kissed her when we got to the top of the mountain ... that was part of what the priest at Covigliajo called 'my good actions'. But I could just as easily have strangled her – with an entirely steady hand – feeling that dirty, wrinkled skin under my fingers ... The way she stroked the collar of my jacket to brush the dust off, saying, '*Figlio mio! Carino!*' ... Then where did that intense joy come from when I lay down on the moss afterwards – but not smoking – in the shade of that huge chestnut, still sweating? I felt my arms were wide enough to embrace the whole of humanity, or perhaps to strangle it ... What a trivial thing human life is! And how readily I'd risk my own life if there was just some terrific deed, some excellently fearless feat I could gamble it on! ... But I can't suddenly become a mountaineer or an airman ... What would that neurotic recluse, Julius, advise? It's so annoying that he's such a wet blanket! I'd have liked to have a brother.

Poor Julius! So many people writing, and so few of them reading! That's a fact ... people read less and less ... as far as I can see, as the saying goes. It'll all end in catastrophe, some wonderful catastrophe bubbling with horror, and the printed word will be chucked completely overboard. It'll be a miracle if the best doesn't sink to the bottom with the worst.

But curiosity's different: I wonder what the old woman would have said if I'd started to squeeze ... You wonder *what would happen if*, but then there's always a brief moment when the unforeseen can strike. Nothing ever happens exactly the way you'd expect it to ... That's the moment that makes me want to act ... People do so little! ... 'Let all that can be, be!' That's how I explain Creation to myself ... In love with what could be ... If I was in charge, I'd have me locked up.

Rather underwhelming, that correspondence belonging

to a Monsieur G. Flamand that I pretended was mine at the poste restante in Bologna. Dear Gaspard, none of your correspondents had anything to say that was worth saying.

In fact, that's a general rule. God! There are really so few people whose suitcases you'd want to rummage through. But there are also so few that you wouldn't get some weird reaction from, if you said this or did that to them! ... A wonderful collection of puppets, but heaven preserve us from their all too obvious strings! The only people you see on the streets these days are upstarts and halfwits. I ask you, Lafcadio, can a proper person take this world seriously? ... Come on! Let's clear out! Pack our bags. About bloody time! Run away to a new world. Leave our footprints on the shore, leave Europe behind! ... If there's still some late-developing *Anthropopithecus* lurking in the depths of the Borneo forests, we shall go and calculate the odds on a potential new race of humanity to come! ...

I'd like to have seen Protos again. I bet he's sailed off to America. He always used to say that thugs in Chicago were the only people he respected ... Not quite pleasure-loving enough for my taste, that pack of wolves: I'm more the feline sort. Good luck to him.

The priest at Covigliajo was so good-natured he didn't look the slightest bit likely to interfere with the little boy he was talking to. He must have been looking after him. I'd willingly have made friends with him – God, no, not the priest! The boy ... What beautiful eyes he had, looking up and holding my gaze with the same anxiety as I sought his, though then I instantly looked away. Less than five years younger than me. Somewhere between fourteen and sixteen, no more ... What was I like at that age? A stripling,[11] and as greedy as they come. I'd have liked to meet me today, I think I'd have liked me a lot ... To begin with, Faby was confused to find himself so smitten by me. He did the right thing, coming clean about it to my mother. His heart was lighter afterwards. But he did annoy me with his self-restraint ... When I told him so later, in the Aurès, one night when we were in our tent, we had a good laugh about it. I'd like to see him again. It's a shame he's dead. Time to move on.

The truth is, I wanted to annoy the priest. I was trying to think of the most disagreeable thing I could say to him, but I couldn't think of anything that wasn't charming ... Why do I find it so hard to be unappealing! I can hardly brown my face with walnut stain, which is what Carola advised me to do, or start chewing garlic ... Oh God, enough going back to that sad girl! All my most average pleasures I owe to her ... Hello! Where did that strange old man spring from?

Amédée Fleurissoire had just stepped in through the sliding door from the corridor.

Fleurissoire had been alone in his compartment as far as Frosinone. When the train stopped there, an Italian of indeterminate age had got on and started staring at him with such a dark look that Fleurissoire had felt an irresistible desire to bolt.

In the next compartment along, Lafcadio's youthful grace had attracted him.

What a good-looking boy, he thought, not much more than a lad. On holiday, no doubt. How well dressed he is! And a very open expression. What a relief it will be to forget my suspicions for a while! I'd happily chat with him, if he spoke French ...

He sat down facing Lafcadio, in the corner by the door. Lafcadio raised the brim of his beaver hat and ran a glum and apparently indifferent eye over Fleurissoire.

What can this grubby old fart and I have in common? he wondered. Yet he gives every appearance of having rather a high opinion of himself. What does he think he looks like, smiling at me like that? Is he expecting me to throw my arms around him? Can there really be women who don't mind fondling old men? ... He'd probably be rather surprised to know I can read handwriting and printed text, fluently, upside down or reversed on glass, back to front or in a mirror or on blotting paper: three months' study, two years' apprenticeship, and all for the love of art. Now, Cadio, dear boy, *now*, this is your mission: to intervene in this destiny. How? … All right, let's start by offering him a sweet. Whether he accepts or not, we'll find out what language he speaks.

'*Grazio! Grazio!*' Fleurissoire repeated, refusing.

No! It isn't really worth bothering with the old fart, Lafcadio continues to himself. I'd be better off getting some sleep. He tugs his beaver hat back down over his eyes and sits back, trying to conjure a scene from one of his childhood memories. He sees himself in the days when he was called Cadio, in that castle in the Carpathians where he and his mother spent two summers staying with Baldi the Italian and Prince Vladimir Bielkowski. His bedroom is down a long hall, and it's the first time he has slept so far away from his mother. His bedroom doorknob is made of brass, in the shape of a lion's head and attached by a thick nail … How sharp the memories of his sensations are! One night, waking from the depths of sleep, he thinks he must still be dreaming as he sees his Uncle Vladimir standing by his bed and looking even vaster than he usually does, dressed as if in a nightmare, wrapped in a rust-coloured caftan, with his drooping moustache and some kind of flamboyant nightcap balanced on his head like a Persian hat that makes him so tall you can't see where he finishes. He has a smuggler's lamp in his hand that he puts down on the bedside table next to Cadio's wristwatch, nudging a bag of marbles out of the way to make room for it. Cadio's first thought is that his mother is dead or ill. He is about to question Bielkowski when the prince places a finger on his lips and gestures to him to get out of bed. The boy quickly puts on the bathrobe that his uncle has picked up off a chair and is holding out to him, with furrowed brow and a look warning that he is utterly serious. But Cadio trusts Vladi so implicitly that he is not afraid for a moment. He puts on his slippers and follows him, deeply intrigued by his behaviour and, as always, relishing the thought of something amusing happening.

They go out into the hallway. Vladimir walks solemnly and mysteriously ahead, holding the lantern at the end of his outstretched arm. They look as if they are performing a rite or following a procession, Cadio tottering slightly because he is still sleep-fuddled, but curiosity is making short work of his dreams. Outside his mother's bedroom door they stop and listen: not a sound. The castle is fast asleep. Reaching the landing, they hear the snoring of a servant whose room opens onto the attic floor. They go downstairs. Vladi steps with feather-light feet on the treads, and at the slightest creak spins round with such a furious look that Cadio finds it hard not to laugh. He points to one tread in particular, signalling that he should step over it, with as much seriousness as if it represented a real peril. Cadio does not spoil his enjoyment by wondering whether these precautions, like everything else they are doing, are strictly necessary. He enters into the spirit of the game and slides down the banister to avoid the step ... He is so hugely entertained by Vladi that he would walk through fire to follow him.

When they reach the ground floor they sit down on the second to last step to get their breath back. Vladi nods and expels a little breath from his nose, as if to say, Ah! That was a narrow squeak. They set off again. More precautions outside the drawing-room door! The lamp, which Cadio is holding now, lights up the room so strangely that he hardly recognises it. It seems exaggeratedly large, and a shaft of moonlight slips in through a crack in the shutters. Everything is bathed in a supernatural calm, like the calm of a lake just before a net is to be cast, and as he recognises individual objects in their place he understands their strangeness for the first time.

Vladi walks over to the piano, half opens it and strokes several of the keys with his fingertips. They respond softly. Suddenly the lid slips out of his hand and falls, the sound exploding in the silence (Lafcadio jumps again at the memory of it). Vladi dashes to the lamp and closes its shutter, then slumps into an armchair. Cadio hides under a table. The two of them stay like that for a long time in the dark, not moving, their ears pricked ... but there are no answering sounds: in the castle nothing moves. In the distance a dog yelps at the moon. So slowly, gently Vladi raises the lamp's shutter again.

In the dining room Vladi's prudence redoubles: how cautiously he turns the key to the sideboard! The boy is well aware by now that this is only a game, but his uncle seems completely immersed in it. He sniffs as if to locate where the most delicious smells are coming from, selects a bottle of Tokay and pours two small glasses that they dip biscuits into. With a finger to his lips he raises his glass to Cadio's and the crystal chimes almost inaudibly ... The midnight refreshments at an end, Vladi goes around putting everything back where it should be, takes Cadio with him to rinse the glasses in the sink in the butler's pantry, dries them, re-corks the bottle, puts the lid back on the biscuits, meticulously sweeps up the crumbs, gives a final glance at everything in its place in the cupboard ... The eye hath not seen, nor the ear heard ...

Vladi accompanies Cadio back to his room and with a deep bow takes his leave. Cadio goes straight back to sleep and to his dreams, and the next morning wonders if he might not have dreamt it all.

A queer game for a little boy. What would Julius have thought of it?

Lafcadio is not asleep, though his eyes are closed: sleep eludes him.

He thinks: I can sense the old man there across from me. He believes I'm asleep. If I were to half open my eyes, I'd see him looking at me. Protos used to claim that it's particularly difficult to pretend to be asleep when you want to be alert. He boasted that he could always recognise when people weren't really asleep by the minute fluttering of their eyelashes ... which at this moment I am suppressing. Protos himself would be taken in ...

The sun, meanwhile, had set. The glories of its last rays were fading, and Fleurissoire gazed out at them, moved by the sight. Suddenly the electric light in the carriage's curved ceiling flooded the compartment with a brightness brutally at odds with the melting twilight outside and – anxious too that his fellow traveller's sleep should not be disturbed – Fleurissoire turned the switch off, which did not plunge the carriage into complete darkness but diverted the current from the central light to a blue-coloured nightlight. Fleurissoire, feeling that this blue bulb still shed too much light, twisted the switch a second time: the nightlight went out and two wall-lights came on that were even more unpleasantly bright than the overhead light. Another twist, and the nightlight came on again. He gave up.

Has he quite finished playing with the lights? Lafcadio wondered, losing patience. Now what's he doing? No, no, keep my eyelids closed. He's standing up ... Has my suitcase caught his eye? Oh, well done! He's noticed that it's open. Having instantly lost the key, it was awfully clever of me to have got that complicated lock fitted at Milan that I then had to have picked in Bologna! At least a padlock can be replaced ... Bloody hell! Not taking his jacket off now, is he? All right, come on, let's see.

Paying no attention to Lafcadio's suitcase, Fleurissoire was busy with his new collar, having put down his jacket to be able to button it more comfortably, but the heavily starched cotton, as stiff as cardboard, resisted his most strenuous efforts.

He doesn't look at all happy, Lafcadio thought. He's got to be suffering from a fistula or some other hidden affliction. Shall I help him? He's not going to get there on his own ...

He was wrong. The collar eventually allowed itself to be fastened to its stud. Fleurissoire then picked up his tie from the seat cushion where he had placed it, next to his hat, jacket and cuffs, and moved over to the door where, like Narcissus peering into the pool, he stared at the glass, trying to make out his reflection in the dark landscape.

He can't see.

Lafcadio switched the main light on. The train was steaming along an embankment that could be seen through the window, lit up by the light coming from each compartment, forming a series of bright squares that danced along the track, each one changing shape identically in turn with every unevenness in the ground.

In the middle of one of the squares danced Fleurissoire's nondescript shadow. The other squares were empty.

Who'd see him? Lafcadio thought. Just here by my hand, right by it, a two-stage lock that's child's play to open, and the door would suddenly give way and he would lose his balance and topple forward. A little push would do it: he'd fall out into the dark like a stone. Nobody would even hear him call out ... And then tomorrow the islands! ... Who would ever know?

Fleurissoire had his tie on now, a little ready-made sailor's knot, and had picked up a cuff and was applying it to his right wrist and as he did it was examining, above the seat where he had been sitting a moment before, a photograph (one of four that decorated the compartment) of some seaside palace.

An unmotivated crime, Lafcadio went on to himself: what a hell of a quandary for the police! On this embankment anyone might, from a neighbouring compartment, notice a door opening and the old fortune cookie tumbling out. At least the curtains are closed on the corridor side ... It's not so much the way events turn out that I'm curious about, but myself. So and so thinks himself capable of anything, and then, faced with doing it, chokes ... What a distance there is between imagining something and doing it! ... And with no more right to retract your move than you have at chess. You know something? As soon as you start foreseeing all the risks, the game's not worth it any more ... Between imagining and ... Hold on! We're at the end of the embankment. We're on a bridge. A river ...

The window had darkened, and the reflections appeared much more clearly. Fleurissoire leant forward to straighten his tie.

Right here by my hand, a two-stage lock – while he's distracted and staring into the dark in front of him – opens – yes! – even more easily than you'd have thought. If I can count to twelve, nice and slow, before I see a light in the dark out there, the old fart's safe. Go. One. Two. Three. Four (slow down!). Five. Six. Seven. Eight. Nine ... Ten ... A light!

II

Fleurissoire made no sound. On the receiving end of Lafcadio's shove, and facing the abyss that suddenly yawned in front of him, he lunged wildly to stop himself falling. His left hand clutched at the smooth surface of the doorframe while, half-turned, he threw his right hand way back over Lafcadio's head, sending his second cuff, which he had been putting on at that moment, shooting underneath the seat on the far side of the compartment.

Lafcadio felt a horrible hand gripping the back of his neck, ducked and gave a second shove more impatient than the first. Fingernails clawed at his collar, and then Fleurissoire could not find anything else to hang on to, except for Lafcadio's beaver hat, which he grabbed frantically and took with him as he fell.

'Now keep calm,' Lafcadio said to himself. 'Don't slam the door. They might hear in the next compartment.'

He dragged the door towards him – the wind was against it – and pulled it gently shut.

'He's left me his hideous boater, which I was just about to kick out after him, but he's taken my hat. It was a wise precaution to unpick the initials! … But the lining's still got the hatter's name on it, and I don't suppose beaver hats like that are ordered every day … Too bad, it's done now … People might think it was an accident … No, because I shut the door afterwards … Shall I stop the train? … Come on, Cadio! No retouching after the event. Everything's exactly the way you intended it.

'Let's prove I'm in complete control of myself. First let's examine calmly what's on this photograph the old man was looking at just now … *Miramar!* I haven't the slightest desire to go and see that … It's stuffy in here.'

He opened the window.

'The pig scratched me … I'm bleeding … He really hurt me. I need to dab some water on it: the toilet's at the end of the corridor, on the left. Let's get another handkerchief.'

He pulled his suitcase off the luggage rack above his head and opened it on the seat where he had just been sitting.

'If I bump into anyone in the corridor I've got to stay calm … It's all right, my heart's stopped pounding. Let's get cracking! … Oh look, there's his jacket. I can hide it under mine. And there are some papers in the pocket: something to read for the rest of the journey.'

It was a shabby, threadbare jacket, made of thin low-quality cloth the colour of liquorice. Lafcadio felt faintly disgusted, holding it away from him as he locked himself in the narrow toilet and hung it on a coat hook. Turning to the washbasin, he inspected himself in the mirror.

His neck had two unsightly gashes. A thin red scratch

that started at the nape of his neck continued around to the bottom of his left ear. The second one, which was shorter but deeper – a genuine wound – was two centimetres above the first: running straight up to his ear, it had torn his earlobe, which was bleeding, although less than he might have feared. The pain, on the other hand, which he had not felt at first, was now starting to sting. Soaking his handkerchief in the washbasin, he dabbed both cuts and stemmed the trickle of blood, then rinsed the handkerchief.

Not enough to stain my collar, anyway, he thought, making himself presentable. All's well.

He was about to unlock the door, but at that moment the locomotive whistled and a string of lights flashed past the frosted glass of the toilet window. They were coming into Capua. He was so close to the scene of the accident that he could get off the train and run back in the dark to retrieve his beaver hat … The thought suddenly struck him as a terrifically clever idea. He was disconsolate at the loss of his soft, light, silky, uncreasable hat, which was simultaneously warm and cool and so understatedly elegant. He never yielded to his desires straight away, however: it was not in his character to give in, even to himself. But he disliked indecision most of all, and for several years had kept, like a fetish, a dice from a backgammon game that Baldi had once given him. He always had it with him: it was in the fob pocket of his waistcoat now.

'If I throw a six,' he said to himself as he took it out, 'I'll get off!'

He threw a five.

'I'll get off anyway. Quick! The jacket! ... Then my suitcase ...'

He ran back to his compartment.

Ah! How futile all exclamations seem in the face of a fact's sheer strangeness! The more astonishing the event, the more simply I shall tell it. So I'll say only this: when Lafcadio got back to his compartment to collect his suitcase, the suitcase was not there.

At first he thought he had made a mistake and went back out into the corridor ... There was no mistake. It was certainly this compartment where he had been sitting. There was the photograph of the Miramar ... and then? ... He sprang to the window and thought he must be dreaming: on the station platform, just a few steps from the carriage, his suitcase was calmly disappearing in the custody of a tall man carrying it away at a leisurely pace.

Lafcadio was about to race after him, but as he reached to open the door the liquorice-coloured jacket fell at his feet.

'Blast! Blast! One more false move like that and I will be in the soup! ... But wouldn't that joker be getting a bit more of a move on if he thought I was coming after him? Might he have seen ...?'

At that moment, as he remained bending over, a drip of blood trickled along his cheek.

'Too bad about the suitcase! The dice was right: I mustn't get off here.'

He closed the door and sat down again.

'No documents in the suitcase, and none of my clothes are labelled: what have I got to worry about? Whatever! Time to ship out, as soon as possible. It may be a bit less fun, but it'll be a lot more sensible.'

The train was pulling out.

'I don't mind so much about the suitcase ... but I do mind about my beaver, which I'd really have liked to get back. I must stop thinking about it.'

He stuffed his pipe with dried juniper, lit it, then, digging his hand deep into the liquorice-coloured jacket's inside pocket, pulled out a letter from Arnica, a Thomas Cook agency wallet and a padded envelope, which he opened.

'Three – four – five – six thousand francs! Nothing there for honest folk, then.'

He put the notes back in the envelope and the envelope in the jacket pocket. But when he examined the Thomas Cook ticket wallet a moment later, he reeled. On the first page was written 'Julius de Baraglioul'.

Am I going mad? he thought. What was the connection with Julius? A stolen ticket? No, it couldn't be. A borrowed ticket, it must be. Blast! Blast! Maybe I have made a mess of this: these old boys are better connected than you think ...

Shaking from the unanswered questions that crowded in on him, he opened Arnica's letter. What had just happened seemed far too strange, and it was hard to concentrate. It was impossible to work out what relationship there might be between Julius and the old boy, but he did grasp one fact: Julius was in Rome. His decision was made. He was filled with an urgent desire to see his brother again, and an unbridled curiosity to witness the reverberations of this affair on his calm, logical mind.

All sorted! I'll stay in Naples tonight. I'll get my trunk back, and then tomorrow I'll catch the first train back to Rome. It'll be a lot less sensible, for certain, but perhaps a bit more fun.

III

At Naples Lafcadio booked into a hotel next to the station. He took care to have his trunk brought with him, because travellers without luggage are suspicious and he wanted to attract as little attention as he could. He then hurried to buy himself the few toiletries he needed and a hat to replace the ghastly boater (too tight at the front in any case) that Fleurissoire had left him. He had also decided to buy a revolver, but had to postpone that purchase till the morning, as the shops were already closing.

The train he wanted to catch the next morning left early. He would be at Rome in time for lunch ...

He intended to announce his presence to Julius after the newspapers had reported the 'crime'. *Crime!* The word seemed bizarre, and the word criminal, applied to him, totally inappropriate. He preferred *adventurer*, a word as flexible as his beaver hat, whose edges could also be reshaped at will.

The morning newspapers carried no news of the *adventure*. He waited patiently for the evening papers, eager to see Julius and to feel the game start. Like a child playing hide and seek, who does not want to be found but does want to be looked for, he became bored with waiting.

He was in an intermediate state, neither one thing nor the other, that he had not known before. The people he jostled in the streets seemed particularly mediocre, disagreeable and hideous.

When evening came, he bought the *Corriere* from a vendor on the Corso and went into a restaurant, but as a sort of challenge to himself and as if to sharpen his desire, he forced himself to dine first, leaving the newspaper folded up on the table next to him. Then he went out onto the Corso again, where he stopped in the light from a shop window, opened it, and on page two saw this headline above one of the news stories:

CRIME, SUICIDE ... OR ACCIDENT

Underneath he read this, which I translate:

A man's jacket containing six thousand francs was found yesterday on a Naples-bound train. At Naples station, railway staff discovered a dark-coloured jacket in the luggage rack in a first-class compartment of a train from Rome, the inside pocket of which contained an open yellow envelope with six one-thousand-franc notes inside. There were no other documents to identify the jacket's owner. Police have not yet commented on whether they are treating the find as suspicious, although the presence of such a

*large sum in the victim's jacket makes it likely that,
if crime was involved, theft was not the motive. There
was no sign of a struggle in the compartment, apart
from the discovery under a seat of a man's shirt-cuff
with the cufflink attached, in the form of two cat's
heads joined by a silver-gilt chain, cut from a semi-
transparent quartz known as opalescent smoky agate
or moonstone.*

*A thorough search is being conducted along the length
of the railway track between Naples and Rome.*

Lafcadio's hands clenched on the newspaper.

'What the hell? Now it's Carola's cufflinks. Who would have thought the old man had so many coincidences in him?'

He turned the page and saw:

STOP PRESS
BODY FOUND NEXT TO RAILWAY TRACKS

He did not read on, but ran to the Grand Hotel.

Asking the desk clerk for an envelope, he wrote under the name on his visiting card,

LAFCADIO WLUIKI
*wishes to know whether Count Julius de Baraglioul is
in need of a secretary*

put it in the envelope and asked for it to be sent up.

A page eventually came to collect him in the lobby where he was waiting, led him down long corridors, and presented him.

Looking around the room, Lafcadio saw a copy of the *Corriere della Sera* thrown down in a corner. On the table in the middle of the room a big unstoppered bottle of eau de Cologne spread its powerful scent. Julius opened his arms.

'Lafcadio! Dear friend … how very happy I am to see you!'

His mussed hair wafted agitatedly around his temples, and he seemed oddly excited. He had a handkerchief with black polka dots in his hand and was fanning himself with it.

'Well, you're one of the last people I expected to see. But the one I'd most have liked to be able to talk to this evening … Was it Madame Carola who told you I was here?'

'What a queer question!'

'Why? As I've just met her … Although actually I'm not certain she saw me.'

'Carola! Is she in Rome?'

'Didn't you know?'

'I've just this minute got here from Sicily and you're the first person I've seen. Her I don't have any desire to see.'

'I thought she was looking remarkably pretty.'

'You're not hard to please.'

'I mean, much prettier than in Paris.'

'That's your love of the exotic coming out – but if you're feeling frisky …'

'Lafcadio, such language is inappropriate between us.'

Julius tried to look stern, but only succeeded in making a face. He went on, 'You find me extremely agitated. I'm at a turning point in my life. My head feels as if it's on fire and my whole body is in the grip of a sort of giddiness, as if I were about to evaporate. I've been in Rome for three days, having come here for a sociology conference, and it has just been one shock after another. Your arrival, although of course very welcome, is the last straw … I hardly know myself any more.'

He was pacing up and down. Stopping at the table, he picked up the bottle, liberally splashed scent over his handkerchief, pressed it to his forehead like a compress and left it there.

'Dear young friend … allow me to call you that … I believe I have cracked my new book! What you said to me in Paris about *The Air on the Heights*, although I thought you went too far, makes me feel that you won't find this one unappealing.'

His feet performed an almost balletic little jump, and the handkerchief fell on the floor. Lafcadio quickly bent over to pick it up, and, as he did, he felt Julius's hand rest gently on his shoulder, exactly as he remembered old Juste-Agénor's hand resting there. He smiled as he straightened up.

'I've known you for such a short time,' Julius said, ' but tonight I can't help speaking to you as if to a …'

He stopped.

'I am listening to you like a brother, Monsieur de Baraglioul,' Lafcadio said, emboldened, 'since you see fit to invite me to.'

'Can you see, Lafcadio, that in the circles I move in in Paris, out of all the people I frequent – the worldly, the clergy, men and women of letters, Academicians – I don't really have anyone I can talk to, I mean anyone to whom I can confide these new preoccupations that have taken hold of me. The point being that since our first meeting – yours and mine – my point of view has completely changed.'

'A good thing too, I'd say!' Lafcadio said cheekily.

'I don't think you can really understand, not being a writer yourself, how much an erroneous outlook can inhibit the free development of your creative faculties. That's why nothing could be further from my earlier work than the novel I'm planning today. All the logic and consistency that I demanded from my characters, I also used to insist on from myself, in order to make them genuine. It wasn't natural. We so often prefer to lead lives that aren't authentic rather than fail to live up to the portrait we drew of ourselves right at the beginning.

It's absurd – and by doing it we run the risk of distorting what's best in us.'

Lafcadio was still smiling, waiting to hear what would come next and amused to see the effect his earliest remarks to Julius had had.

'How can I explain it to you, Lafcadio? For the very first time I feel I can give myself free rein ... Do you understand what those words mean: free rein? ... I say to myself that I had free rein before. I tell myself I still do, and that all that's held me back are impure considerations about my career, public opinion, and all those unappreciative judges whose approval the poet hopes for in vain. From now on I shall hope for nothing, except from myself. From now on I shall expect everything from myself: I shall expect everything from the man of sincerity, and I shall expect anything, because I also sense the strangest possibilities growing in me. And since it's only on paper, I have no qualms about letting them out. We shall see what we shall see!'

He was breathing heavily, his shoulder thrown back, arching his shoulder blade almost like a wing, as though these new perplexities were half stifling him. Continuing irrelevantly, he said in a lower voice, 'And since they don't want me, those Messieurs at the Académie, I'm about to provide them with several good reasons not to admit me, which incidentally they did not have before. They did not.'

At the last words his voice abruptly became almost shrill and sing-song. He stopped, then said more calmly, 'So, this is what I'm thinking about … Are you listening?'

'You have my undivided attention,' Lafcadio said, still grinning.

'And are you following me?'

'To the ends of the earth.'

Julius moistened his handkerchief again and sat down in an armchair. Lafcadio straddled a chair opposite him.

'It's about a young man, whom I want to turn into a criminal.'

'I can't see any difficulty with that.'

'Wait! Wait!' Julius, who rather liked difficulty, said.

'Well, who's stopping you, Monsieur-the-novelist? And from the minute you begin imagining things, from imagining everything you want?'

'But the stranger the thing I imagine, the more I have to provide motive, explanations.'

'It's hardly arduous to think up a motive for a crime.'

'I'm sure you're right … but that's precisely it, I don't want a motive for the crime. All I want is to motivate the criminal. Yes: I want to bring him to the point where he commits the crime quite gratuitously, where he wants to commit a completely unmotivated crime.'

Lafcadio started to listen more closely.

'Let's start with him as an adolescent: I need that starting point so that we see the elegance of his character, that everything he does is for the sake of play, and that he consistently puts his pleasure ahead of what's good for him.'

'That's fairly unusual, wouldn't you say?' Lafcadio ventured.

'Isn't it?' Julius said delightedly. 'We should also add that he enjoys exercising self-control ...'

'To the point of dissembling.'

'So we need to give him a love of risk.'

'Bravo!' Lafcadio said, more and more amused. 'And then, if he knows how to listen to the demon of curiosity, I think your pupil is ready for the wide world.'

With the thoughts of each vaulting over the other's, and each of them overtaking and being overtaken by the other, their conversation started to sound like a game of mental leapfrog.

JULIUS: I see him practising first, becoming an expert at petty theft.

LAFCADIO: I've often wondered why there isn't more petty theft. It's true that the opportunity mostly arises for those who aren't in need and aren't particularly susceptible to temptation.

JULIUS: Who aren't in need — exactly. He's one of those. But he's only drawn to opportunities that demand some skill from him, some cunning ...

LAFCADIO: And those that expose him to some danger, probably.

JULIUS: As I said, he enjoys risk. The point being that he loathes crookedness: he's not a thief in the ordinary sense, he just enjoys moving objects surreptitiously from one place to another. He has a magician's talent for making things vanish.

LAFCADIO: And the fact that he goes unpunished eggs him on ...

JULIUS: But irritates him at the same time. If he isn't getting caught, it means he must be playing too easy a game.

LAFCADIO: So he urges himself on to riskier and riskier scenarios.

JULIUS: Yes, I make him reason along exactly those lines ...

LAFCADIO: Are you quite sure that it's a process of reasoning?

JULIUS (*going on*): It's through the need he has to commit the crime that the perpetrator gives himself away.

LAFCADIO: We've established that he's very clever.

JULIUS: Yes, all the cleverer for acting completely coolly. Think about it: a crime unmotivated by either passion or need. His reason for committing the crime is precisely that of committing it without a reason.

LAFCADIO: *You're* reasoning out his crime. *He* just commits it.

JULIUS: There's no reason to suppose someone's a

criminal because he commits a crime without having a reason to.

LAFCADIO: You're being too subtle. When you take him that far, he surely becomes what we call 'a free man'.

JULIUS: At the mercy of the first opportunity.

LAFCADIO: I can't wait to see him at work. What do you plan to suggest to him?

JULIUS: Well, I hadn't quite made up my mind. Yes – until this evening I hadn't decided … Then suddenly tonight the paper broke some news that gave me exactly the situation I was looking for. Providential – but frightful too. I can hardly believe it. Someone has just murdered my brother-in-law!

LAFCADIO: What? The old man on the train was—

JULIUS: He was Amédée Fleurissoire, to whom I'd lent my ticket and whom I had just seen off at the station. An hour earlier he had cashed a cheque for six thousand francs at my bank, and because he had the money in his pocket he was nervous when we said goodbye. He was nursing dark thoughts, black thoughts – how can I describe it? Forebodings. Then in the train … But you've seen the paper.

LAFCADIO: Only the headline.

JULIUS: Let me read it to you (opening the *Corriere*). I'll translate:

'The police, who have been searching the length of the railway track between Rome and Naples, have this afternoon, in the dry bed of the Volturno river five kilometres from Capua, recovered the body of the man they believe was the owner of the jacket found yesterday evening in the carriage of a Naples-bound train. The man is of average height and build and approximately fifty years of age. ['He looked older than he was.'] *No documents were found with the body that offered any clues to its identity.* ['Fortunately that gives me the time to collect myself.'] *He had apparently been thrown out of the carriage with sufficient force to clear the parapet of a bridge whose stonework was undergoing repairs and had been replaced by wooden scaffolding.* ['What a prose style!'] *The bridge stands more than five metres above the river, and the victim is thought to have died as a result of the fall, his body carrying no trace of other wounds. He was discovered in shirtsleeves, and on his right wrist wore a shirt-cuff similar to the cuff found on the train, although the cufflink was missing* ... ['What's the matter?']

Julius stopped. Lafcadio had been unable to suppress a start at the thought that the cufflink had been removed after the body had landed in the river bed. Julius continued.)

'His left hand was still clutching a soft felt hat ...'

'*Soft felt*! Philistines!' Lafcadio muttered.

Julius stuck his nose over the top of the newspaper.

'What strikes you as so surprising?'

'Nothing, nothing! Go on.'

'*… soft felt hat which was much too large for his own head and may belong to his aggressor. The manufacturer's name had been carefully removed from the lining, out of which a piece of leather the shape and size of a laurel leaf was missing …*'

Lafcadio got to his feet and stood behind Julius, to read over his shoulder and perhaps also to conceal his pallor. It was irrefutable: his crime had been retouched. Someone else had been at the scene and had cut the name from the lining, probably the same stranger who had made off with his suitcase.

Julius read on:

'*… which seems to indicate that the crime was premeditated.* ['Why specifically this crime? My hero had perhaps taken his precautions entirely at random …'] *As soon as the police had made their report at the scene, the body was transferred to Naples to establish the man's identity.* ['Yes, they've the means to do that, and are used to preserving bodies there for a long time …']'

'How can you be sure it was him?' Lafcadio's voice shook slightly.

'It can't be anyone else. I was expecting him for dinner this evening.'

'Have you informed the police?'

'Not yet. I need to put my thoughts a little more in order before I do. I'm already in mourning, so from that side of things (I mean, the dress side) I'm all right, but you have to understand that as soon as the victim's name is released I shall have to let all my family know, send telegrams, write letters, put it into the papers, arrange the funeral, go to Naples to claim the body … Oh! My dear Lafcadio, with this conference going on, which I've committed myself to taking part in, would you mind very much acting as my representative and collecting the body instead of me?'

'Can we decide that later?'

'Assuming it doesn't upset you too much, of course. In the meantime I'm saving my poor sister-in-law some cruel hours of uncertainty. It's very unlikely that she would connect her husband with these vague newspaper reports … I return to my subject.

'So, when I read the *Corriere* report I said to myself: This crime, which I can visualise so easily, which I can reconstitute, which I can see – I'm positive I know what made the perpetrator do it, and I know that if it hadn't been for the lure of those six thousand francs, the crime wouldn't have been committed.'

'But suppose, though, that—'

'Yes, exactly: let's suppose for a moment that there had been no six thousand francs or, better still, that the criminal hadn't taken them: he's my man.'

Lafcadio had already got to his feet. He retrieved the newspaper that Julius had dropped and opened it at page two.

'I see you haven't read the earlier edition: in fact the … criminal didn't steal the six thousand francs,' he said, as coolly as he could. 'Here, read this: "This makes it likely that, if crime was involved, theft was not the motive."'

Julius snatched the page that Lafcadio was holding out to him and read it eagerly, then rubbed his eyes with his hand, sat down, stood up again abruptly, stepped over to Lafcadio and seized both his arms.

'Theft not the motive!' he exclaimed, and as if in the grip of a fit shook Lafcadio fiercely. 'Theft not the motive! But then …' He pushed him away, rushed to the other end of the room, fanning himself, hitting his forehead and blowing his nose. 'Then I know, good God, I know why this scoundrel killed him … Oh, my unlucky friend, oh, poor Fleurissoire! He was telling me the truth all along! And I thought he'd gone mad … This is absolutely dreadful.'

Lafcadio waited, astonished, for the attack to subside. He felt faintly annoyed: it seemed to him that Julius did not deserve to be let off the hook so easily.

'I thought that was exactly what you—'

'Be quiet! You don't know anything about it. And here I am wasting my time with you, making up ridiculous scenarios … Quickly! My stick and my hat!'

'Where are you rushing off to?'

'To inform the police, of course!'

Lafcadio blocked the doorway.

'Explain it to me first,' he said commandingly. 'Good Lord, anyone would think you'd gone mad.'

'No, I was mad before, I've just woken up from my madness … Oh, poor Fleurissoire! Unlucky friend! Saintly victim! His death has stopped me on the path of disrespect and blasphemy just in time. His sacrifice has saved me. And to think I mocked him!'

He had started pacing up and down again. Suddenly stopping and putting his stick and hat down on the table next to the bottle of eau de Cologne, he stood squarely in front of Lafcadio.

'You want to know why the scoundrel killed him?'

'I thought he did it without a motive.'

Julius said furiously, 'First and foremost, there is no crime without a motive. He was eliminated because he knew a secret … which he'd entrusted me with, a secret of considerable magnitude and certainly too important for him to deal with. They were afraid of him. Do you understand? So … Oh, it's easy for you to laugh, you who understand nothing of the ways of faith.'

Then, very pale, standing very straight: 'And I am the one who has inherited this secret.'

'Be careful then! It's you they're going to be afraid of now.'

'Now you see why I must go and warn the police immediately.'

'One more question,' Lafcadio said, stopping him again.

'No. Let me go. I'm in a frantic hurry. The continual surveillance that almost drove my poor brother-in-law mad will be focused on me from now on, you can be quite certain. You have no idea whatsoever how clever these people are. They know everything, I tell you … It becomes more opportune than ever that you should go and collect his body instead of me … Watched as I am at this moment, it's impossible to say what might become of me. I ask you to do this as a personal favour to me, Lafcadio, dear friend.' He put his hands together imploringly. 'At this moment my head is spinning, but I'll make some enquiries at the *questura*, to provide you with the proper authorisation. Where can I send it to you?'

'It'll be more convenient if I take a room here. I'll see you tomorrow. Goodbye. Hurry!'

He let Julius go. A feeling of deep disgust rose in him and almost a kind of hatred, against himself, against Julius, against everything. He shrugged his shoulders, then took out of his pocket the Thomas Cook ticket wallet in the name of Baraglioul that he had removed from

Fleurissoire's jacket, put it on the table where it would be seen, next to the bottle of eau de Cologne, switched off the light and went out.

IV

Despite all the precautions he had taken, despite his representations to the *questura*, Julius de Baraglioul was unable to stop the newspapers both divulging his relationship to the victim and identifying the hotel where he was staying.

The previous evening he had, without question, experienced several minutes of extreme apprehension when, returning from the *questura* around midnight, he had found in his room, clearly visible, the tickets from Thomas Cook issued in his name which he had given to Fleurissoire to use. He had immediately rung the bell and, walking straight back out into the corridor, white and trembling, requested the page to check under his bed because he did not dare check himself. The enquiry he instituted there and then produced no answers, but how could you have confidence in the staff of large hotels? After a good night's sleep behind a solidly bolted door he had woken up more at ease, remembering that the police were now protecting him. He wrote a number of letters and telegrams and took them to the post office himself.

As he returned, he was informed that a woman had been asking for him. She had not given her name but was waiting for him in the reading room. Julius went to find her, and was more than a little surprised to discover Carola there. Not in the main room, but in another, more private space that was smaller and less well lit. She was sitting at an angle, at the corner of a far table, and distractedly leafing through a photographic album for appearance's sake. Seeing Julius come in, she stood up, more nervous than glad. The black coat she wore opened to reveal a dark, simple, tailored dress that was almost in good taste, but her exuberant hat, despite also being black, gave the game away.

'You will think me very forward, Monsieur le comte. I don't quite know how I found the courage to come to your hotel and ask for you, but you greeted me so nicely yesterday ... And what I have to tell you is too important.'

She remained standing, with the table between them. It was Julius who made the first move, going over to her and unceremoniously holding out his hand across the table.

'To what do I owe the pleasure of your visit?'

Carola looked down.

'I know what you must be going through.'

Julius did not understand at first, but as Carola took out a handkerchief and dabbed her eyes he said, 'Forgive me! Is this a visit of condolence?'

'I knew Monsieur Fleurissoire,' she went on.

'I beg your pardon?'

'Oh, not for very long at all. But I liked him. He was

so kind, so good … In fact it was me who gave him those cufflinks: you know, the ones whose description they gave in the newspaper. They were how I knew it was him. But I didn't know that he was your brother-in-law. I was really surprised to hear that. You can imagine how glad I was … Oh, I'm sorry! That's not what I wanted to say.'

'Don't worry, dear Mademoiselle, what you doubtless wanted to say is that you're happy to have this opportunity to see me again.'

Without answering, Carola buried her face in her handkerchief. She was racked by sobs, and Julius felt he should hold her hand.

'I also,' he said, in a ringing voice, 'I also, dear lady, believe me when—'

'That very morning, before he left, I told him to take care. But it wasn't in his nature … he was too trusting, you know.'

'A saint, Mademoiselle, he was a saint,' Julius said feelingly, and took out his own handkerchief.

'Yes, that was just what I thought,' Carola exclaimed. 'At night, when he thought I was asleep, he got up, he knelt at the end of the bed and …'

This unthinking admission added to Julius's disturbed state. He put his handkerchief back in his pocket and, moving closer, said, 'Please take your hat off, dear lady.'

'Thank you, but it's not bothering me.'

'But it is bothering me … Allow me …'

But as Carola took a deliberate step backwards, he pulled himself together.

'Allow me to ask: do you have any particular reason to feel worried?'

'Me?'

'Yes. When you told my brother-in-law to take care, I'm asking you if you had any reason to suppose ... You can speak openly: no one comes here in the mornings and we can't be overheard. Do you suspect someone?'

Carola lowered her eyes.

'Understand that it's of particular interest to me,' Julius continued excitedly, 'and put yourself in my position. Yesterday night, coming back from the *questura* where I had been to give a statement, I found in my bedroom, on the table – right in the middle of the table – the train ticket poor Fleurissoire had used. It was in my name: these return tickets are non-transferable, obviously. I was wrong to lend it to him, but that's not the point ... In that act of cynically taking advantage of a moment when I was out and returning my ticket to me, right to my room, I feel a challenge, a brazen piece of bravado, almost an insult ... which would not bother me, needless to say, if I didn't have good reason to believe myself targeted in turn, and I shall tell you why: poor Fleurissoire, your friend, was in possession of a secret ... an outrageous secret ... a very dangerous secret ... which I didn't ask him to reveal ... which I had absolutely no desire to know ... which he, in the most irritatingly reckless manner, confided to me. So now I must ask you: the person who has been perfectly ready to commit murder in order to suppress this secret – do you know who it is?'

'Set your mind at rest, Monsieur le comte. Yesterday evening I told the police his name.'

'Mademoiselle Carola, I expected nothing less of you.'

'He promised me he wouldn't hurt Monsieur Fleurissoire. All he had to do was keep his promise, and I'd have kept mine. This time I've had enough: he can do what he likes to me, I don't care.'

Carola was flushed with excitement. Julius walked around the table and stood close to her again.

'We would perhaps be better off talking in my room.'

'Oh, Monsieur,' Carola said, 'I've told you everything I had to say to you. I shouldn't like to hold you up any longer.'

Retreating again, she edged around the table towards the exit.

'It will be better if we take our leave of each other here, then,' Julius replied with dignity, determined to claim the credit for her resistance. 'Oh yes, there is one other thing I wanted to say: if you feel inclined to come to the funeral, which will be the day after tomorrow, it will be better that you don't know me.'

On these words they went their separate ways, without once having mentioned the name of the unsuspected Lafcadio.

Lafcadio collected Fleurissoire's body from Naples. It was transported in a mortuary van that was coupled to the rear of the train, although he had not felt that it was vital for him to travel with the corpse. Even so, his sense of decorum made him take a seat in a compartment that while not absolutely the closest he could find – because the last carriage was second-class accommodation – was as close to the body as the first-class carriages would allow. Having left Rome in the morning, he was due back in the evening of the same day. He was nevertheless reluctant to accept a new feeling that crept up on him as he travelled, for there was nothing he despised more than boredom, that secret affliction he had so far been saved from by the fine, careless appetites of his youth and then by harsh necessity. And so, quitting his compartment with a heart empty of both hope and joy, he paced moodily up and down the carriage corridor, nagged by an ill-defined curiosity and doubtfully looking for he knew not what new and absurd project to test himself on. Nothing seemed to match up to his aspirations. He had stopped thinking about taking ship for the East and unwillingly acknowledged that Borneo now seemed as profoundly dull as did the rest of Italy. Even the ramifications of his adventure failed to interest him: it just seemed compromising and peculiar to him now. Angry with Fleurissoire for not having struggled more, he railed inwardly at the pitiful figure of his victim and would have liked to erase him from his mind.

On the other hand, he would very much have liked to bump into the fellow who had made off with his suitcase again. A serious prankster! ... And as if he might just be waiting there to be glimpsed at Capua station, Lafcadio leant out of the window, scouring the deserted platform. But would he even recognise him? He had only seen him from behind, already some way away and disappearing into the darkness ... In his imagination he followed him into the night, as far as the Volturno's river bed, coming across the hideous corpse, robbing it and, in a defiant gesture, cutting out of the lining of the hat, his own hat, Lafcadio's, that piece of leather 'the shape and size of a laurel leaf' as the newspaper had so elegantly phrased it. Lafcadio was nevertheless extremely grateful to the suitcase thief for having removed such an incriminating piece of evidence – his outfitter's name – from the police's scrutiny. Doubtless the aforesaid corpse robber himself had every reason for not wanting to attract attention to himself – and if, despite everything, he decided to make use of his leather souvenir, then, good Lord! it might be rather amusing to confront him.

Dusk had fallen. A waiter from the restaurant car came

past, informing first- and second-class passengers up and down the train that dinner was being served. Not feeling hungry, but with the prospect of being rescued from his idle state for an hour, Lafcadio trailed in the wake of several others, though a long way behind them. The restaurant car was at the head of the train. The carriages Lafcadio passed through were empty. Here and there various objects on the seats indicated and reserved the diners' places: shawls, pillows, books, newspapers. A lawyer's briefcase caught his eye. Certain of being the last, he paused outside the compartment, then went in. To tell the truth, the briefcase itself was of little interest to him. It was mainly so as not to overlook the slightest opportunity that he rifled through its contents. On an inner label, in inconspicuous gold letters, the briefcase bore the name:

DEFOUQUEBLIZE
Faculty of Law, Bordeaux

It contained two pamphlets on criminal law and six copies of *La Gazette des Tribunaux*.

More bumf for Julius's conference, Lafcadio thought. Dull, dull, dull. And he put it all back in the briefcase before stepping out to catch up with the line of passengers on their way to the restaurant car.

A frail-looking young girl and her mother stood at the back of the queue, both in mourning clothes, and directly in front of them was a man in a frock coat and top hat with long straight hair and thick, greying sideburns: Monsieur Defouqueblize himself, probably, the briefcase's owner. The passengers made their way forward slowly and unsteadily with the swaying of the train. Just where the corridor turned at the end of the carriage, as the professor was about to step into that sort of accordion that connects one carriage to the next, a more pronounced jolt made him lurch. Jerking backwards to try to regain his balance, he sent his pince-nez, its ribbon pulled free, flying into the corner of the narrow corridor space in front of the door of the WC. As he bent down to try to retrieve it, the woman and her daughter stepped past him. For a few moments Lafcadio watched his efforts with amusement. Impotent and defenceless, he groped feebly and with anxious hands across the floor of the corridor: he looked as though he was performing the shuffling dance of a bear or had regressed to his childhood and was playing 'Heads, shoulders, knees and toes'. Come on, Lafcadio! Be decent. Listen to your heart, which has not been entirely corrupted yet. Give the poor man a hand. Pick up his glasses, you know he can't do without them, and nor will he find them on his own. Another step in that direction and he'll tread on them … At that moment a fresh jolt threw the unfortunate man head first against the door of the WC. His top hat absorbed the impact, but was half flattened and ended up jammed over his ears. Monsieur Defouqueblize groaned, straightened, and tugged his hat off. Lafcadio, meanwhile, judging the joke had gone far enough, picked up the pince-nez, placed it in the hat the man was holding out as though asking for alms, and made his escape, deaf to all thanks.

Dinner had started. Lafcadio sat down at a table for two next to the glass door, on the right-hand side of the car. The seat opposite was vacant. On the other side of the aisle, level with his table, the widow and her daughter had sat at a table for four, two seats of which were vacant.

'How dull these places always are!' Lafcadio said to himself, his languid gaze straying over the other diners and not finding a single face interesting enough to rest on. 'All these cattle treating life as if it were an endlessly tedious chore, instead of the entertainment it really is, or can be … And so badly dressed. But they'd be even uglier naked! I'll have died of boredom before the dessert course if I don't get some champagne.'

The professor came in. He must have gone to wash his hands after dirtying them in the search, and was now examining his nails. A waiter sat him opposite Lafcadio. The wine waiter was going through the car. Lafcadio, not speaking, pointed to a Montebello Grand Crémant for twenty francs and Monsieur Defouqueblize ordered a bottle of Saint-Galmier water. He was now holding his pince-nez between two fingers, gently breathing on it and cleaning it with the corner of his napkin. Lafcadio watched him, fascinated by his mole-like eyes blinking beneath heavy, reddened eyelids.

'Fortunately he doesn't know that it's me who gave him his sight back! If he starts thanking me, I shall move tables immediately.'

The wine waiter came back with the Saint-Galmier and the champagne, which he uncorked first and placed between the two diners. The bottle was no sooner on the table than Defouqueblize reached for it without checking which it was and poured himself a glassful that he swallowed in a single gulp ... The wine waiter was about to intervene, but Lafcadio stopped him, laughing.

'What on earth am I drinking?' Defouqueblize exclaimed, pulling a horrible face.

'This gentleman's Montebello,' the wine waiter said stiffly. 'This is your Saint-Galmier water!'

He put down the second bottle.

'I'm extremely sorry, Monsieur ... My eyesight is so poor ... I'm covered in confusion, believe me—'

'You would give me great pleasure, Monsieur,' Lafcadio interrupted, 'if you would stop apologising – and then accept another glass, if of course you enjoyed the first one.'

'Alas, Monsieur, I'll admit to you that I thought it was quite loathsome, and I do not understand how, in my distracted state, I was able to swallow a whole glass. I was so thirsty … Tell me, Monsieur, if you wouldn't mind, that wine is extremely strong, is it not? … Because I must tell you, I never drink anything but water … The slightest drop of alcohol always goes straight to my head … Good heavens! Good heavens! What is going to happen to me? … Perhaps if I went straight back to my compartment? … I'm certain that I'd better lie down.'

He made a movement as if to get to his feet.

'Stay! Do stay, Monsieur,' Lafcadio said, beginning to enjoy himself. 'On the contrary, you'd be better off eating your dinner and not worrying about the wine. I'll take you back to your compartment in a little while if you need some help getting there, but don't worry: what you've drunk wouldn't make a baby's head spin.'

'I'd like to believe what you say. But truly I don't know how you … Might I offer you a glass of Saint-Galmier?'

'I'm obliged to you, but will you forgive me if I prefer my champagne?'

'Ah! So it really was champagne! And … you're going to drink all that?'

'To set your mind at rest.'

'You're too kind, although in your place I—'

'Suppose you ate something now?' Lafcadio interrupted, turning to his own food and finding Defouqueblize tiresome. His attention had been attracted by the widow.

Definitely Italian. Her late husband probably an officer. What dignity in the way she carries herself!

What tenderness in her eyes! How pure her complexion is! How intelligent her hands are! What elegance there is in her clothes, and simplicity too ... Lafcadio, when you can no longer hear in your heart the harmonies of such deep refinement, may that heart have ceased to beat! Her daughter looks like her, and with what nobility – tinged with seriousness, almost sadness – the child's excess of grace is tempered! With what loving solicitude her mother leans towards her! Before beings like those two, even the devil would bow down. For beings like them, Lafcadio, there is no question that your heart would devote itself wholeheartedly ...

The waiter had come to serve the next course. Lafcadio relinquished his plate, which was still half full, because at that moment he was suddenly dumbfounded by what he saw: the widow, his delicately refined widow, had leant out into the gangway and, deftly hitching up her skirt with the most natural movement, revealed a scarlet stocking and an exquisitely shaped calf.

So unexpectedly did this provocative note break into the dignified gravity of the symphony ... had he dreamt it? The waiter, meanwhile, had returned with a clean plate. Lafcadio was about to serve himself, and his gaze went to his plate, and what he saw there finished him off.

There, in front of him, clearly visible in the middle of his plate, fallen from heaven knows where but hideous and instantly recognisable ... do not doubt it, Lafcadio, do not doubt it for a moment: it is Carola's cufflink! The one with the two cat's heads, missing from Fleurissoire's second cuff. The whole business is turning into a nightmare ... But the waiter is bending over the dish. Adroitly Lafcadio wipes his plate, sweeping the ghastly trinket onto the tablecloth, puts his plate back down over it, serves himself generously, fills his glass with champagne, gulps it down and refills it. For now, if the man who has not eaten is already having drunken visions ... No, it's no hallucination: he can hear the cufflink crunch against his plate. He tilts it, scoops out the cufflink, slips it into his waistcoat pocket next to his watch, and feels for it to reassure himself: yes, it's there, safely hidden away ... But who can say how it got to be on his plate? Who put it there? ... Lafcadio looks at Defouqueblize: the professor is eating unconcernedly, his nose in his food. Wanting to take his mind off things, Lafcadio glances again at the widow, but everything in her gestures and dress has gone back to being decent and mundane. He finds her less pretty than before. He tries hard to conjure up her provocative gesture again, her red stocking, and cannot. He tries hard to visualise the cufflink on his plate again, and if he could not feel it there, in his pocket, he would definitely doubt ... More to the point, though, why did he pick up the cufflink? ... Which did not belong to him. By making that instinctive, absurd gesture, what an admission he had made! As if he had owned up ... identified himself to whoever it was, and perhaps also to the police, who are doubtless lying in wait, watching him … He has blundered into this crude trap like an amateur. He feels himself turning pale. He turns round sharply: there is no one behind the glass door into the corridor … But perhaps someone saw him just now! He forces himself to carry on eating, but his teeth are clenched in annoyance. Poor Lafcadio! It is not his dreadful crime that he regrets, but being haplessly caught off guard … What's wrong with the professor now? Why is he smiling at him like that? …

Defouqueblize had finished eating. He wiped his lips. With both elbows on the table, nervously twisting his napkin, he began to stare at Lafcadio. His lips shifted in a queer sort of grin. Eventually, as if unable to restrain himself any longer, he said, 'Dare I ask for just a little more, Monsieur?'

He shyly pushed his glass towards the almost empty bottle.

Lafcadio, distracted from his anxiety and glad of the diversion, poured him the last drops.

'I'm afraid I can't give you much … But would you like me to order some more?'

'Well, I think a half-bottle ought to be enough.'

Defouqueblize, already distinctly tipsy, had lost all sense of propriety. Lafcadio, for whom champagne held no terrors and who was amused by the other's unworldliness, asked the waiter to open a second bottle of Montebello.

'No! No! Don't give me too much,' Defouqueblize said, raising his swaying glass, which Lafcadio had just filled to the brim. 'It's odd that I should have thought it so unpleasant to begin with. One makes monsters out of so many things like that, just because one doesn't know them. There I was thinking I was drinking Saint-Galmier, and so I thought it had a decidedly peculiar taste for Saint-Galmier, you see. It's as if someone poured you some Saint-Galmier when you were expecting to drink champagne, and you'd say, wouldn't you, that tastes decidedly peculiar for champagne!'

He laughed at his own joke and then leant across the table towards Lafcadio, who was also laughing, and said in a low voice, 'I don't know what's making me laugh like this: it must be your wine's doing. I suspect it's definitely a bit more potent than you say. Haha! But you'll help me back to my carriage, won't you? We agreed, didn't we? We'll be alone there, and if I misbehave you'll know why.'

'When you travel,' Lafcadio averred, 'you don't need to worry about consequences.'

'Ah, Monsieur,' Defouqueblize replied, 'if only one could be certain that there was no need to worry about consequences, as you put it so neatly, where everything one did in life was concerned! If only one could guarantee that it didn't embroil one in anything else ... Look, precisely these things I'm saying to you, here and now, and which after all are perfectly natural thoughts, do you think I'd

292

dare say them so unguardedly if we were in Bordeaux? I say Bordeaux because that's where I live. I'm known and respected there. Although I'm unmarried, I have a nice quiet life there, and my profession is well regarded: I'm a professor at the law faculty – yes, comparative criminology, a new chair … But you see, I'm not allowed, there I'm not actually allowed to get tipsy, not even once and not by accident. My life must be respectable at all times. Imagine if one of my students were to meet me drunk in the street! … Respectable at all times, and without appearing to be in any way constrained. That's the snag: one must not arouse any suspicion. "Monsieur Defouqueblize" (that's my name) "does a jolly good job of keeping himself in check!"… One must not only never do anything out of the ordinary, but also persuade others that one couldn't do anything out of the ordinary even under the severest provocation, that one simply has nothing out of the ordinary inside one, wanting to get out. Is there a little wine left? Just a drop, dear partner in crime, just a drop … An opportunity such as this occurs once in a lifetime. Tomorrow in Rome, at the conference we are all attending, I shall find dozens of colleagues, serious, civilised, restrained men, as stuffy as I shall also become the moment I'm back in harness. People who are public figures, such as you or I, Monsieur, are duty-bound to live inauthentic lives.'

Dinner was coming to an end. A waiter came past, settling diners' bills and collecting tips.

As the restaurant car emptied, Defouqueblize's voice deepened and got louder. There were moments when his animation began to make Lafcadio feel uneasy. He went on, 'And if society did not exist to keep us in check, that group of our relations and friends whom we can't bring ourselves to upset would do its job for it. Holding up against our uncivilised authenticity an image of ourselves that we're only half responsible for, that bears little resemblance to who we are, but which it's profoundly improper to cast aside. At this moment – I can't deny it – I've cast aside that image, escaped from myself … Oh, giddy adventure! Oh, delicious peril! … I'm sorry, am I boring you to tears?'

'I find you curiously interesting.'

'I can't stop talking, talking … I can't help it! Even when one's drunk, one is still a professor, and the subject is close to my heart … But if you have finished eating, perhaps you'd be so kind as to offer me your arm to help me back to my compartment while I'm still capable of standing. I'm afraid if I stay on here much longer, I shan't be able to get up at all.'

As he said it Defouqueblize made a sort of lunge as if to extricate himself from his chair, but fell heavily back down and half slumped across the empty table, the upper part of his frame sprawled close to Lafcadio. He started speaking again, this time in a softer, half-confidential voice.

'Here's my thesis. Do you know what it takes to turn

an honest man into a rascal? All it takes is a change of scene, forgetting where you once were! Yes, Monsieur, one's memory goes blank, and authenticity emerges! ... A cessation of continuity, a simple disruption of the current. Naturally I don't say that when I'm teaching ... But between ourselves, what an advantage it gives to the child born out of wedlock! Think about it: the being who owes his very existence to a misdemeanour, to a flaw in the family's straight line of descent ...'

The professor's voice had become louder again. He was now staring at Lafcadio with a strange look in his eyes that was alternately vague and piercing and beginning to worry him. Lafcadio's next thought was to wonder whether the man's short-sightedness was feigned, and almost whether he recognised his look. More uneasy than he would have liked to admit, he got to his feet and said abruptly, 'Let us go, Monsieur Defouqueblize. Take my arm. Stand up. Enough talking.'

Defouqueblize, with a great stumbling effort, got up from his chair. Staggering, the two men made their way down the corridor to the compartment where the professor had left his briefcase. Defouqueblize went in first, and Lafcadio sat him down and took his leave. He had just turned to go, when a powerful hand landed on his shoulder. He spun round. Defouqueblize had leapt to his feet ... but was it still Defouqueblize who was exclaiming, in a voice that was simultaneously mocking, commanding and jubilant, 'You really ought not to try to abandon a friend so quickly, Monsieur Lafcadio Whoeveryouareski! So …? Is it true? Were you just going to run away?'

Of the tottering, tipsy, buffoonish professor of a few moments ago there was now no sign in the tall, well-built, vigorously youthful man whom Lafcadio no longer had any hesitation in identifying as Protos: a bigger, broader, larger Protos, who gave an impression of daunting force.

'Ah. It is you, Protos,' he said simply. 'I like that better. I couldn't decide whether it was or it wasn't.'

Because, however ominous it might be, Lafcadio preferred reality to the outlandish nightmare he had been struggling to deal with for the last hour.

'Not badly made up, was I? I made a special effort for you … Even so, you're the one who ought to be wearing glasses, my boy. You'll go getting yourself into serious trouble if you can't recognise "the subtle" better than that.'

What half-submerged memories that word 'subtle' brought to the surface of Cadio's mind! A 'subtle', in the slang he and Protos had used from the time when they had been at boarding school together, a subtle was a man who, for whatever reason it might be, did not present to everyone and in every situation the same appearance. The two of them had created numerous categories of 'subtle', all more or less elegant and praiseworthy, and in contrast to them had designated an opposing, unified and more numerous force known as 'the mossbacks' whose members, whatever walk of life they came from, behaved as if it belonged to them by entitlement.

Our schoolfriends took two tenets for granted:

1) The subtle recognise each other.

2) Mossbacks do not recognise the subtle.

All of this came back to Lafcadio, and as it was his nature to throw himself into the spirit of any game, he smiled.

Protos went on, 'Even so, the other day you were glad I was there, I think I'm right in saying … It wasn't perhaps entirely by chance. I like to keep an eye on the novices: they're imaginative, they're enterprising, they have style … But they're a bit too fond of supposing that they can do without advice. Your disguise was famously in need of some retouching, my boy! … What was the idea of wearing a titfer like that when you were on the job? With the maker's name on that nice bit of evidence, they'd have fingered you within a week. But I keep a soft spot for old friends, and I'll prove it. You do know, don't you, Cadio, that I was very fond of you? I always thought we might make something of you. With your good looks we could have made a clean sweep of all the women, and for that matter one or two of the men into the bargain. I was so pleased to hear news of you after so long, and to hear you were coming to Italy! And, you know, I was all ears to hear what had happened to you since the days we went to that little tart of ours. You're not so bad-looking even now, you know. Ah, that Carola, she was an uppity little minx!'

Lafcadio's annoyance was becoming more and more evident, as were his efforts to conceal it, all of which amused Protos greatly, even as he pretended not to be aware of it. From his waistcoat pocket he pulled out a piece of leather and examined it.

'I did a nice job of cutting that out, didn't I?'

Lafcadio could have strangled him. He clenched his fists until his nails dug into his skin. Protos continued to needle him.

'And a nice favour, I'd say! Easily worth the six thousand francs that … Well, you tell me, why didn't you trouser them?'

Lafcadio was rigid with indignation.

'Do you take me for a thief?'

'Hear this, my boy,' Protos went on calmly, 'I don't like amateurs much: it's better that I tell you that straight up. And in any case, with me, you know, there's no point your being full of yourself or playing dumb. You show promise, I grant you, extraordinary promise, but—'

'That's enough of your condescension,' Lafcadio interrupted, unable to contain his anger. 'What's your point? I made a mistake the other day – do you think I need to be reminded of it? Yes, you've got something on me now, but let's not go into whether it would be wise for you to use it, shall we? You want me to buy back that bit of leather? Then say so! Stop laughing and leering at me like that. You want money. How much?'

His tone was so resolute that Protos stepped back, but recovered.

'Easy, easy!' he said. 'What was unfair about what I just said? We're talking as friends here, calmly. It's nothing to get worked up about. You know, you're even younger than you were, Cadio!'

He stroked Lafcadio's arm in a conciliatory gesture. Lafcadio pulled away with a jerk.

'Let's sit down,' Protos went on. 'It'll be more comfortable to talk.'

He settled himself in a seat next to the door into the corridor and put his feet up on the seat opposite.

Lafcadio decided that he was intending to bar the exit. Protos was no doubt armed. He himself was not carrying a weapon. He reflected that, if it came to a struggle, he would come off worse. At the same time, if he had considered for a moment trying to escape, his curiosity had already got the better of him – that passionate curiosity over which nothing else, not even his own safety, had ever been able to prevail. He too sat down.

'Money? Oh, for heaven's sake!' Protos said. He took a cigar from his cigar case and offered one to Lafcadio, who shook his head. 'The smoke bothers you? ... All right, hear me out.'

He took several puffs from his cigar, then said calmly, 'No, Lafcadio, my friend, no. It's not money I'm expecting from you, but compliance. Because, my boy, you don't seem – and you'll excuse my frankness – to realise exactly what your situation is. You need to face up to it, and boldly. Allow me to help you.

'So, a youth wanted to break out of that social fabric that constrains us. A likeable youth – indeed one very much after my own heart – artless and appealingly spontaneous – because he didn't, I presume, think it necessary to do it in a very scheming fashion … Cadio, I remember how hot you once were with numbers, but that where your own expenses were concerned you always refused to count the cost.

'In short, the mossbacks' world disgusted you. Surprise, surprise … But what does surprise me is that intelligent as you are, Cadio, you should have believed that you could distance yourself from a society just like that, without walking straight into another one, or that any society can do without a set of laws.

'"Lawless" – do you remember? We read that somewhere:

Two hawks in the air, two fishes swimming in the sea not more lawless than we [12]

What a beautiful thing literature is! Lafcadio, my friend, learn the law of the subtle!'

'You could oblige me and get on with it.'

'What's the hurry? We've plenty of time. I'm only getting off at Rome. Lafcadio, my friend, it does happen that a crime gets past the police, and I shall tell you why: we are cleverer than they are, because our lives are on the line. Where the police fail, we sometimes succeed. Good God, Lafcadio, that's what you wanted, and now the thing's done and you can't get away from it. I should prefer you to comply with my instructions, because quite frankly I should be very sorry indeed to have to hand over an old friend like you to the police. But what can be done? From now on you're either in their hands – or ours.'

'To hand me over would mean handing yourself over too …'

'I had hoped we were talking seriously. So try to take this in, Lafcadio: the police lock up those who transgress, but in Italy they're happy to come to an understanding with the subtle. "Come to an understanding" – I believe that's the phrase. There's something of the police in me, my boy. I've got an eye for it. I help to keep order. I'm not an actor, I'm a producer – I make others act.

'Come on, Cadio! Stop fighting it. There's nothing so terrible about my law. You exaggerate these things to yourself – you're so naïve, so impetuous! Don't you see that you're already falling in with it, snatching Mademoiselle Venitequa's cufflink off your plate at dinner? You did it because I wanted you to. Aha! An entirely unthinking gesture, an instinctive gesture! Poor

Lafcadio! Have you done cursing yourself for that one tiny act yet, eh? The bloody annoying thing of course is that I wasn't the only one to see it. Pah! Don't get yourself in a state but the waiter and the widow and the little girl are all in on it. Delightful people! It's all up to you whether you have them as your friends or not. Lafcadio, my old pal, be sensible. Give in?'

Perhaps out of extreme shamefacedness, Lafcadio had decided to say nothing. He sat stiffly, lips pressed together, eyes staring fixedly ahead. Protos continued with a shrug of his shoulders.

'Strange fellow! And actually so relaxed! ... But perhaps you'd already have acquiesced if I had told you at the outset what we expect from you. Lafcadio, old friend, enlighten me on one point. For you – who, when I left you, were so poor – not to pick up six thousand francs that chance had thrown at your feet, do you think that's natural? ... Monsieur de Baraglioul died, according to what Mademoiselle Venitequa tells me, the day after Count Julius, his noble son, came to visit you, and that same evening you dumped Mademoiselle Venitequa. Since that time your relations with Count Julius have become, and I believe there's no other word for it, highly intimate. Would you care to explain why? ... Lafcadio, old friend, once upon a time your life was filled with numerous uncles. Subsequently your family tree seems to have become more than somewhat embaragliouled ... No, no, don't get cross, I'm only joking. But what is one supposed to think? … Unless, however, you owe your current fortune to Monsieur Julius himself, which, if you don't mind me saying so, handsome though you are, Lafcadio, would seem distinctly scandalous to me. Anyhow, whatever the real reason, and whatever you would like us to imagine, Lafcadio, old pal, the whole thing is unambiguous to us and your duty is clear: you must blackmail Julius. Don't get huffy! Blackmail is a virtuous business, necessary for the maintenance of morals. Hey! What? Are you leaving?'

Lafcadio had stood up.

'Let me get past, won't you!' he exclaimed, stepping over Protos's body. Protos, outstretched legs extended from one side of the compartment to the other, made no move to stop him and Lafcadio, surprised not to find himself restrained in any way, opened the door into the corridor.

Turning to leave, he said, 'I'm not running away, don't worry. You're welcome to keep me under observation. But anything is better than listening to another word from you … Forgive me for preferring the police. Go and let them know. I'll be waiting.'

VI

On the same day, the evening train brought the Armand-Dubois from Milan. As they were travelling third-class it was only as they arrived that they met the Countess de Baraglioul and her elder daughter, who had come from Paris in the sleeping car on the same train.

A few hours before the arrival of the telegram announcing Fleurissoire's death, the countess had had a letter from her husband. In it the count had spoken fulsomely of his pleasure at having an unexpected visit from Lafcadio, although doubtless without the faintest hint of that half-brotherhood which, in Julius's eyes, endowed his young sibling with such treacherous appeal (Julius, faithful to his father's command, had not explained the situation to his wife, any more than he had done to Lafcadio), yet certain allusions and certain gaps in his account had told the countess all she needed to know. Indeed I cannot be completely sure that Julius, who lacked for diversions in the routine of his bourgeois existence, was not amusing himself by fluttering around the flame of scandal and singeing his fingertips there. Nor am I certain that Lafcadio's presence in Rome, and the hope of seeing him again, was not a factor, even rather a large factor, in

Geneviève's decision to accompany her mother there.

Julius was at the station to meet them. He swept them off to the Grand Hotel, having perfunctorily greeted the Armand-Dubois, whom he was to meet the next day in the funeral cortège. They made their own way to the hotel in Via di Bocca di Leone where they had stayed on their first visit.

Marguerite brought her novelist husband good news. Nothing now stood in the way of his election. The day before yesterday, Cardinal André had informed her unofficially: it was not even necessary for the candidate to make another round of visits. Of its own accord, the Académie had opened its doors: the Quai de Conti was expecting him.

'There you are!' Marguerite said. 'What did I say to you in Paris? Everything comes to those who wait. In this world that's all one need do.'

'And remain constant,' Julius finished up self-importantly, raising his wife's hand to his lips and unaware of his daughter's eyes filling with scorn as she watched him. 'Faithful to you, my thoughts, my principles. Perseverance is the most invaluable virtue.'

The memory of his recent swerve into fantasy was fading, as was every thought bar conventional ones and every plan bar respectable ones. Now that he knew he would be where he wanted to be, he recovered his aplomb effortlessly. He even admired the subtle consistency with which his mind had, for a moment, gone off the rails. *He* had not changed: it was the pope who had changed.

'No, on the contrary, what constancy there has been in my thinking,' he said to himself. 'What logic! The difficulty is deciding where you stand. Poor Fleurissoire died because he went too far and found himself behind the scenes. The simplest thing – when you're as simple as he was – is to stick with what you know. He discovered a ghastly secret and it killed him. Knowledge only strengthens the strong … Never mind! I'm glad Carola was able to warn the police. It means I can think more freely … All the same, if Armand-Dubois knew it was not the *real* pope who was to blame for his misfortune and exile, what a consolation it would be – what an encouragement to his faith – what comfort!… Tomorrow, after the funeral, I must have a word with him.'

The ceremony did not draw much of a crowd. Three carriages followed the hearse. It was raining. In the leading carriage Blafaphas offered Arnica his friendly support (as soon as she comes out of mourning he will marry her, no question about it). They had both travelled from Pau two days earlier – the thought of abandoning the new widow to her sorrow and leaving her to undertake the long journey alone was too much for Blafaphas to bear, and in any case why would he? He might not be family, but he had also gone into mourning. Was any family member as loyal as such a friend? – but they had only arrived at Rome a few hours earlier, having missed one of their connections.

The count travelled with Anthime Armand-Dubois in the second carriage, and Madame Armand-Dubois brought up the rear with the countess and her daughter.

No reference was made over Fleurissoire's grave to his unfortunate adventure. But on the way back from the cemetery, as soon as they were alone, Julius de Baraglioul spoke to Anthime.

'I promised you I would intercede for you with His Holiness.'

'As God is my witness, I did not ask you to.'

'That's true. I just found myself so outraged by the destitution in which the Church had left you that I could only listen to the promptings of my heart.'

'As God is my witness, I never complained.'

'I know! … I know! … You've vexed me more than enough with your resignation! And since you invite me to return to the subject, I'll confess to you, my dear Anthime, that I see rather more pride than saintliness in your attitude, and that this excessive resignation of yours last time I saw you in Milan seems to me closer to insubordination than genuine piety. As a Christian it deeply antagonised me. God doesn't demand so much from us, for heaven's sake! Let us speak frankly. Your attitude shocked me.'

'And yours, my dear brother, I may then also admit to

you, saddened me. Wasn't it you who actually incited me to rebel and—'

Julius, who was becoming incensed, interrupted him.

'I have experienced enough in my own life – experience I have passed on to others throughout the course of my career – to believe that one can be a perfectly good Christian without dismissing the legitimate advantages conferred on us by the station in life in which God has been pleased to place us. What I reproached about your attitude was precisely that in its affectation it claimed to be superior to mine.'

'As God is my witness—'

'Oh, do stop God-is-my-witness-ing!' Julius interrupted again. 'He's got nothing to do with this. I'm simply pointing out that when I say your attitude was close to rebellion … I mean rebellion as I see it, and that is precisely what I reproach you for – that in accepting the injustice done to you, you've let others rebel for you. While I, personally speaking, refused to accept that the Church herself was in the wrong, you, with your holier-than-thou airs, put her in the wrong. So then I felt I had to complain in your place. You'll soon see how right I was to be infuriated.'

Beads of perspiration were starting to form on Julius's forehead. He placed his top hat on his knees.

'Shall I give us a little air?' Anthime obligingly let down the window on his side.

'As soon as I got to Rome,' Julius went on, 'I requested an audience. It was granted. And my gambit was to be crowned by a very odd kind of success ...'

'I see,' Anthime said indifferently.

'Yes, my friend. Because even though I obtained in a material sense nothing of what I had come for, I at least took away from my visit an assurance ... that placed His Holiness safely beyond the reach of all the injurious suppositions we had formed in respect of him.'

'As God is my witness, I have never formulated anything injurious in respect of our Holy Father.'

'I formulated for you. I saw you injured and I was outraged.'

'Come to the point, Julius. Did you see the pope?'

'Well, actually ... no, I didn't see the pope!' Julius finally burst out. 'But I came into possession of a secret – a barely credible secret initially but one that, with the death of our dear Amédée, was soon to be suddenly corroborated – a horrifying, bewildering secret, but one in which your faith, dear Anthime, will know how to take solace. So I am here to tell you that in this denial of justice of which you have been a victim, the pope is innocent ...'

'Huh! I never thought otherwise.'

'Anthime, listen to me. I didn't see the pope, because no one can see him. The person who is presently seated on the pontifical throne, whom the Church listens to and who pontificates, the person who spoke to me, the pope one sees at the Vatican, the pope I saw IS NOT THE REAL POPE.'

At these words Anthime's whole frame began to shake with guffaws of loud laughter.

'Laugh! Yes, go on, laugh!' Julius went on, stung. 'I laughed too at first. And if I had laughed a bit less, Fleurissoire would not have been murdered. Oh, our saintly friend! Our poor victim!' His words dissolved into sobs.

'Good God! Do you mean to say that this drivel of yours is actually serious? ... Well! ... Well! ... Well!' Armand-Dubois said, perturbed at Julius's tearful state. 'I suppose, all the same, one ought to find out ...'

'It was wanting to find out that killed Fleurissoire.'

'Because if in the end I have sold myself short – my property and position, my life as a scientist – if I've let myself be had ...' Anthime said, becoming incensed now himself.

'I tell you: *the real one* is not in any way responsible for all that. The one you've been had by is a stooge of the Quirinal ...'

'Must I believe what you say?'

'If you don't believe me, believe our poor martyr.'

Both men fell silent. It had stopped raining, and a ray of light broke through the clouds. The slowly jolting carriage was entering the city.

'In that case I know what I have to do,' Anthime went on, in his most resolute voice. 'I'm going to let the cat out of the bag.'

Julius stared at him.

'Dear friend, you fill me with alarm. They'll excommunicate you.'

'Who will? If the pope's not the real one, who gives a damn?'

'And here I was, thinking that by passing on this secret I could help you to feel strengthened in your faith,' Julius went on, shocked.

'Are you joking? ... And then what? Who's going to tell me Fleurissoire didn't arrive at the pearly gates and find out after all that his Lord God wasn't *the real one* either?'

'Come on, Anthime! You're going too far, dear friend. As if there could be two of them! As if there could ever be ANOTHER.'

'Well, frankly, it's all very well for you to talk, when you haven't actually given up anything *for Him* – you profit both ways, whether it's true or false ... No, really! I must get some air.'

Leaning out of the carriage door, he touched the coachman's shoulder with the tip of his stick and made the carriage stop. Julius made a move to follow him.

'No! Leave me alone. I know everything I need to know now. Keep the rest for one of your novels. As for me, I shall be writing to the Grand Master of the Order this evening, and from tomorrow I shall resume my science columns for *La Dépêche*. It'll be great fun.'

'But,' Julius said, surprised to see him favouring one leg, 'you're limping again!'

'Yes. I've been having pain again for a few days now.'

'Oh, well. Now I know what this is all about,' Julius said, and without watching his brother-in-law go, settled back into the carriage's upholstery.

VII

Did Protos intend to hand Lafcadio over to the police, as he had threatened to?

I don't know. The incident at least proved that not all gentlemen of the police were to be counted his friends. Those who were not, and had been tipped off by Carola the day before, had set their mousetrap at Vicolo dei Vecchiarelli. They had been aware of the house for some time and knew that its top floor offered easy communication with the adjoining building, so those exits were also watched.

Protos was not at all afraid of the constables. Neither the prospect of charges being brought nor the apparatus of justice held any terrors for him: he judged that it would be hard to arrest him, since in reality he was not guilty of any crime, merely of a few peccadilloes so trifling that no law enforcement officer would bother with them. He was therefore not wildly alarmed when he realised he was cornered, which he did very rapidly, having a practised eye for identifying police, whatever form their disguises took.

At first, little more than mildly puzzled, he locked himself in Carola's room and waited for her to come back.

He had not seen her since Fleurissoire's murder. He was keen to ask her advice, and to leave her some instructions in the likely event of his ending up in jug.

Carola, meanwhile, deferring to Julius's wishes, had not shown herself at the cemetery. From behind a distant mausoleum and under an umbrella she watched the sad ceremony, alone and unobserved. Patiently and humbly she waited until the mourners left the newly dug grave and the procession re-formed. She watched as Julius and Anthime climbed into their carriage and the cortège rolled away in the drizzle. Then she went up to the grave, took out a large bouquet of asters from inside her shawl, laid them down far from the family's wreaths, and stood there for a long time in the rain, not looking at anything or thinking about anything, and crying instead of praying.

When she got back to Vicolo dei Vecchiarelli, she noticed the two unfamiliar figures standing outside, but did not realise that the house was being watched. She was in a hurry to find Protos: not doubting for an instant that it was he who had committed the murder, she hated him now.

A few minutes later, the police rushed into the house in response to her screams – but too late. Exasperated at finding out that Carola had turned him in, Protos had strangled her.

This took place at around midday. The evening papers ran the story, and as the police had found the piece of leather from the beaver hat's lining on Protos's person, no one doubted that he was guilty of both crimes.

Lafcadio, meanwhile, had spent the afternoon in a state somewhere between expectancy and fear, not of the police, despite Protos having threatened him with them, but of Protos himself or some other force against which he no longer had the will to defend himself. An unspecified listlessness weighed him down. Perhaps it was just tiredness. He gave up.

The day before, he had only seen Julius briefly, when Julius had met him off the Naples train and taken delivery of the body. Afterwards he had walked around the city for a long time, going nowhere in particular, to dispel the anger he still felt following his encounter with Protos and the feelings of dependency it had aroused.

Yet the news of Protos's arrest did not bring Lafcadio the relief he might have expected. It was almost as if he felt disappointed. Strange creature! Just as he had expressly rejected any material benefit from the crime, so he was also reluctant to relinquish any of the risks associated with it. He could not accept that the game was over so quickly. He would willingly, as he had done in his chess-playing days, have sacrificed a rook to his opponent, and with the turn of events having suddenly given him the match too easily and thus stripped it of its interest, he felt he could not stop until he had taken the challenge further.

He dined in a *trattoria* close to the hotel, so that he did not have to dress. Immediately afterwards, walking back through the lobby, he glimpsed Julius through the glass doors of the restaurant, sitting at dinner with his wife and daughter. He was struck by the beauty of Geneviève, whom he had not seen since his first visit. He was loitering in the smoking room, waiting for dinner to be over, when a page came to tell him that the count had gone up to his room and was expecting him.

He went in. Julius de Baraglioul was alone. He had changed back into a jacket.

'Well! The murderer has been apprehended,' he said immediately, holding out his hand.

But Lafcadio did not take it. He remained standing in the doorway.

'What murderer?' he asked.

'My brother-in-law's, for heaven's sake!'

'*I* am your brother-in-law's murderer.'

He said it without trembling, without altering or lowering the tone of his voice and without moving, in such a natural way that at first Julius did not understand. Lafcadio had to repeat himself.

'I'm saying that your brother-in-law's murderer has not been arrested for the simple reason that I murdered your brother-in-law.'

If Lafcadio had looked at all wild or frenzied, Julius

might have taken fright, but his look was more childlike than anything else. He looked younger even than the first time Julius had met him. His eyes were as bright, his voice as clear. He had closed the door, but remained with his back to it. Julius, standing by the table, slumped into an armchair.

'My poor boy,' were his first words. 'Speak more quietly! … What possessed you? How could you have done it?'

Lafcadio looked down, already regretting having spoken.

'How should I know? I did it very quickly. I just suddenly felt like it.'

'What did you have against Fleurissoire? Such a worthy and virtuous man.'

'I don't know … He didn't look happy … How do you think I can explain to you what I can't explain to myself?'

An increasingly awkward silence fell, broken by short bursts of words from each of them, only to fall again more deeply. Snatches of cheap Neapolitan music wafted up from the hotel's lobby. Julius scratched at a small spot of candle wax on the tablecloth with his little fingernail, which he kept long and tapered to a point. He suddenly noticed that this handsome nail was broken, with a crack across it that marred the whole width of its polished, pink-coloured surface. How had it happened? And how had he not noticed it immediately? Whatever the answer, the damage was done, and there was nothing he could do but cut it short. He was deeply irritated: he took great care of his hands and of this nail in particular, which he had tended patiently and carefully and which showed off his finger, emphasising its elegance. The nail scissors were in his dressing-table drawer and he was about to get up to fetch them, but he realised he would have had to walk past Lafcadio. He tactfully decided to postpone the delicate operation.

'So ... what do you plan to do now?' he said.

'I don't know. Hand myself in, possibly. I'm going to sleep on it.'

Julius let his arm fall beside his armchair. Gazing at Lafcadio for a few moments, he sighed in a deeply disheartened voice, 'And there I was, beginning to care for you!'

Lafcadio could not have imagined that it was said with unkind intent, and yet, however unthinkingly the words had been uttered, they sounded just as cruel. He felt them like a knife to his heart. He raised his head, his body rigid with the struggle to overcome the anguish that suddenly washed over him. He looked at Julius. 'Is he really the person I thought of almost as my brother yesterday?' he said to himself. His gaze strayed around the room where, the day before yesterday, he had, despite his crime, been able to talk so cheerfully. The bottle of eau de Cologne was still on the table, nearly empty ...

'Listen to me, Lafcadio,' Julius said. 'I don't see your

situation as entirely hopeless. The person supposed to have committed this crime—'

'Yes, I know he's just been arrested,' Lafcadio interrupted. 'Are you about to advise me that I should let an innocent person be convicted in my place?'

'The person you describe as innocent has just murdered a woman, and moreover one you know …'

'And that sets my mind at rest, does it?'

'That isn't exactly what I'm saying, but—'

'Let's remind ourselves that he's the one person who could give me away.'

'But still everything's not hopeless, surely you can see that.'

Julius stood up, walked over to the window, straightened the folds of the curtains, retraced his steps and, leaning forward with his arms folded on the back of the armchair in which he had been sitting, said, 'Lafcadio, I should not like to see you go without a word of advice. It depends on you and you alone, I am convinced of it, to make an honest man of yourself again, and to take your place in society – as far as your birth permits it, at any rate … The Church is there to help you. Come on, my boy! Be brave: go to confession.'

Lafcadio could not suppress a smile.

'I'll reflect on your kind words.' He took a step forward. 'I'm sure you would prefer not to shake hands with a murderer. All the same I'd like to thank you for your—'

'Don't mention it! Don't mention it,' Julius said, with

a friendly, impersonal wave. 'Farewell, my boy. For now I dare not say it's only a goodbye. Yet perhaps, in future, you'll—'

'You have nothing else to say to me at this moment?'

'Nothing, at this moment.'

'Farewell, Monsieur.'

Lafcadio bowed solemnly and went out.

He went back to his room on the next floor, half undressed, and threw himself on his bed. The late afternoon had been very hot, and nightfall had not brought any cooling freshness. His window was open wide, but there was not a puff of wind to stir the still air. The distant electric globe lamps on the Piazza delle Terme, from which he was separated by the hotel's gardens, filled his room with a bluish, diffuse light that looked like moonlight. He wanted to think, but a strange lethargy numbed his mind terribly. He was unable to think about his crime or about ways of escape. He just kept trying not to hear Julius's awful words: 'I was beginning to care for you …' If he himself did not care for Julius, were Julius's words worth his tears? Was that really what he was crying for? … The night was so balmy he felt all he had to do was let go, and death would steal silently up on him. He reached for a carafe of water next to his bed, soaked his handkerchief, and pressed it to his aching heart.

'There isn't a drink in this world that will ever quench

my parched heart again!' he told himself, letting the tears roll down his cheeks to his lips so he could taste their bitterness. Some lines of poetry – he couldn't remember where he had read them or why – kept repeating themselves in his brain:

My heart aches, and a drowsy numbness pains
My sense ...

He drifted off to sleep.

Is he dreaming? Wasn't that a knock at his door? The door, which he never locks at night, opens gently on a slim figure dressed in white who steps into the room. He hears a voice call faintly, 'Lafcadio ... Are you there, Lafcadio?'

In his half-asleep state he nonetheless recognises that voice. But does he still doubt the reality of such a welcome apparition? Does he fear that a word or gesture might scare it away? He stays silent.

Geneviève de Baraglioul, whose room was next to her father's, had been unable to help hearing every part of the conversation between her father and Lafcadio. An unbearable anguish had driven her to Lafcadio's door and now, convinced because her call had gone unanswered that Lafcadio had just killed himself, she ran to his bedside and fell to her knees, sobbing.

Lafcadio, seeing that she was not moving, sat up and

leant bodily over her, still not daring to press his lips to the lovely brow he saw gleaming in the half-light. As he moved towards her, Geneviève felt all her will drain from her body. Throwing back her forehead, on which she could feel the warmth of Lafcadio's breath, and not knowing where to turn for help to resist him, except to him himself, she murmured, 'Have pity on me, dear friend.'

Lafcadio recovered his self-control, recoiling from her and simultaneously pushing her away from him.

'Get up, Mademoiselle de Baraglioul! And get away from me! I'm not ... I cannot be your friend any longer.'

Geneviève sat up but did not step away from the bed, where the person she had thought dead half lay, instead stroking Lafcadio's burning forehead as if to assure herself that he was still living.

'But, dear friend, I heard every word you said to my father tonight. Don't you understand that that's why I came?'

Lafcadio half sat up and stared at her. Her untied hair fell around her shoulders. Her face was entirely in shadow, so he could not see her eyes, but he felt her gaze engulfing him. Unable to bear its gentleness, and hiding his face in his hands, he groaned.

'Oh, why did I take so long to meet you? What did I do to make you care about me? Why are you saying these things to me when you know I'm not a free man or worthy to care about you any more?'

Geneviève protested miserably, 'You're the one I came

to see, Lafcadio. Not someone else. You, the criminal! How many times have I whispered your name, since that first day I saw you as a hero? More than a hero: you were too reckless ... I can't keep it to myself any longer. I was secretly yours the moment I saw you risk your life for others so unthinkingly. But what happened then? Is it possible that you've killed someone? What have you let yourself turn into?'

As Lafcadio just shook his head without answering, she went on, 'Didn't I hear my father say that someone else had been arrested? A bandit who had just killed someone? ... Lafcadio, while there's still time, you must get away. Tonight. Go. Go!'

Lafcadio whispered, 'I can't go on,' and, feeling Geneviève's hair brush against his hands, grasped handfuls of it and passionately pressed it over his eyes and mouth, muttering, 'Escape! Is that what you want me to do? Where do you want me to escape to? Even if I could get away from the police, I couldn't get away from myself ... And then you'd despise me for running away.'

'Me? Despise you, my—'

'I was living without thinking. I killed as if it was a dream, a nightmare I've been struggling in ever since ...'

'Which I want to save you from!' she cried out.

'What's the use of waking me up? If it's only to wake me up as a criminal.' He clutched her arm. 'Don't you see that I can't stand the idea of getting away with it? What is there left for me to do? Apart from giving myself up as soon as it's light?'

'It's God you must give yourself up to, not the police. If my father didn't tell you, Lafcadio, I'm telling you now. The Church is there to determine your punishment and to help you find peace again, once you have repented.'

Geneviève is right. Clearly the best thing Lafcadio can do now is throw himself conveniently on the Church's mercy. Sooner or later he will realise this, when he understands that every other exit is blocked … It's infuriating that it should have been that dope of a father of hers who had given him that advice in the first place!

'Not another sermon!' he said aggressively. 'Is it really you talking to me like that?'

He lets go of her arm, which he was holding, and pushes her away, and as she stumbles back he feels a blind antagonism towards Julius well up inside him and a desire to sever Geneviève from her father, to drag her down, closer to his level. Looking at the floor, in the darkness he catches sight of her bare feet in their little silk slippers.

'Can't you understand? It's not remorse I'm afraid of, but …'

He jumps off his bed and turns away from her. He feels he cannot breathe and walks to the open window to rest his forehead on the glass and his burning palms on the cold iron railing. He would like to put her out of his mind, to forget how close he is to her …

'Mademoiselle de Baraglioul, you have done everything a young woman of good family could do for a criminal – you have gone beyond the call of duty – and I thank you from the bottom of my heart. It will be better if you leave me now. Return to your father, to your habits, your duties … Goodbye. Who knows whether I shall see you again? Believe me when I say that it is in order to be a bit less unworthy of your affection that I shall go and turn myself in tomorrow. Believe me … No! Don't come any closer … Do you think shaking hands would be enough for me?'

Geneviève would have braved her father's condemnation and the world's scorn, but at Lafcadio's icy tone her heart fails her. Can he not understand that to come and speak to him like this at night, to confess her love for him like this, demanded determination and courage from her too, and that perhaps her love deserves more than a thank you? … But how can she tell him that her life was a dream too until today – a dream she could only escape from for short periods at the hospital, where, surrounded by her poor little ones and dressing their real wounds, she could now and then feel in touch with some kind of reality – a low-quality dream in which her parents, fussing around her with their absurd conventions, were never far from her side and in which she could never take their behaviour or their opinions, their ambitions or their principles, or even the way they looked, seriously. Small wonder that Lafcadio had not been able to take Fleurissoire seriously!

... Can this really be how they will part? Love drives her, thrusts her towards him. Lafcadio grabs her, hugs her, covers her pale forehead with kisses ...

A new book starts here.

Desire! Palpable truth of desire! You send the phantasms of my mind racing back into the shadows.

We shall leave our two lovers there, as the cock starts to crow and colour, warmth and life flood triumphantly back at last, after the darkness of the night. Lafcadio raises himself above a sleeping Geneviève. Yet it is not his lover's beautiful face, her forehead damp with sweat, her pearly eyelids, her warm, parted lips, her perfect breasts, her tired limbs – no, it is none of these that he stares at, but, through the wide-open window, the coming dawn and a tree that rustles in the garden.

It will soon be time for Geneviève to leave him. But he waits on, and bent over her, listens above the faint sound of her breathing to the vague clamour of the city that is already shaking him from his lethargy. Across the rooftops, in the barracks the bugles are playing. Hey! Is he going to give up living? And for the sake of Geneviève thinking well of him – Geneviève, whom he thinks a bit less of now that she loves him a bit more – is he still thinking of turning himself in?

Notes:

1. *Vexierkasten* – puzzle boxes.

2. 'The new "Plastic Roman plaster",' announced the catalogue, 'is of relatively recent invention, manufactured to a secret formula by the Blafaphas, Fleurissoire & Lévichon company, and offers a substantial improvement on current materials such as *carton-pierre* and plaster of Paris, whose usage has all too clearly established their defectiveness in many applications.' (Descriptions of the different grades and types followed.) [Text footnote by AG]

3. 'HERE BEGINS THE BOOK OF THE NEW REGIME AND THE SUPREME VIRTUE. "Make of it what you will." BOCCACCIO.'

4. *'Dapprima importa sapere chi è.'* – 'The first thing is to find out who he is.'

5. *'Ma chi sa se vive ancora?...'* – 'But who knows if he is still alive?'

6. *'Importa di domesticare questo nuovo proposito'* – 'I need time to digest this new proposition.'

7. It is time to launch the ship – In English in the original.

8. *Account of the Deliverance of His Holiness Leo XIII, imprisoned in the Vatican's dungeons* (Saint-Malo, printed by Y. Billois, Rue de l'Orme 4, 1893). [Text footnote by AG]

9. Gide's game-playing with his characters' names extends here to a name whose English equivalent might be Arnica Goodfart.

10. *Is fecit cui prodest* – He did it who has profited by it.

11. In English in the original.

12. In English in the original. From 'From Pent-up Aching Rivers' by Walt Whitman.

The meaning of freedom:

The Vatican Cellars a hundred years on

How to live? How to reach meaning? Four hundred years ago Blaise Pascal held that the human being's only answer was through the love of God. By the nineteenth century Søren Kierkegaard had proposed a deep individual subjectivity, backed up by submission to the divine. For Jean-Paul Sartre a hundred years later, God had vanished: the individual must encounter themselves in the world and define meaning out of their own actions.

In the summer of 1914 another French novelist offered his answer. In *Les Caves du Vatican* – *The Vatican Cellars* – André Gide had no recourse to God or to the tone of his previous work. In fact the novel was partly a reaction against his reputation. In his journals of July 1914 he recalls meeting a rich and titled admirer of *Strait is the Gate*:

> At each compliment she pays me, I feel like sticking my tongue out at her or shouting, Shit! 'You so delicately depicted spiritual solitude ... you have discovered a new psychological law that no one had ever stated before' ...
>
> And it goes on and on. ... It was time to write the Cellars.[1]

When it was first published pseudo-anonymously, Gide's story – we would call it a novel but he preferred '*sotie*', originally a medieval satire in which the actors mocked authority – surprised his friends and alienated his critics. Critics on the Catholic right attacked him for the book's attitude to the Church, but many more were appalled by his nihilism, given shape in the book's hero Lafcadio Wluiki and particularly the scene when Lafcadio,

1 *Journals* (translated by Justin O'Brien), vol. II 1914–1927.

without motive, pushes a fellow passenger out of a moving train.

Gide had found the perfect vehicle to make mischief. He sensed that he had mastered a new story and a new way of telling it. Commercially *The Vatican Cellars* was not a success, but its initial failure was in proportion to its newness and its significance. Several years after it was published he wrote in his *Journals*,

> I have scarcely known, throughout my 'career', anything but flops; and I can even say that the flatness of the flop was in direct ratio to the importance and originality of the work, so that it was to *Paludes*, *The Fruits [of the Earth]*, and *The Vatican Cellars* that I owed the worst ones.
>
> (15 July 1922)

The Vatican Cellars may have been an affront to polite readers, but Dadaists and later Surrealists admired its anti-bourgeois, anti-literary values (although Gide later complained that just because he had written a book they liked did not make him a Dadaist). It was a basis of his work that 'each of my books turns against those who were enthusiastic for the preceding one' (*Journals*, 24 June 1924). People should take each work for what it was: a piece of art.

But the Surrealists at least saw part of the book's intention, which was to excavate a deep social and psychological underground beneath the clichés that seeped into public behaviour and paralysed individual freedom. The cellars under the Vatican represented that cavern perfectly.

For Gide the cellars have an allusive part to play in the plot, but their main purpose is to encompass everything that is mysterious, unworked-out and unspoken in the conventional world above ground. The ambiguities of his French title (the Latin '*cave*' counselling caution, the slang French '*cave*' meaning 'coward') begin the reader's journey into a several-sided account that is part anti-Catholic satire, part farce, part thriller and part provocative extravaganza, about those suppressed mysteries at the start of the modern era.

A curiosity of the novel is that almost all its characters are members of the same family by blood or marriage. '*Familles, je vous hais!*' ['Families, I loathe you!'] Gide had written in *The Fruits of the Earth* (1897). '*[F]oyers clos; portes renfermées; possessions jalouses du bonheur*' ['Cold hearths, closed doors, possessions more valued than happiness'], he complained.

And *The Vatican Cellars* is a deliberately familial story. It exploits a confused comedy of family relations while it simultaneously explores the disasters of illegitimacy, rejection, fratricide and incest that family members visit on each other. The only two significant characters who do not belong to the family are the swindler Protos and Carola, a prostitute and Lafcadio's former lover. They stand for the world's spare capacity for evil and good: able to catalyse a chain of events, but its deepest reverberations always occur inside the family.

Lafcadio's adventures are only a part of the farrago of *The Vatican Cellars*, onto which Gide delightedly overlays a chaotic reality. The factually true basis of his narrative gave strength to its outrageousness. A series of reported events dated back to 1892 when, in Lyon in southern France, a trio of confidence tricksters started a rumour that Pope Leo XIII had been incarcerated in the Vatican's cellars by a group of cardinals sympathetic to the freemasons, and that a false pope sat on Saint Peter's throne. The supposed incarceration, recounted to gullible Catholics in great secrecy, was used to extort money from them allegedly to finance a 'crusade' to restore the true pope.

Gide was struck by the story's farcical potential, but the

catalyst for writing a fictionalised account may have been the attempt on his soul by his friend Paul Claudel, a devout Catholic, in 1905. In Gide's version the bogus crusade unfolds in parallel with the biography of the mysterious Lafcadio. The network of family connections that links the stories confirms and undermines the family's integrity: when Lafcadio's father, Juste-Agénor Baraglioul, summons his illegitimate son to his deathbed he concludes with the axiom, 'My boy, the family is a great and closed institution. You'll never be anything but a bastard.' Simultaneously, characters related by legitimate blood and marriage are helpless to control the consequences of their slightest acts on other family members. The family is a non-linear system in which, Gide shows, we are constantly vulnerable. We can spend our entire life playing the family game by one set of rules, and at any moment discover that it is taking place according to another.

The modernity of Gide's *sotie* is not confined to his understanding of the family as a chaos-generating system. The story was widely misunderstood on its first appearance because conventionally minded readers missed that, as in a fairytale, he had given the narrative its own internal logic by paring down the story, compressing the dialogue and switching from scene to scene with such speed that improbabilities were (mostly) dissolved in spontaneity. It is not a particularly linear narrative, built instead from intersecting planes of different perspectives to provide the significance or turbulence Gide was looking for.

First there is the atheist Anthime Armand-Dubois, and his Catholic brother-in-law Count Julius de Baraglioul. Then Lafcadio appears – his behaviour will take the novel and family relations in a new direction. Gide's third plane of narrative begins with the Comtesse de Saint-Prix, Julius's devout widowed younger sister. When the priest Fr Salus visits her with an urgent secret request for financial help to rescue the pope, the plot is set. Salus of course is Protos, leader of the swindlers' gang, and his interview with the Countess is the first of Gide's extended jokes at everyone's expense, Catholics, freemasons, rich and titled ladies.

It is also the prelude to the novel's central comedy, as the Countess rushes to confide in her sister-in-law Arnica Fleurissoire, an act which results in her pious husband Amédée's departure for Rome to save the pope singlehanded.

Gide's comic treatment of Amédée Fleurissoire is harsh. But he risks readers' resentment in order to reveal how we are unable to see reality clearly. From the start, there is a hint of misplaced virility in Fleurissoire's mission to deliver the imprisoned pope. Having been bound by inept ideas of virtue to embark on an unconsummated marriage with Arnica, he rushes to Rome like the hero of a chivalric romance. Virtuous as a friend, virtuous in his religious crusade – twice directed by the doctrine of his faith, he twice misunderstands himself.

The Rome section of the novel – the most comic and fantastic plane of Gide's reality – is titled 'The Millipede': the codename of the conspiracy set up by Protos. The millipede, in the person of Protos and his associates, ubiquitous and irresistible, is however not some personification of Satan, but an expression of our existential vulnerability. Reality is not the world as it appears to Amédée Fleurissoire, Gide's nineteenth-century Mr Bean, or us. Reality is created moment by moment, coming into being (or failing to) in the actions we take (or don't) to confirm our existence.

Now Gide begins to draw together the planes of his narrative. As the overturning of Amédée's sense of reality continues in Rome and then in Naples, he enters a world of misperceptions, coincidence – and gratuity. He goes into Lafcadio's compartment to get away from another traveller. Lafcadio is on his way by stages to Brindisi, to take ship for Borneo in a grand rejection of old Europe, and he is on the lookout for chance opportunities.

Spontaneity has already shown Lafcadio capable of good actions, as when he rescued a young mother's children from a fire and carried an old woman's bag on his hike across the Apennines. He has also committed the odd modestly bad act. But the sap of moral relativism is rising in him: he considers what might have happened if he had strangled the old woman whom he kissed instead at the top of the hill.

As his relative from Pau ties his necktie in his reflection in the window-glass, he realises that his opportunity has come. The door handle by his hand, the door swinging open, a man falling. A crime without motive.

Lafcadio is determined to taste the intensity of experience, to master events: to retain his freedom. An outsider, in the entire *sotie* he is one of only two characters – Protos is the other – who are free of fear and limitation, while almost everyone else is comically shut off from reality by their fears and manias.

The novel's last pages describe a chaotic collision between the worlds of real and apparent meaning, and convention and freedom, most notably when, following Protos's arrest, Lafcadio confesses the crime to Julius. Julius, with his usual opportunism, points out that the presumed murderer is already in custody and Lafcadio only need confess himself to God, conveniently avoiding the law.

Honesty puts in an appearance when Julius's daughter Geneviève comes to Lafcadio's room to beg him to escape, and he announces that he will give himself up to the police the next day. But the story ends with the lovers in each other's arms at sunrise, and Gide's final provocation as Lafcadio contemplates the dawn and a bugle sounds in a nearby barracks.

Hey! Is he going to give up living? And for the sake of

Geneviève thinking well of him – Geneviève, whom he thinks a bit less of now that she loves him a bit more – is he still thinking of turning himself in?

Is Gide, finishing the novel this way, delving into immorality, approving the lovers and Lafcadio's crime? Or is he offering a happy ending as fully ironic as life is: life as a loose end enlivened by desire and hope, a union of two characters denied the promise of 'happy ever after' but offered the shelter of here and now?

Lafcadio's escape from censure was another reason for Gide's critics to condemn his supposed endorsement of young men who spend their leisure hours defenestrating harmless middle-aged bourgeois from trains. But how could he offer judgment or justification without negating a central purpose of the novel, which was to uncover the imposed, convention-bound, external nature of *all* judgments?

From a narrative viewpoint, Lafcadio's 'gratuitous act' is a marvellous 'Stop' sign, wrecking the novelistic chain of cause and effect. It is a *coup de théâtre*. Yet at another level it is best read as a theory of possibility – a symbol of our need for liberty – rather than a real act championed by the novelist. It remains a potent concept. If the bastard is a theoretical case of pure freedom – beyond the family circle, beyond the reach of inherited morality and imposed motivation – the motiveless act is his counterpart, freedom of action in its purest form. Nietzsche and Dostoyevsky had made free with aspects of gratuity in their work before Gide; thirty years later Sartre finally formalised his ideas on motivation.[2] But in *The Vatican Cellars*, with immense delicacy, Gide is already playing out the puzzle in full. Lafcadio's act, to be truly motiveless, would be without meaning, so the meaning of gratuity could not be ascribed to it. If it is to be understood by the reader as part of

2 In *Being and Nothingness.*

the novel's pattern of action it requires, or acquires, a motive –
and is immediately purged of gratuity.

That motive, I believe, is the bastard's riposte to convention
(and perhaps for Gide the homosexual's riposte to convention):
the riposte of Lafcadio, bright, resourceful, nihilistic and rich,
butting like a young bull at the bourgeois world of credulous,
pitiable Amédée Fleurissoire. Lafcadio's need for fatherly
love and contact emerges in rejection and a delinquency that
is possibly temporary, possibly not. We cannot know. 'A new
book starts here.' And that new book is *the* new twentieth-
century novel, of alienation from social and formal norms; the
novel of revenge against the nineteenth century.

There is one more element. Lafcadio also offers us a
metaphor for the forces that lie outside ourselves. In his version
of existence's gratuity – his defenestration of Amédée – we
glimpse the protean disorder of our universe: a prophetic
statement at the outset of a gratuitous century.

Out of this Gide does not make a philosophy. His characters
just convey the world's absurdity, like Anthime's rats scuttling
from place to place, trying to make out, blinded or with limited
vision, the meaning of it all. Simultaneously the novel becomes
a part of what the essayist Lakis Proguidis has called 'the Europe
of laughter'. The *Cellars* is part of the underground stream
of the comic picaresque that has watered the European novel
since its inception. Gide is of the party of Rabelais, Cervantes,
Voltaire and Sterne, his laughter an emblem of his liberty – his
refusal to be categorical a refusal to compromise his liberty.

The world is not how Don Quixote read about it in books, or
how Candide (another bastard) sees it through Leibnizian-tinted
spectacles, or how Amédée Fleurissoire imagines it outside Pau
or Lafcadio outside the fortress of his adolescent sullishness or
Julius outside his fortress of timid conventionality. The world
is funny: dangerous, deceptive, farcical. There is always 'la

part du diable'. Gide replaced his own conditioned belief in a Christian universe by a human-made, flawed, incomplete social and ethical landscape, refusing to commit himself to philosophy or judgment. His critics have long fought to systematise his writing and judge him, before giving up in a kind of despairing derision.

But a hundred years have passed and the *Cellars* are still here. Indirection, non-commitment and doubt are good insurance: Gide's insistence on remaining inexplicit in his work has made it last. Justifying to Paul Valéry in July 1914 his reason for removing an explanatory preface he had written, he said, 'I don't like to be discovered too soon.' Valéry replied, 'You've done the right thing ... One must never take away or soften a book's sting. That's what makes people pick it up again.'

Valéry was right. The impact of Gide's *sotie* has been wide and continuing: on the Dadaist Jacques Vaché who carried it to the trenches in the First World War, on the Surrealists, on Jean Cocteau and Jules Romains, Anouilh and Ionesco, on all the characters for whom Lafcadio is a prototype in the novels and films that narrate some of his future careers: Mathieu Delarue in *The Age of Reason*, Meursault in *The Outsider*, Holden Caulfield, Tom Ripley, Vincent Corleone, Patrick Bateman, Tyler Durden, Jean-Baptiste Grenouille ... But let us also reserve some of our admiration for Gide's creation of one of the first and most comic expressions of the modernism that would shake Europe in the 1920s and, in the episode of Lafcadio the murderer, one of the most completely expressed formulations of that revolt.